TOMATO SLICES

TOMATO SLICES

Edited by Iscah

Amoeba Ink

Front Cover Design by Iscah
Back Cover Photograph by Christopher Woods

Edited by Iscah

www.amoebaink.com

ISBN-10: 0-9835519-8-7
ISBN-13: 978-0-9835519-8-0

To tomato lovers everywhere…

Table of Contents

Short Stories

Nonfiction

Poetry

Recipes

Illustrations

The Illustrious Society of Tomato Lovers International and My Adventures Therewith, by E.G. Rumpuddle III, Esq.

Bret James Stewart

Surely, the tomato is the noblest of fruits. It is obvious to even the most casual observer. As the eagle is the proudest of birds, as Shakespeare is foremost among writers, as Barry Manilow is the standard against which all other entertainers are measured, so is the tomato the grandest among fruitkind.

I say 'fruitkind' because the tomato is, indeed, a fruit—not a vegetable as the maligned, ignorant, or flora-

challenged imply. The tomato has been viciously slighted in the past by wrongful classification. It is hard to believe, in this time of modern advancement, that such prejudice could exist. It is my sorrow to affirm such atrocities do still occur. Fortunately, each passing year finds the tomato more respected and it is not too difficult to envision a time in the near future wherein the tomato will enjoy perfect liberty.

History demonstrates the perseverance of the tomato. The tomato (*Solanum lycopersicum*) is native to Mexico, was brought to Europe by the Spaniards, and then boldly conquered the world despite early misgivings (totally unfounded) over its placement in the nightshade family. In the face of all opposition, the tomato has not only survived, but thrived. Its dominance over the fruit scene grew until, now, it is foremost among fruits. The tomato reigns supreme.

For this reason, I assembled other adorers of the lofty fruit, true believers of the blessed fructose, and created The Illustrious Society of Tomato Lovers International. Such perseverance cannot but be commended. Such zeal is inherently appreciated. Such strength is naturally desired. Is it any wonder, then, that the tomato's most ardent admirers should band together? Destiny and shared adoration brought a few men together and, from this nucleus, was born The Illustrious Society of Tomato Lovers International, of which I have the honour of being president, or Top Tomato as we lovingly term it.

My adventures with the Society have been varied and deeply profound. None, though, have been more life affecting than the incidents dominating the first week or so of my tenure as president.

The very day I was sworn in for my first term, my life was changed. Flushed with elation over my success, I decided to celebrate. Nothing is more festive than a nice tomato

medley salad. Therefore, on my way home, I stopped by the grocery store to pick up the luscious fruit.

There, amid the bright lights and shiny display cases, I experienced one of the most abominable atrocities ignorance or malice could ever hope to orchestrate. There, amidst the asparagus and lettuce and broccoli, sat a bin full of tomatoes. *With the vegetables!* True, they shone like diamonds in the rough; as visible as a splendidly garbed king amongst peasants, but such callousness was inexcusable. My wrath was kindled seeing the tomato relegated to the vegetable bins.

Fortunately, the produce man (a boy, really) was a few bins over watering the artichokes. He barely acknowledged me when I approached and it went downhill from there. I told him of the grave, though probably inadvertent, crime being committed regarding their tomatoes. He grunted something unintelligible and noncommittal. When I pursued the matter, he referred me to the store manager.

The manager was a swarthy, beefy man with a flat top haircut who stood very, very straight. Here, I thought, is a no-nonsense man, a man of action, a man who gets things done. With him, it would have to be straight to the point.

"Sir," said I, "I must report a crime of the cruelest nature. I'm sure you can see that, probably inadvertently, you have slighted yon ripe red tomatoes."

"What?" he bantered skillfully.

"Your bright, delicious tomatoes have been cast, carelessly cast, amongst the lowly vegetables."

"So?" he countered.

"I'm sure you can see and will readily agree the tomato is actually a fruit!"

"Yeah," he responded intellectually.

"Therefore," I continued, "since you agree, the tomatoes, glorious tomatoes, should be delivered from

3

their present plight and restored to their rightful place amongst the fruit."

"You're a fruit," he replied, and he and a couple of bagboys promptly escorted me out of the store and bade me (in a rather rude manner) never return.

Later that night, still smarting from the rude and totally uncalled for treatment from the grocery store chain, I was given my chance for immortality. I was studiously composing a rather harsh letter to the CEO of the store chain and watching a game show I had never seen at that point called Triviamaster. Contemplating a particularly climactic sentence, I stared blankly at the TV screen. Gradually, I became aware of a solicitation for contestants in my area. At a loss for the sentence and momentarily unencumbered, I called the toll-free number. Imagine my surprise when I was chosen to appear on Triviamaster the following week. I never did finish the letter.

The next week was a blur. I studied all the oddball trivia I could get my hands on. My friends read questions off Trivial Pursuit cards to me at work. I watched Jeopardy religiously and even slept with the History Channel on so I might learn subliminally while I slept. To say I was nervous and excited doesn't even come close to describing it—I was absolutely wired up.

Finally, the Day arrived. I put on a nice suit, had a good breakfast (tomato omelet), took my lucky Thomas the Tomato keychain, got into my car, looked at myself in the rearview, realized I had forgotten to comb my hair, got out of the car, went back inside, combed my hair, viciously berated myself for forgetting to comb my hair, got back into my car, and drove to the studio for my Triviamaster date with destiny.

The game consists of a contestant (me) and a host (not me). The host (not me) asks the contestant (me) various trivia questions. Twenty questions answered correctly and

you win $100,000.

I was a little nervous. Perhaps slightly concerned about making myself out to be an idiot in front of the audience and millions of home viewers, but nothing I couldn't handle. After all, I'm a confident guy. Also, a half bottle of vodka and my lucky Thomas the Tomato keychain didn't hurt.

Anyway, everything went well during round one. I missed none and the ten minutes or so covered by the round was enough time for me to get relatively comfortable. It's all a matter of focus. You focus on yourself, the host, and the question as if nothing else exists; as if everything else in existence was a barren wasteland and your very survival depended upon the correct response to that one tiny, all consuming question. My God—the stress is almost shattering.

Round two. After a little nonsensical chitchat about my hometown for the benefit of the audience (though I don't think they *really* care), we began in earnest. Let me not say it was easy, there were several nail-biting instances when I wasn't really sure about an answer, guessed anyway, and got it right (the applause was truly thunderous). The third and final round and daytime TV immortality awaited.

You can only imagine the total elation I felt when Mr. Smiley, the host, asked the final question:

The tomato is: A—a fruit, B—a vegetable, or C—a Scandinavian polka.

My heart leapt. Fate, warm and benevolent, smiled upon me. Right before she shattered me like a sheet of glass.

Under the circumstances, I think one can understand why I felt a little overconfident. I remember thinking to myself, secure in my knowledge, how funny it would be if I said the tomato is a vegetable.

"Oh…I'm sorry," said the host.

5

"What?" I said, blinking.

"That's incorrect!" he flashed his plastic smile.

"What's incorrect?"

"The tomato is not a vegetable, it is actually a fruit."

"I didn't say it was a vegetable."

"Yes, you did," his smile never faded.

"I did not! Everyone knows the tomato is a fruit!"

Let's just say things got a little ugly. I had apparently been musing aloud. I was upset over my little blunder. I know I shouldn't have said those things about his mother. I'm sure she's a nice person. Really. Anyway, I was ejected and dejected. I slowly made my sad, despairing way home, lost in the bitter irony of my situation.

Shambling along, I wasn't really paying attention to where I was going. I was crossing the street when I heard a horrible screeching sound. I looked up just in time to see the blur of a grocery truck and feel the intense pain of impact. The next thing I knew, I was lying in a hospitable bed.

It seems like the perfect ending to my really bad day. In actuality, it was perfect. It turns out the driver of the truck (who was hauling a load of yellow tomatoes!), was somewhat intoxicated. The short of it is the driver's company settled for a large undisclosed amount that more than made up for the incident on Triviamaster.

Now, I live a life of luxury. I spend my time heading the Illustrious Society of Tomato Lovers International and penning articles vital to the progression of tomatokind. It's amazing how the seemingly negative is truly a blessing in disguise. The tomato, of course, takes care of its own.

A Tomato Walks Into a Bar

Mark L. Levinson

A tomato walks into a bar
and says, "Pour me a Beaujolais noir."
But the man says, "Get lost.
You're too readily sauced,
and you're red in the face as you are."

Tomato Invasion

Alarie Tennille

Tomatoes march single file across the windowsill, then close ranks, parading over the kitchen counter for inspection. Daddy surveys his troops with obvious pride— says, "Follow me," and leads me down the hall. In the guest room, another platoon of tomatoes stands at attention. A few balance right on a ledge, like paratroopers ready to leap. *"As a master sergeant, I was always the last one out of the plane,"* says Daddy, *"I was supposed to shoot anyone who refused to jump, but I never had to."*

Now he is general of his own tomato army. I think, "Twenty-five tomato plants—that's a lot for two people." Then I see him prepare the first convoys. Bulging in their khaki sacks, tomatoes soon line Daddy's car, making room at home for fresh recruits.

He provided for his men. He provided for his family. Now Daddy sets off to supply cousins, neighbors, friends, even friends of friends from his victory garden. It will be a short mission—over by first frost, then Daddy can rest for winter. But as he gazes out the kitchen window, I know he is already planning next year's campaign.

Fried Green Tomato BLT
Amanda Rotach Huntley

Remoulade:

2 tablespoon parsley, finely chopped
1 shallot, finely chopped
1/2 lemon
1 tablespoon hot sauce
3/4 cup mayonnaise
2 teaspoon Dijon mustard

Combine shallot, parsley, the juice of lemon, hot sauce, mayonnaise, and mustard; set aside.

Sandwiches:

1 narrow 24" loaf of crusty French bread
Olive oil
1 dozen slices bacon
Butterhead lettuce (enough for 4 sandwiches)
2 large green tomatoes
2 cup buttermilk
4 tablespoon canola oil

1 cup cornmeal
1 cup flour
Garlic powder (to taste)
1/2 teaspoon cayenne powder
Salt and pepper (to taste)

1. Preheat oven to 350 degrees.

2. Cut one loaf of French bread into quarters, and then cut each quarter horizontally.

3. Brush the cut surfaces with olive oil and then place, oil side up on a cookie sheet. Toast in the oven for 5-8 minutes on the middle rack, until golden brown. Set aside.

4. Fry bacon until crisp, reserving 2 tablespoon drippings.

5. Prepare the dredge by combining cornmeal, flour, and garlic powder, cayenne, salt, and pepper.

6. Slice the green tomato into thick slices.

7. Dip the slices in the buttermilk, then the dredge.

8. Fry in reserved drippings plus canola oil until golden brown.

9. Spread toasted bread with remoulade.

10. Place fried green tomatoes, 3 slices of bacon, and lettuce on the toasted bread.

Yield: 4 sandwiches

My Sister, The Tomato Lover

Wendy Kennar

Tomatoes make me think of my younger sister. She'd often reach into the refrigerator searching for a snack and grab a handful of cherry tomatoes, as if they were grapes. She'd ask for extra slices in her dinner salad each night.

Symbolic of our differences, I detested tomatoes. It's an aversion I haven't outgrown. However, I recognize that tomatoes play a key role in condiments and sauces that I thoroughly enjoy. Think French fries and ketchup. Spaghetti and meat sauce. As much as I might not want to admit it, the tomato is pretty essential to certain meals.

Appearances are deceptive, when it comes to tomatoes and my sister. On the outside, a tomato may appear firm and smooth. Cut it open, it's somewhat squishy and juicy with seeds squirting out. My sister was always tall and thin, and looked rather weak. But, she was surprisingly strong, and held onto my mom with a death grip when she didn't want to go into her kindergarten class. She looked sweet and innocent, with long brown hair and a full smile. At home, though, her anger took on violent tendencies, and I was often on the receiving end of her bites, her scratches, her hits, and her punches.

And I do think there's a parallel between the strained relationship I have with my sister and my dislike for tomatoes. In terms of science, we are sisters; we share common genes. In terms of reality, we have grown up to be very different women, women who don't consider each

other friends. She lives in the suburbs; I'm happy to be in an urban setting. She's a homeowner; I'm a renter. She drives a mini-van, purchasing a new one every few years. I drive an eleven-year-old sedan. She's on Facebook. I read books. She texts. I write. She's Coach. I'm Target.

For all our differences, though, there's no denying that my sister and I have shared some profound experiences. We participated in each other's weddings. I was with her for the birth of her first son; she was with me for the birth of my son.

I don't buy tomatoes on a regular basis. They're not a necessary part of many of my meals. And, I don't need my sister on a daily basis, not the way that I need my mom (my closest friend) and my husband. But, there are times when tomatoes are needed, such as when making spaghetti sauce. And my sister was incredibly helpful to me before I became a mother. Because my sister became a mother seven years before I did, she had some insight and advice to share, which she generously did. She gave suggestions about car seats and even provided the contact information for an expert car seat installer. I asked her about diapers and bottles, and she answered all my questions.

There's a general ambivalence when it comes to a tomato's classification: is it a fruit or is it a vegetable? (Personally, I consider it a vegetable, but the question remains open for debate.) This ambivalence extends to my feelings about my sister. On the one hand, she's not someone I consider a friend. And although we share a history, families do not always share a future. However, she is my son's aunt; the mother of his cousins. My son is an only child. His two cousins provide him with an opportunity to interact and play with two older boys, boys he has fun with.

As kids, my sister preferred tomatoes while I always opted for avocados. The two food items are very different;

it's not possible to confuse them. However, they do have similarities—they're both technically identified as fruits although some people consider them vegetables. They are both used as ingredients in guacamole and salads. They can peacefully coexist. But, tomatoes and avocados can also stand on their own and be enjoyed separately. Just like my sister and me.

Tomato Face
Rick Eddy

I was shy and bashful,

a pale-skinned redheaded boy,

so much so that the teasers, and even

friends, called me "tomato-face."

I didn't understand,

so somebody had to tell me that

when surprised or embarrassed, my face

got so flushed that

it was as red as a tomato.

Thus I learned the connection between

things as ubiquitous as ketchup and red sauce

and the rare involuntary excitement of my facial capillaries.

"Tomato-faced" is not such a bad thing to be—

who knew that identity would show in the

complexity of a blush?

Under Mother's Bed

Catherine Moore

It was at least three months after she died that we discovered the boxes under mother's bed. There was one for each child. My box originally held Waverley Wallpaper, at least until that was crudely X-ed out and renamed with thick black marker. Inside was a cornucopia of kid artifacts. Elementary school report cards, long-forgotten accolades, student handbooks, and artwork in the way of fingerpainted Pilgrims and Indians chasing down a handprint turkey. I cringed at the stacks of paintings. I laughed at the handwritten notes my teachers made, like my kindergarten teacher, "Lizzie has very good hygiene."

Deeper still was the three-dimensional treasure, clay paper weights, a jar of baby teeth and my Campbell's Kids mug. I won it in 1977 by collecting the most Campbell soup labels from family and neighbors, then submitting them in the schoolwide soup label drive. Rolled up inside the mug was a faded Kodachrome of my award acceptance, along with the dusty ribbon, and a wad of hastily torn soup labels pinched under a hardened rubber band. I suppose those were the few I forgot to turn in and then oddly saved in the orphanage of my childhood. The mug was white and red with gold like the soup mom served; steaming tomato soup drizzled with cream and crumbed with crushed Ritz crackers. I remembered the welcoming smell of that soup after we burst in the back door to shut out the snowy wind. And the way mother looked summer flushed in the

16

kitchen even during January. Her love was always food. A hot hug on a winter's day.

I looked for the 'Mother of the Year' card I made her. The matching headbands I had crocheted for us. I sighed. In the end, I recognized very little of my own relics. What of these things she chose to keep? Honestly, I was simply a runner in the Campbell soup label scheme. A patsy to others who did the purchasing, the preparing, the soaking, the shearing. So this was my great feat? Where was my science project ribbon or my first poem in the school newsletter? I wondered if the items we treasure are simply an accident of time and space. Created in that brief moment a busy mother gets to grab nearby objects and time capsule them away. It would be a mere coincidence if these snatched items represented the biography.

I placed the Campbell's mug aside and knew as I sorted items into an ever-growing toss pile that somewhere, right now, there's a mother placing childhood scribbles into a stylized tote from the Container Store. And somewhere a Mrs. Warhol wishes the child would stop painting soup cans.

"Lycopersicum"
The Black Rabbit

Tomato Surprise

Randall Lemon

Bright and early Monday morning Mort showed up in his dependable but beat-up old Ford pickup at Daisy's to take Henry out to the farm. Henry whined and dragged his feet saying he didn't want to go with Grandpa. But before Henry could launch into a full-blown tantrum, Mort grabbed Henry and threw him onto his Grandpa's shoulders. Startled and slightly out of breath, Henry forgot he was about to have a fit and viewed the world from his new perspective, taller than anyone else in the room.

Mort started out the screen door, onto the porch and down the steps to the truck. Daisy trailed along carrying Henry's bag of clothes and tossing it into the back of the truck while Mort secured Henry into the front seat.

Jumping into the seat next to Henry, Grandpa waved. "Goodbye, Daisy. We'll see you on Friday. Okay, Henry, prepare for *adventure*!"

Mort turned the key in the ignition, the truck sputtered to life and off they drove spewing gravel behind them.

Henry turned his head to see his Mom but she was already heading back into the house. He wondered what was going on. "*Adventure.*" The word stuck in his head. He had heard of adventures in the storybooks Daisy read to him in an attempt to get him to settle down for bed each night. Though he often paid little attention when his Mom tried to read to him, he seemed to remember that adventures could involve giants or wolves or geese that laid golden eggs.

"Grandpa, what kind of adventure am I going on? Will I have to battle monsters?"

Mort thought for a moment. "Well, maybe in a way. Did your Ma ever tell you the story of Jack and the Beanstalk?"

Henry nodded his head gravely, "Yes, that's the one with Giants who try to squish him, right?"

Mort looked very serious. "That's correct, Henry. And that is precisely the kind of adventure you'll be having. Do you remember at the start of story how Jack had to get the magic beans and plant them and water them and care for them before the beanstalk grew and he got the treasure?"

Henry was a little uncertain about this. Mom might have told him that part. But he was usually arguing and complaining about having to go to bed, especially at the start of a story, but it did sound a little familiar. "Maybe..."

Mort whispered conspiratorially to Henry, "Well, I've gotten some magic seeds. I'll give you some and I'll keep some and we'll plant them on the farm. I'll take care of mine and show you how to take care of yours. It won't be easy. Scary looking creatures might show up and try to destroy our plants before they can grow to the point where we can obtain our treasure. We'll have to fight them off and kill those scary monsters in order for us to save our defenseless plants. It'll take a pair of real heroes. I'm not sure if I can do it alone. But your Dad wrote me and said you had been taking care of and protecting your Mom. So I thought maybe with your help, we could make the magic plants grow and find the treasure at the end."

"Monsters," said Henry, his voice filled with awe. "Will we have swords and spears to fight them with?"

Grandpa scratched his head, "Well, unfortunately I'm fresh out of swords and spears, but I do have rakes and shovels we can use as our weapons. And I can even teach you some special tricks we can use to help kill off the monsters."

Almost despite himself, Henry found himself looking forward to getting to the farm and starting his battle to gain the treasure.

When Mort's pickup arrived at his farm Henry tried to tear open the seat belt himself. "C'mon Grandpa. Let's go get the treasure!"

"Whoa there, young man. There is much we have to do first to prepare. A knight doesn't go into battle without his armor, sword, and shield. Does he? We have to plan our battle first and we have to get the dirt ready to receive our magic seeds. March on into the kitchen and Grandma will give us some breakfast to build up our strength for the coming adventure."

Henry could hardly contain himself, but still, if he was going to have to fight a giant or dragon, he wanted to be as strong as possible. Grandma had prepared quite a breakfast for the three of them and Henry had to admit that he liked that breakfast almost as much as the idea of the adventure.

After breakfast, Grandpa got out a large piece of paper and a pencil and spread them out on the kitchen table. He called Henry over. "Okay, Henry. It's time we started planning our strategy for the upcoming adventure."

He drew some large rectangles on the paper. "This is our farm and these are our fields." Then he drew an x on one of the smaller rectangles. "This is the garden where we will plant our magical seeds. I will need you to personally handle one of our magical plants and I will handle the rest. Now, I want you to place a circle where you want your magical plant to be."

Grandpa handed the big pencil to Henry, who scrunched up his forehead and stared fixedly at the piece of paper. After a very few moments, Henry reached tentatively forward and drew a circle at the bottom right hand corner of the garden rectangle. "I think I want my magic plant right here!"

Grandpa rolled up the paper. "You have chosen an excellent spot, Henry. Now we must prepare the earth so that the magic seeds will take hold in the soil and grow straight and strong."

Grandpa led Henry out to a shed and started pulling things out and handing them to Henry until his little arms were full. When Grandpa closed the shed door, he had some final items in his hands. "These are the knightly gauntlets we will wear when utilizing our tools." He had one big pair of gloves and one far smaller pair. The pair walked over to the garden area and put on the gloves. Grandpa showed Henry how to use the rakes and spades and hoes. Then Grandma came out of the house carrying shiny new Henry-size examples of the tools.

"We got these special for you, Henry. These will be your personal weapons in the adventure ahead. You must keep them clean and shiny when you are done using them so they will serve you in good stead when you need them the most. They belong to you now," said Grandma.

Henry took the tools almost reverently from his Grandma. "These are really mine now and no one else's?"

Grandma nodded gravely to Henry, then turning slightly, winked at her husband. "I'll need to head back into the house and bake some cookies. I'll leave you men-folk to your adventure." With that she walked back into the house.

Grandpa showed Henry how to use the tools to prepare the ground, but he left the area in the lower right-hand corner of the garden untouched. "Alright, Henry, you go ahead and prepare the ground for your magical plant." Henry tried to do everything to his land just like Grandpa had done. While Mort worked, he kept an eye on Henry and offered him suggestions whenever Henry looked

confused or ran into a problem. Henry raked stones out of his garden plot and threw them away. He turned over the dirt, bringing the fresh loam to the surface. Then they watered the overturned earth. Finally they added plenty of compost.

Henry was fascinated and the time flew by. Eventually Grandma called from the kitchen that it was time to come in and wash up. "You two get in here. I'm going to need some help eating all these cookies. I made way too many."

So Henry and Mort went in, washed and enjoyed big glasses of fresh milk and Grandma's homemade cookies.

The week flew by and one day Grandpa said, "It's time we planted our seeds, Henry. Late February is the best time to help these beauties grow." He held out a small bag of seeds on which Grandma had sewn the word, "*Magic*." Grandpa opened the bag and dropped some of the seeds reverently into Henry's open hand.

"Grandpa, will these seeds grow a beanstalk?" asked Henry.

Grandpa shook his head and opened a book to a beautifully colored page. "No, Henry. Our magic seeds will bring us a different golden treasure. Instead of a beanstalk, our seeds will grow into tangerine tomato vines that look just like these."

The picture in the book showed beautiful large, round, orange-golden tomatoes. Dozens of them hung from the green vines which were held off the ground by a metal wired cone.

"After we plant the seeds, the battle will just have begun. We will need to water and fertilize them. We will have to keep weeds from trying to choke the life out of them. Animals will try to dig them up. A variety of bugs will try to devour them. It will be a constant struggle: you and I versus all of them. I cannot do it alone without you. Do you think you are up to this struggle?"

Henry felt a pang of doubt and disappointment. "But these just look like funny colored tomatoes. They are not really made of gold, are they? How are they a magical treasure?"

Grandpa closed the book and then opened it to the first page. "Do you see this name, Henry? That is your father's name, Drake Enright. This was *his* book and the tangerine tomato was his very favorite kind of plant. The magic of you growing this plant will bring your Daddy home safely. He will return and you will give him your delicious tomatoes, and once he tastes them, he will never want to leave you and your Mommy again. That is the real magic. We'll all live here on the farm together and one day the farm will belong to you.

In the following weeks, Mort and Henry planted, watered, and fertilized the tomatoes. Every seven days, they soaked the soil to a depth of four to six inches, and soon Henry saw the green start to sprout from the deep, black soil. Grandpa gave Henry a tomato cage of his own and Henry carefully wove the vine through the metal latticework to keep the leaves off the ground.

"Those tomato cages are like armor for your plant. Using one will lessen the chance of spreading disease and aid it in developing heavier foliage," Mort explained to Henry.

Twice they drove off rabbits that wanted to devour their plants. The cages were separated by about three feet so the plants got plenty of sun and one could easily see if the soil around them had been disturbed by some critter.

When Henry came home on weekends, Daisy was surprised by how much he had changed. He still enjoyed playing video games and watching cartoons on TV, but at the end of a day he seemed much more ready to go to bed without a fight, and he looked forward to the stories his Mom would tell him. Whenever Daisy asked Henry what he was doing at Grandpa's farm, he would get a twinkle in his eye and then in a hushed voice he would just say, "It's a magical secret that will bring us the greatest treasure of all."

The greatest threat to Henry's plant appeared in April. One Wednesday morning when Henry scooted out to check his plant before Grandpa came out, he noticed that some of the leaves near the top of his plants looked damaged, as if they were missing parts. He ran back inside the farmhouse and dragged Mort out to see. Grandpa inspected some of his plants and turned to Henry.

"Remember when I warned you about the monsters who would try to eat your treasure? Well, I think they're here. Kneel next to your tangerine tomato plant and turn the leaves over one at a time and let me know if you see any bugs."

The first few Henry turned over revealed nothing, but then as he turned a leaf over...

"Ew!!!!"

"Tell me what you see, Henry," said Gramps. "Give me a good description so we know exactly what it is. Then I'll know how we can best fight it."

As Henry stared at the creature, he realized that in a way, it did look a little like a monster.

"It's about three inches long and shaped like a caterpillar. It's green but has some v-shaped yellow strips on it and there looks to be a dark blue horn at one end. It's kind of scary-looking."

"Wait right here."

Grandpa walked into the house and moments later came out with two full buckets. He walked over and set the smaller one down next to Henry's plant. Henry could see that the bucket was filled with soapy water. Steam rose from the surface of the water so Henry knew the water must be hot.

Grandpa Mort turned to Henry. "We could use pesticides like Spinosad to try to kill these monsters, but I don't like to use chemicals. There's another way to kill them off, but it will require you to be very brave. Are you ready to fight for your treasure?"

This was the moment Henry had both looked forward to and dreaded. "Yes, Grandpa, what do I need to do, hit them with shovels?"

Mort knew that this was the moment-of-truth for young Henry. "You are going to need to check each side of every leaf on your plant and the vines as well. Each time you see one of the hornworms, you need to pull it off the plant and drop it into the bucket. The soap and hot water will kill the bugs. We'll need to come out here every morning first thing and catch them while they are still trying to feed. If that doesn't work, we'll need to come out here in the night with lights because hornworms like to feed between dusk and dawn. We need to do this every day until they stop feeding on the tangerine tomatoes. Are you ready?"

Henry looked a little sick. "You mean I have to touch these yucky, wormy things?"

"Yep," said Grandpa. "They may look ugly, but they really can't hurt you. And besides, you'll be wearing your gauntlets so you won't actually have to touch them. Watch me."

Grandpa knelt down next to one of his many plants and before long found one of the predators. He called Henry over and showed him how he pulled the bug free from the leaf and then dropped it into the bucket. "Okay, Henry. That's how you do it. Now you need to go fight the monsters in order to gain the treasure."

Henry walked back over to his tomato plants and knelt next to it. As Grandpa watched him, he began to examine the vine and leaves working from the top down just as Mort instructed him. Finally Henry spotted one of the worms. He stared fixedly at it for a few seconds but as he looked at the damage the creature had already done to the leaf, he made up his mind. He reached gingerly forward and tried to pinch the critter between his gloved fingers. His first couple efforts failed. He couldn't quite seem to manipulate the bug because of the cloth of the glove, but gradually, he got better at it. He finally pulled the creature free from the leaf, but then he dropped it to the soil and it tried to burrow away from him. Henry reached down and grabbed it before it could dig its way to freedom. He looked at it as it struggled to worm away from his fingers and then dropped it into the bucket. He couldn't quite make himself watch what happened to the hornworm once it was in his small bucket. He went back to searching for more hornworms. By the time he was done, Henry had found four more trying to devour his tomato plant. Then he went over to help Grandpa Mort who had many more tomato plants to liberate.

Finally after hours at their task, they reached the final plant. They straightened up and Grandpa took the buckets to dispose of the worms.

Tired, but happy, Henry said, "Well, we beat them, Grandpa."

"Remember what I told you, Henry. This was only the first battle of the war. We'll have to come out here just before sunset tonight and check the plants again. And we'll have to come out twice each day until there are no more worms and no more damage to the plants. Only then will the battle be won."

As they washed their hands, Henry managed a small grin. "I never knew there was so much work to being a hero. Did Jack have to go through just as much as we did?"

Mort couldn't resist a small chuckle, "Oh, yes, beanstalks can be even a bigger problem."

Not very long after they had seen the last of the

hornworms, the tomatoes themselves began to appear on the vines, getting bigger and heavier every day. To Henry, they looked like they were indeed made of shiny orange-gold. Finally in May, they were vine-ripened. They were firm to the touch and around four inches in diameter. The caged tomato vines had grown to a height almost equal to Henry himself. It stood about thirty-eight inches tall.

Henry wanted to pick the tomatoes. But Grandpa, who was privy to some information that Henry didn't have, said to wait for a day.

The next morning Grandma gave each of them a bushel. Grandma had written "Henry's magic tangerine tomatoes" on one of the bushels. After a big farm breakfast, they went outside and Grandpa gave Henry his last lesson, showing him how to gently pluck the tomatoes from the plant and which ones were ready now and which ones still needed to ripen some more. Henry picked the fruit from his vine almost filling his small bushel. Then he went on and helped Grandpa to fill his basket from the other plants. Henry was so intense he never heard the gravel crunching on the farm's driveway.

The two farmers picked up their bounty of fruit and headed into the farmhouse's kitchen. Henry was surprised to see his Mom sitting at the kitchen table with Grandma. Daisy had finished her first semester of college classes and had wanted to be present for the big day. She pretended to be surprised when Henry showed her the special "treasure" he had been working on all these weeks. Daisy *oohed* and *aahed* over the basket of Henry's tomatoes.

Henry picked one out of the basket and handed it to his mother. "These are special, magical tomatoes, Mom. Did you know that these were Daddy's favorite fruit?"

Daisy smiled broadly, yet there were tears at the corners of her eyes. "Well then, why don't you give him one?"

With that Drake stepped into the kitchen from the hallway where he had been hiding. His tour of duty was over and his enrollment was up.

Henry was stunned at the sight of his Daddy. He knew that the tomatoes were magical but he had never expected them to work so quickly. He grabbed a tomato from the bushel and leaped into his father's waiting arms. All of the time he had spent planting and watering and raking, chasing off rabbits, and killing off hornworms was now worthwhile. This was the greatest surprise he had experienced in his young life. It was indeed, a tomato surprise!

my prize-winning plants
plundered by tomato thieves
cannabis ignored

- *Tracy Davidson*

Gardening

Richard Koreen

Agnes slipped her wrinkled hand into a white glove. Mother had insisted a lady wear gloves on all occasions, not just on Easter Sunday when everyone wore them. Memory of past occasions tickled a giggle that bubbled to the surface. But perhaps Mother wouldn't have classified today's excursion as an *occasion*. She giggled again.

Agnes loved gardening. She walked down her apartment stairs and out through the security doors. It was a perfect day for gardening, not overly hot and yet not too cool. Agnes didn't have a garden plot, but regularly visited neighborhood gardens, closely following the progress of a few selected vegetables. She thought of each of them as individuals. Each was her special friend. "Oh Agnes, what a silly idea," she giggled to herself.

Agnes was off to visit a particular friend. Mr. McGarrity was a kindly, older man about her age and not too ill mannered, even given to moments of politeness. Mother would have approved. The friend she was visiting was his tomato. She lusted after the beefsteak beauty. She thought of cutting into the inviting flesh, the red juice spurting, pouring out. She smiled the smile of a fulfilled gardener, proud of a perfect item from the year's crop.

"Hello, Mr. McGarrity. Lovely afternoon."

"Yes, hello, Agnes. I only have a small plot, but look at what has grown. This cabbage is the best I've ever seen."

33

"Oh, you probably have favorites, all gardeners have their favorites. I really love the look of your carrots. Straight row, good bushy tops, they must be delicious." *But not as beautiful as that beefsteak*, she thought to herself.

Mr. McGarrity couldn't pass up a compliment, and besides, he liked Agnes. "Here, let me pick one."

Agnes really didn't like carrots; in fact she never ate them. Her eye was already stroking the tomato of her dreams. "Oh, yes, I'd love a taste, but not a big one. I just had a bite at home and I really couldn't take one of your prizes."

Mr. McGarrity's smile split his face as he picked his biggest and best. "Here's one, a middling-sized one, a Nelson carrot. Last year I planted Mokum. You had to dig them out, the tops just pulled right off. Now these are real carrots, pull 'em out by the top."

Agnes' eyes bugged and she forced a smile. "Oh, I'm so embarrassed. I have a small problem with one of my teeth. But that carrot looks so good. Would you mind if I took it home and cooked it?"

"No problem, Agnes. Here, take a few more." He pulled two, slightly smaller but still larger than any she'd seen at the grocery store.

"Now over there is my real pride and joy." His hand swung halfway down the tomato row to his prized Celebrity beefsteak tomato plant, the main stem staggering under the weight of Agnes' tomato friend.

"Oh, that is a nice tomato. I hadn't noticed it, maybe because my favorites are carrots. It looks quite big. Is it ready yet?"

"Tomorrow I'll pick that one. I've been watching over it all summer. Tomato fruit worms became a problem in early July. I don't like to spray, so I picked them off daily. Too little water could lead to blossom rot, but too much water will cause the skin to split. To boost the ph I added ashes. I've pampered it all summer."

Agnes walked up the steps to her apartment knowing she'd need dinner and a rest before going out again. She sat at the dining-room table and ate a small sandwich from a china plate. In her mind she was eating thick slices of beefsteak tomato bleeding rich juices into fresh Italian bread. Mother had taught her that eating properly didn't refer to nutrition. She dabbed the corners of her mouth with a linen napkin and rose from the table.

After her rest, Agnes pulled on a black long-sleeve 'T' shirt, overlapping a pair of black denim jeans. Gloves completed the encasement in black. She slipped outside into the darkness and disappeared.

Mr. McGarrity's garden was much closer than in daylight. Agnes' heart pounded as she crouched by the hedge. She reached up from darkness and unlatched the gate. Noiselessly she entered the forbidden space. The brightness of Mr. McGarrity's veranda light flooded the yard. *Thoomp, thoomp, thoomp*, her heart beat on the inside of her rib cage.

She scooted along, her crouched side rubbing the fence wire. Her sleeve snagged, the fence swayed, her shirt tore. Mr. McGarrity opened his front door and stepped out onto his veranda. Agnes froze.

He stepped over to the veranda railing. "Who's there?" He was looking right at her. "Who's that?"

Agnes knew she was caught. Her main concern was how to explain the ninja gardening outfit she had on. She lifted her head to face the most humiliating moment in her life. Mr. McGarrity turned away and went back inside. Agnes had stopped breathing, felt faint. She gasped in a breath. Her head cleared. She thought, *I can't believe I escaped.* She backed up slowly to free the sleeve. The prize tomato was inches from her nose.

Agnes slipped her hand into the white glove. She was heading out to see Mr. McGarrity. It was another sunny, good gardening day.

"Hello, Mr. McGarrity. Why so sad?"

"Someone stole it! My prize."

"Your carrots?"

"My tomato. I can't believe it."

"That's so sad. I know how much you cared for that tomato. Come with me. I'll make you a sandwich."

Agnes loved gardening, especially harvest season.

"Now I know this store-bought tomato isn't what you would have had, but it does have some juice."

She sliced into the McGarrity prize tomato and thrilled as the juices spurt and then ran onto the cutting board. She cut two generous slices and laid them on a thick slab of Italian bread. She thought he'd appreciate the exotic bread sandwich served on a proper china plate. The plate's green and red flower pattern accented the richness of the tomato. Mr. McGarrity managed a smile as he bit into the treat.

"You know I thought I grew good tomatoes, but this one has such rich flavor."

Agnes had trouble containing her giggle and just managed to reply, "Well, I guess it depends on where you shop."

Agnes' mind drifted to the firm head of lettuce she'd seen in Mrs. Hillory's garden. Maybe tomorrow a lettuce and tomato sandwich...

Spaghetti Nap

Peter Goulding

Spaghetti Nap, boys, we're in luck!
Oh, what a frabjous day!
Let's have three cheers for the cook–
Hip, hip, puree!

Note: The way my mother used to make it, Spaghetti Napolitana was spaghetti, mince, fried onions, and tomato puree.

Spaghetti The Wrong Way

Gerri Leen

The wrong way is how I learned to eat spaghetti: the sauce cooked into three-inch noodles, with lots of Parmesan—the grated kind, from the green *Kraft* bottle—on top. I never called it Mom's spaghetti or weird spaghetti; it was just spaghetti.

Then I went to a youth outing where they made spaghetti for dinner. Because it was so easy. You know, the real kind: a plate with a big heap of noodles and a dollop of sauce.

I ate it. The sauce was heavy and strong and so... present. Raw and thick and wrong. The noodles were like eating cardboard and so long, so unmanageable.

Ugh.

I went back home and told Mom about it. She laughed. Her way was the only way she knew to make spaghetti. Her mom had taught her. Her family wasn't Italian. She was Norwegian and Scottish and English. This was some strange form of Italian, but it tasted right, it tasted good.

I never tried to cook it when I was still in Seattle. Cooking was a pain, and Mom was close by. But once I moved away from home, far away, where Mom's spaghetti wasn't an option, I had to learn to make it myself.

I learned it's not easy, this spaghetti in a pan, spaghetti all together: it makes a holy mess.

But you're curious now, aren't you? You'd like to know what this wrong spaghetti is like.

You start with the meat. Or sliced baby eggplant if you don't want meat. You fry it up in a big pan in olive oil and onions and garlic. You don't want too much oil, just enough to get the job done, to keep the meat or the eggplant from sticking.

Once it's cooked—and it needs to be nearly done through, no thinking it will finish as you cook the rest—it's time for any other vegetables. Mushrooms—mom used canned; I use fresh—and maybe some plum tomatoes cut up small. They cook fast, so once they're looking ready, you pour over the sauce.

The sauce is pedestrian. It's low rent and it's easy. Tomato sauce. Ketchup. Red Wine. That's it. Pour it over the meat and vegetables. The tomato sauce first—probably two little cans—and then dump in some ketchup. You can tell this is scientific, right? It's all by sight and taste and feel. Then the red wine. Doesn't matter what kind as long as it's not something heavy or sweet—no port or sherry or dessert wine. A nice zinfandel works, or a cheap cabernet. Don't spend much money on this wine; you're cooking it away. In fact, any open bottle should do if you've got some older stuff around that hasn't turned yet. But it must be red because you want heart for this. You want something that can stand up to ketchup and not back down—even if I've always suspected the wine is secretly horrified to be included in this recipe.

You can add spices if you like. Oregano is good; I crush it in my hands. Basil's good, too. If you have some other Italian spice you like, that's fine. The first time, don't go nuts adding cumin or curry. You can play with this once you've made your first batch. Respect the tradition—and then shake it up once you know what you're doing.

Once the sauce is simmering nicely, and you've stirred it around and over the meat and vegetables, then take your spaghetti and break it up into thirds and drop it into the sauce. You want enough spaghetti to fill the pan, I usually end up using about half a box or so.

The first time you try to stir it into the sauce, you will make a mess. This is a given. Don't worry about it. You'll have plenty of time to clean as you go.

Did I mention this takes forever to cook and you can't leave it?

The sauce will cook down, and as you stir it occasionally, you'll see it soaking into the noodles. Don't let it get too dry at first if the noodles aren't soft yet. You may need to add some water with some ketchup and more wine mixed in. It's fine, really. Just pour it over and stir it.

Eventually, the noodles will become soft. This will not happen as quickly as it does in boiling water. You will get tired of stirring. You will get bored. You will want to wander away from the stove.

Don't.

You will have to try the noodles periodically to see how they taste, how the texture is. If the sauce tastes bitter, add more ketchup. If it's dull, add wine.

Eventually, it will taste right. You'll serve it with garlic bread, maybe. You'll grate a nice parmigiano reggiano—or be lazy and buy it already shredded from the grocery. Or be really lazy and do like we did back then, get that old green *Kraft* shaker out and go nuts.

It will taste pretty damn good, even if you do say so yourself. But you won't be sure it was worth all that work.

And here's the secret: it will taste so much better the next day. You'll put the leftover spaghetti in the fridge, and you'll heat it up the next day in the microwave, maybe for lunch, and it will be so good you'll want to cry.

And you'll wish you had more. I always do.

When my mother died, when there was absolutely

no chance of getting her spaghetti again, this became *my* spaghetti. I taught it to a friend because I have no child to pass it on to.

And now I give it to you.

Take good care of it.

And pass it on.

Fire and Ice Tomatoes

Catherine Moore

Salad:
6 small tomatoes, quartered
1 onion (any color), sliced
1 green pepper, cut thin strips
1 cucumber, sliced

Toss salad ingredients together in a large bowl; set aside.

Marinade:
3/4 cup vinegar
1/4 cup water
4 1/2 teaspoons sugar
1/8 teaspoon red pepper
1/8 teaspoon black pepper
1 teaspoon mustard seed
1 1/2 teaspoons celery salt
1/2 teaspoon salt

1. In a medium saucepan combine marinade ingredients; heat to boiling.

2. Continue to boil for 1 minute.

3. Immediately pour marinade over salad ingredients; toss well.

4. Cover and refrigerate for 2 to 3 hours, or until ice cold.

Yield: 12 servings.

Note: Recipe is adaptable to taste. Tomato quarters can be bite sized or slightly larger.

Personality Test

Sarah Doebereiner

"I have one last question. If you were a fruit, what kind of fruit would you be?" the woman across the table asked. She lounged against the back of her chair. I wondered if the posturing was designed to put me at ease. It didn't. It made me feel like a bug about to be crushed.

What kind of question is that to ask in an interview? What am I supposed to say? Think—think of fruits. It has to be a fruit. You need this job. Come on, Tiffany; you can do this! Fruit, fruit, fruit, I thought.

"That's a great question, may I have a moment to consider it?" I asked. My focus shifted to controlling my breathing. Heat pooled in my hands and armpits despite that extra strength deodorant with the dryness guarantee. My cheeks flushed with pale pink. The more I tried to push the color away, the redder they became.

"Sure," the interviewer responded. She smiled gently in my direction. The woman was at least ten years younger than me. Her skin smoothed without gobs of makeup to fill in the cracks. I smiled back at her. My lips tugged at the corners in a thin line that was nothing like her plump pucker. The edge of my grin sagged after a moment. My eyebrows crept together as I considered it.

I wasted two weeks researching the company, looking up sample interview questions, and rehearsing the most commonly asked queries. All of that should tell you what kind of person and employee I would be. Is she is making fun of me? Okay, Okay. Settle down. Positive attributes: wholesome, dependable, trustworthy—odd, anxious, doesn't fit in. Crap. It was supposed to be positive attributes, but really people find me abrasive, even acidic.

That's it! A tomato. Wait, is a tomato a fruit? I think it is. Arrogant people always say so because of the seeds. If she isn't smart enough to know that, then I'll look like a show off. She doesn't look very intelligent. If she knows, then we could laugh about it. That's me. I'm a stem growing, food pyramid misfit—who really wants this job. No, that will never work. What's the opposite of a tomato?

"An apple," I lied. Apples were sweet and beloved. This woman probably was the apple of the company's eye.

"And why?" The woman nodded through the same congenial smile.

"They are versatile and they go well with anything. Apple pie, apple slices, baked apples, cobbler, fresh apples, apple sauce, apple juice," I rambled.

The woman scribbled a few notes on my resume. We moved into the goodbye dance. She noted: questions, pleasantries, and when I'd hear back. That flawless, frozen smile reassured me. We shook hands. Her skin was soft and firm as a woman who had never held a menial job or worked in difficult labor.

I'm not going to get this job, I thought. She didn't say it. I didn't say it. It wasn't because I was older or underqualified. It wasn't my attitude, resume, or experience. I was a tomato, and no one would put a tomato in a bushel of apples.

What You Grow

Heidi Morrell

It wasn't enough that he was self-centered and selfish, sometimes Barry Cranston acted downright arrogant. Certainly his younger girlfriend Cherie knew this. They had an off and on relationship, which at the moment was off. Barry had passed the fourth decade with not much to show for it other than his skill as an electrician. He liked soccer and was a fairly good cook; in fact, that was what intrigued Cherie in the beginning, that and Barry's outdoorsy, thick haired good looks.

Often Barry would shop in the local organic grocery store to further his cooking endeavors. He frequently wandered the fresh produce section looking for inspiration, buying just the right plump tomatoes and fresh basil for his favorite bruschetta. That was where he came across an older arthritic woman, rather hunched over, rummaging through the Fuji apple section.

"These are good eating," she ventured to anyone nearby enough to hear. Barry glanced around for a friend, and seeing no one, he answered her.

"Yeah they are, and they're consistently that way. Sometimes the red ones aren't crisp, you can't rely on them."

"That's right, mister!" the woman confirmed.

Eight days later, Barry ran into the same elderly woman again, close to the red onions this time. He actually brightened a bit seeing her, surprising himself. This time, he

45

said the first words, "When I cook, I like to use the sweeter red onions."

"Me too, although I don't cook much anymore. I still just do mushrooms and onions sautéed, suits me fine."

"You must live nearby; I saw you here last week, right?"

"That's true. You're not gonna come rob me are you?"

Barry didn't know whether she was joking or not, and he felt tinged with what could only be called dismay. Barry offered, "No no, I live just around the corner from here; not so good doing that sort of thing."

"You never know." She looked him over fully.

"Let me tell you, the tomatoes look great at the moment, pretty sure they're hot house ripened."

They jousted like this for a few minutes, and Barry somehow felt he was defending his integrity, which he was. He thought of Cherie saying, "Sometimes you come across as a suspicious type."

He didn't want to come across that way with the old woman for some reason; to this charming lady with the intense orange-flecked brown eyes. Something compelled him to be understanding and gentle with this woman.

"I'm Barry, and you must be?" He had framed it wrong.

Not missing a beat she answered, "Well, I must be June!"

They chatted more and suddenly Barry said he'd be back on Saturday morning to buy ingredients in order to cook a special dinner for his girlfriend; for which he hadn't yet called regarding this, nor had he any idea if she'd be willing to anyhow. For an instant, he felt a wash of guilt that he had deceived his new acquaintance. But he did want to see the ol' gal again. That's why he awkwardly spurted the fib. Of course why would June return so soon just because he was planning to.

"Maybe I'll see you then, on Saturday," June pronounced.

On Saturday, that's just where June pushed her walker, the produce area of the Natural Foods Emporium. Barry spotted her reaching in the organic carrots, and after greeting her, she soon asked about his girlfriend: whether she had a job, a family, how long he knew her and more.

That someone was so interested in his doings warmed him, so much so that he found himself offering to give June a lift home.

"Well, I won't get in any car with a stranger, quasi or not, but if you'll take my groceries, the juice is heavy... I suppose you can follow me home, because I really don't have much, you know, by way of belongings, so…"

Barry followed her as she inched along the pavement pushing her walker, suddenly realizing the effort June had expended by just showing up at the grocery store. He was touched by this, and that guilt returned because of his earlier deception about his girlfriend and dinner. Maybe he was self-centered.

When they arrived at the small cottage, he immediately saw it needed painting. But what he didn't see right away was behind the house. She said, folding the recycled bags, "Here, let me show you something." She led him to the back door and opened it. Stretching out before them was nearly half an acre of land, only part of which was planted. A tiny vegetable garden of three tomato and three or four eggplants, a patch of flowers, mostly marigolds and roses, and some fruit trees dotted around.

"Zow," exhaled Barry. "That's a lot of land to use. Are those plum trees?"

"Yes and yes those are. Been thinking about this since the second time we met. You can see it's much more turf than I can handle, so, I was wondering if you want to plant some tomatoes, maybe some squash or melons. It's still early enough to plant."

"I could use some seedling starts," Barry agreed without realizing he was. "And come after work to water."

"The only thing I want for using my garden, is to come out here and pick some of your results." She winked.

Barry came over every day for the next month, planting, watering, tending. He relaxed and enjoyed himself chatting with June about nearly everything. He confessed about his not really having a date with Cherie, but June didn't mind. Instead, she encouraged him to call his girlfriend and tell her about the big garden. So he did call her. And right away she said how he wasn't sounding so tense anymore, and he told Cherie about how he met June and the big garden. Cherie exclaimed, "She's a good influence; I don't care where you met her!"

As Barry's tomatoes and yellow neck squash grew and ripened, so too did Barry's awareness of how other people felt, and his empathy blossomed like June's fruit trees in spring. But by late September, June had developed bronchitis, coughing so endlessly, it wore her out. It quickly turned to pneumonia.

Barry brought by extra blankets, and while he was there, he made her hot tea. He felt her forehead and knew she had fever. It rained and thundered, coming down in sheets. June looked pale and gaunt. "I think you need a doctor. Let me take you, there's a clinic on Spool Street not seven minutes from here." June grimaced and shook her head, coughing and gasping as she pulled the blankets higher.

"June, listen, I've used it myself." He didn't tell her it was for a migraine headache. But it did change her mind.

Eventually June got better from the medication but was never again as strong as she was before. Somehow Barry sensed this, causing his more regular visits.

He began to call her every morning, just a quick exchange to hear June's voice answer, "Hello, Barry, I'm a-okay." or "Hello, Barry, gonna rain today, torrents they say."

One morning in late February with heavy frost, she answered brightly, "I had a great night's sleep. Feel good for a change. Don't bother visiting today, don't need a thing."

"Good to hear, but I visit on Wednesdays."

"No need, dear."

But, Barry saw through this. He quit work early, eager to confirm his suspicions about June's cheeriness. He arrived at her house and she wasn't breathing. He called 911, and pumped her chest, blew in her mouth. But she was gone. After the EMTs took her body away, Barry drifted outside and sat in the big garden.

He had made a simple bench for June last summer, for her to gaze out on the tomato and squash plants and tangerine trees while he pulled weeds or watered, jabbering with her. But this evening, he hung his head, hands to face, and wept.

Torn from the Vine

David Elliott

If I smell a tomato
long enough, I always
land in that tiny
New York apartment
the year I was five,

teaching my father
to like them, the traffic
of Amsterdam Avenue
five stories below,
odor of exhaust breezing

through the kitchen window.
The rest of the building
is gone—stairs, hall—
was there an elevator?
memories unformed

as the half-jelled fluid
these seeds are suspended in,
with their fragile
thread-like connections.
Now tomatoes grow

in my backyard and I try
to teach my son to like them.
Look, how juicy! I say.
Dad, they're not done,
he replies, thinking of eggs.

Nothing is ever done,
I suspect, the only
tomato lover in my family,
as I slice again
to add to my sandwich,

memories and fruit
torn from the vine,
and eat my way back
to New York, juice
dripping down my wrist.

The Essex Street Garden

Wayne Scheer

On a warm Brooklyn weekend, near the end of the 1955 school term, Wayne, a skinny ten-year-old boy with glasses that kept slipping down his nose, heard a noise he had never heard before. He had grown used to the sounds of honking automobiles, whining police sirens and the calls of neighboring women hanging their laundry on clotheslines that connected like umbilical cords the neighborhood apartment buildings.

"Sylvie," a woman would shout.

"What, Rosa? You need something?"

"You got some talcum powder? The baby got a rash and Anthony don't get paid till tomorrow."

A few minutes later, Sylvie would call back. "It's on the line. Take what you need but send it back. My Sammy needs it for his feet." And Wayne would look down from his fifth-story window and see a cloth pouch hung by a wooden clothespin being pulled from Sylvia Kaplan's apartment on the third floor to Rosa Santini's place across the way.

But on this day, in the cement courtyard formed by the neighboring apartments, littered with fallen laundry, girlie magazines and who-knows-what-else that occasionally came streaming out of a window, Mr. Burman was doing something Wayne couldn't understand.

Mr. Burman was not only the owner of the apartment house, but he and Mrs. Burman were Wayne's adopted

grandparents. The Burmans' two sons had committed the worst sin children in the neighborhood could ever commit against their parents. They grew up, married and moved away, taking the grandchildren with them. True, they only moved to a Brooklyn suburb, but for the Burmans, who didn't drive, they may as well have moved to Timbuktu.

Wayne became their surrogate grandson and Mrs. Burman took it upon herself to fatten him up. She baked sugar cookies and apple strudel and regularly slipped him a brisket sandwich on fresh rye bread with a sour pickle.

"Don't tell your mother," she'd say. "On what she cooks, a boy could starve."

Mr. Burman, who wore his keychain and tool belt as proudly as a young doctor might wear a stethoscope, took it upon himself to show Wayne how to fix things, like a running toilet or a short in the electrical wiring.

"So what are you doing, Mr. Burman?" Wayne asked, watching the wiry old man with thinning white hair take a sledgehammer to a small area of concrete he had chalked out in the middle of the courtyard.

"I'm making a garden," Mr. B said.

"What's that?"

Mr. Burman looked at Wayne with a mixture of sadness and dismay. "You don't know what is a garden?"

"I think I do. Is that with flowers and stuff?"

"That's right, boychik," he said, patting Wayne's head. "But we're gonna grow vegetables—tomatoes and peppers." Then he handed the sledgehammer to the boy. "Here, you do it. I need a rest."

Wayne could barely lift the sledgehammer. Still, he managed to slam it against the concrete a few times before the old man took it back. Wayne could see large perspiration stains under the arms of the blue work shirt Mr. B always wore. Mud caked his baggy pants held up by suspenders. After a few hours, the patch of concrete was broken to expose rock-hard soil. "Now, for you I have a job. The burlap sacks I keep in the cellar near the wine barrels, bring them. We have to pick up all these pieces of cement."

It took the rest of the day to load the cement pieces into the sacks and drag them to the cellar. Mr. Burman made a place for them along the wall where he kept a rusted bicycle, pieces of pipe and other odd items. "They may come in handy someday," the old man explained. "You should never throw away."

The next day, he showed Wayne how to loosen the encased soil with a shovel. Later, they added sand, sawdust and horse manure from the police stable not far from the neighborhood. Something about the smell of the sawdust made the manure odor seem less unpleasant.

"When do we plant the tomatoes?" the boy asked.

"When the soil is ready," Mr. Burman explained. "What? You in some kind of hurry?"

The next thing Mr. B did was build a wrought iron fence around the small garden. He included a gate with a heavy iron lock. He gave Wayne a key and showed him how to open the lock. "Me and you, boychik, we got the only keys to the Essex Street Garden. You, I trust. The others," he slapped at the air with the back of his hand, "pppfffttt."

This was the only time Wayne could remember a compliment from Mr. B, directed towards him or anyone for that matter.

When the soil was ready, the following spring, they planted six tomato plants.

"Is that all we're growing?"

"All you need is tomatoes. Fresh tomatoes from the garden, not bought in a store. You have real tomatoes, you don't need treasure or peppers or eggplants. Pffffft"

Mr. Burman showed the boy how to fertilize the plants and how to weed the garden without getting too close to the plants' roots.

The vegetables never grew as large as Wayne's Jack-in-the-Beanstalk imagination, but for the next three years—until his own parents, too, committed the unpardonable sin and moved the family to Long Island—this would be Wayne's favorite place. All summer, he'd put on his old Brooklyn Dodgers cap, and work in the garden, often carrying pitchers of water from Mrs. Cusick's basement apartment. When the vegetables came in, he and Mr. Burman enjoyed tomato and pepper sandwiches on rye bread—with a little mustard and, of course, a sour pickle. A tomato never tasted so good.

A few years after his family moved to the suburbs, Wayne heard that Mr. B had passed away and later the old neighborhood was torn down and replaced with a low-income housing project, which was then torn down and replaced with single-family homes.

Wayne Scheer, now a man nearing seventy, with trifocals that keep slipping down his nose, still remembers the taste of the tomatoes he and Mr. Burman picked from the Essex Street Garden.

Garden Casual

G.L. Francis

Cultivars—fancy
word for what grows in gardens
of small farming towns.

Late planting—Fourth of July. There was no way to transport the garden from one state to another in a moving van. Dad dearly loves his tomatoes, and a year without any fresh from the garden is like a year without holidays.

He tills a quarter of the backyard, works a concoction of amendments into the sandy soil, then disappears. When he returns, Ol' Blue's extended bed is lined with flats of drooping plantlings.

Beefsteak—we know this
type; the rest are real big, big,
medium, little.

Scattered showers predicted, but the sky roils with heavy charcoal clouds. We're each handed a flat and a coffee can for watering in the plants.

The sky dumps a deluge, and our clothes plaster to us. Up the row, some of what we've already put in the ground starts floating.

Dad outshouts the thunder. "Make sure you use a full can of water on my 'maters!"

Soil, water, weeding—
experts say we do it wrong;
harvests say it's right.

Other people's gardens are more orderly than ours.

56

Grandma and Grandpa staked the tomatoes in their garden. Later came the cages for the bigger plants, but the little tomatoes thrived in barrel containers on the patio.

Our garden's first month or so receives obsessive attention to weeding. This segues into occasional watering when the weather's been too dry too long.

It doesn't matter. We'll live with overabundant harvest for months.

Ever notice how
Mom's eyes glaze at garden time
when she counts the plants?

The tomatoes are especially enthusiastic. Hundreds of fruits will be sliced, diced, stewed, sandwiched, juiced, dehydrated, pasted, sauced, and frozen as well as given away. Late tomatoes still green on the vine ripen slowly in brown paper sacks, but some will be baked in pies or crisps.

Trick or miracle?
Green tomato crisp tastes like
savory apple.

Preheat oven to 350° F.

For filling, combine:
4 cups sliced green tomatoes
(Use firm ones, not too juicy, and don't slice too thin unless you want slime.)
3-ish tablespoons packed brown sugar
(Honestly, Grandma, how do you pack sugar on a spoon?)
2 teaspoons lemon juice
2 teaspoons wheat or tapioca flour

For topping, combine:
3/4 cup rolled oats
3/4 cup almond meal or wheat flour
(If home grinding almonds, can add an additional 1/8 cup
very coarsely ground almonds for extra crunch.)
1/4 cup + 2-ish tablespoons lightly packed brown sugar
1 teaspoon cinnamon (more for heavier cinnamon flavor)
pinch of nutmeg
5 tablespoons softened butter

Place filling in 8" square greased baking dish. Cover with topping.
Bake approximately 45 minutes (give or take—until tomatoes are tender) in 350° F oven.
Can substitute a fourth of the tomatoes with baking apple slices for more apple-y flavor.
Can add raisins to taste.

Back to the garden—
vital autumn clean-up, but
will we plant next year?

The plants' stems thicken to sapling diameters, and their shoots intertwine into impassable tangles. Ferocious if they were thorny, but with effort, we can harvest.
And harvest.
And harvest.
By fall, we'll need hatchets and chainsaws to clear these botanical monsters.

Casual neglect:
ultimate secret to grow
trunks like sequoias.

I miss Grandma's little tomatoes. Because of them, I

learned the words *determinate* and *indeterminate*.

The red ones now available aren't so different from what she grew, but the yellow varieties have skins too thick and flesh too mealy.

The yellow ones she had were sweeter.

And fun.

Hey! Are you watching?
Don't let Grandma catch us 'fore
we eat our thieving.

The tiny reds are ducks, and the slightly bigger yellows make great shooters. Draw a circle on the ground behind Queen's huge doghouse. Best to play keepsies with little tomatoes. Just dust off each win with your shirt and pop it in your mouth.

Keep a sharp lookout. We'll all get a swat with the butter paddle if Grandma finds out we raided her plants. She has special plans for them.

Canning jars filled with
sweet saffron sunshine—yellow
tomato preserves.

The Ache of New Muscles

Holly Schofield

Julie gripped the base of the plastic pot and hurled another of the tomato plants down the hill behind the woodshed. The plant, complete with root ball and soil, landed at an angle on the compost pile next to the other broken-stemmed Early Girls. She turned away, fighting tears.

The northern British Columbia wind, howling last night throughout the late spring storm, had pushed her to the limit. She had huddled in bed, listening to the creaks and groans of the old cabin and the occasional mysterious thumps in the surrounding forest. By the time she heard the crash of breaking greenhouse glass, she'd already made up her mind to return to the city.

In the raw morning light, the metal braces and glass shards of the former greenhouse glittered under the huge fallen alder. She poked at a bent strut dispiritedly but didn't even try to rescue the smashed greenery underneath. A month ago, she'd painstakingly hammered together old windows from the recycle center, ending each day with aching muscles that matched her aching heart. As ramshackle as the greenhouse had looked, she'd been proud of it.

Now, only broken woodwork and glass, ripped plastic, and the miraculously-intact rain barrel remained. For the past seven weeks she'd nurtured the tomato plants, carefully following a gardening website's instructions.

She'd started them inside the cabin next to the warmth of the woodstove. Waking up at four a.m. to load in more wood had been a small price to pay for the growing sprouts. She'd moved them into the unheated greenhouse last week, as soon as the weather had warmed. Now, the handsome two-foot-tall plants lay dying and scattered on the gravel, their astringent green smell filling the air.

The website said that if more than two branches of a plant got damaged the plant was not salvageable. She picked up a broken pot and its wilting contents, preparing to make yet another trip to the compost pile.

The rumble of a pickup truck interrupted her thoughts. By now, after two months in her newly adopted community, she could recognize the sound of her nearest neighbor's rattling old Ford. Deb had driven the quarter mile at her usual breakneck speed and now the metallic purple truck barreled down the driveway toward her.

Julie lowered the pot and brushed potting soil off her hands as Deb screeched to a halt and climbed out. The ache in Julie's chest eased a little. Deb was now the closest thing Julie had to a friend and, today, she needed one.

"Just popped by to see how you lasted the storm," Deb said, in her usual almost-shout. The older woman wore embroidered Chinese slippers and a multi-colored poncho. A blue beret perched on her spiky white hair. She trotted past Julie, inspecting the remains of the greenhouse. "Shame, that. But glad the cabin made it through!"

Julie nodded. A few small fir branches had pattered down on the cabin roof but it had survived perfectly well. But then it would, wouldn't it? It'd been built by experienced craftspeople with years of experience, not by a born-and-bred city dweller like her.

"I know I should count my blessings." Her throat tightened and she swallowed. "It's just that, you know? It's the one thing I tried to do myself around here."

"You did a fine job. Can't help that particular tree falling. And we can trust in Mother Earth to help you revive the crop"—she took a harder look at the limp plant at Julie's feet—"or plant a new one."

No, she couldn't have predicted the alder crashing down, but she could have built the greenhouse stronger or in a more protected location or something. Maybe her ex-husband's opinion was right. She didn't seem to have the experience or the judgement to succeed at *anything*.

That might include living up here, where she knew nothing about the community or the lifestyle. Buying the cabin had seemed like karma at the time. It was sheer chance that the realtor had listed the off-grid cabin on the same day Julie and Tim's townhouse had sold. Her sense that it was "fate" had grown as the realtor enthused about the romantic look of the moss on the cabin's cedar-shingled roof. She'd taken out her checkbook when he said that the furnished cabin's price was *exactly* the amount she'd received in the divorce settlement from Tim.

She had to face it, her decision to move hundreds of miles from the city and purchase a cabin sight unseen was fiscally irresponsible and completely illogical. Even her new part-time job was a result of nothing more than a whim as she passed the hardware store's "help wanted" sign the day she'd driven up, the cabin's purchase papers on the seat beside her.

For once, as her life with Tim crumbled around her, she had wanted to go beyond logic, beyond common sense. And, now, that approach too had failed.

She had failed.

Deb must have seen the look on her face because she patted her on the arm, murmured something further about Mother Earth, and took her leave.

Julie stood watching the truck's blue cloud of exhaust smoke drift away on the breeze for a very long time.

The next day dawned cold and gloomy. Julie woke up with clenched fists and a renewed determination. She lay in bed and straightened her fingers slowly, planning her day—buck up the alder with her brand new chainsaw, stack it for firewood, then see if the greenhouse could be fixed. It was already early June but there was time, barely, to start seeds again and bring in a tomato crop before the short northern growing season ended. The seed catalogue sported some varieties with fewer "days to maturity", boasting rapid production. They should know what worked.

She re-read the chainsaw manual over breakfast. The steps to start it were clear but the starting cord required a terrific pull. When she'd first bought it, she'd managed to start it once after numerous tries, then had hit the kill switch, unsure what to do next. She was determined this time would be different.

Miraculously, the saw roared into life on the first pull. Julie braced her feet and touched the whirling chain to the first of the alder limbs. The teeth bit in and she focused on cutting a straight line through the thigh-thick wood. The limb fell into two and she let out her breath. Maybe she *could* do this.

She began to enjoy the vibration through her gloves, the spurting sawdust, and the growing stack of logs. When she caught a glimpse of bright purple flicking through the trees, she was almost reluctant to stop.

As Deb's wheels skidded on the driveway gravel, Julie switched off the saw and flexed her shoulders.

"Got you some replacements." Deb, clad today in red and orange, clambered into the back of the truck box and

swung an old wood-framed window over the side.

Julie stepped forward and grabbed it, sending paint chips fluttering. "Thanks, Deb. You're a true friend."

"Neighbors got to be friends here, not like the city, eh?"

They worked for a few minutes, unloading more windows, scraps of lumber, and scratched sheets of hard plastic, before Julie thought to invite Deb in for tea. Was she losing her social skills, spending so much time alone?

Deb plopped down on the old sofa "There's one more thing we have to do today." She hauled her large purple purse up beside her.

Julie set mugs and plates of store-bought cake on the coffee table. "I'm beginning to realize there's *always* one more thing to do, up here."

As Deb continued to rummage through the bag, Julie forked up a mouthful of cake. It was so stale it caught in her throat, so she hastily sipped the too-hot tea.

Deb looked up. "Shoulda done it the first time around. A settling ceremony. You know—for Mother Earth's peace of mind."

"A what?" Julie almost coughed again.

Harry, her new boss at the hardware store, had once made a comment about Deb "having a lot of raisins in her granola", and the other customers had given knowing laughs—all except Julie. Maybe this was why.

Deb drew out a long thin tool of some kind—a carved wooden handle tipped with a metal hook. That was followed by some clear pieces of Lego, a few glass-topped threaded fuses, and a computer ink cartridge. Her voice lowered as she leaned forward. "My grandmother spent winters up here in a log cabin without seeing another soul for months. She developed a theory that a new building, even a greenhouse, needs to be settled in the landscape, blessed by Mother Earth herself. The longer I live, the more I see her ceremony is as true and as pure as the first snowfall."

Julie didn't want to offend, but it sounded nuts. "Like breaking a bottle of champagne over a new ship?" she ventured.

"Exactly!" Deb beamed. "And more! It's science, really. The buttonhook grabs the rain down to the rain barrel, the fuses will lock in the earth's magnetism, and the Legos are the updated version of crystals—my own little modernizing touch since some of your next greenhouse will be plexiglass. Crystals attract sunlight in the precise wavelengths necessary, don't ya know. Grandma was a bit of a scientist."

Julie managed to keep her eyes off the cuckoo clock above Deb's head, telling herself that she needed to rest her muscles anyway and surely this wouldn't take too long. "And the ink cartridge?"

"Updated that as well. Grandma used a fountain pen cartridge—remember them?—and blotter paper. I figure the cartridge will increase your soil fertility even better. Now, give me your hand."

Julie reached her somewhat-grubby hand across the coffee table, hoping her reluctance didn't show. It was almost one o'clock and she still had lots to do.

Deb took her cell phone out of her bag and pressed a button. A high-pitched tune began to warble out. Was that whale song? Deb cleared her throat, pursed her lips, and burst forth with an accompanying chant—all nonsense syllables as far as Julie could tell.

The ceremony actually didn't take that long. Some waving of the buttonhook, a twirling of the fuses on the coffee table, a casting of the crystals as if they were dice, and finally, a black smear across Julie's palm.

"Don't you feel better now? I do!" Deb wiped beads of sweat off her forehead with the ends of her crimson scarf and took a large bite of cake.

Julie jumped up as soon as Deb started coughing. "That store-bought cake is truly awful, isn't it?" she said, patting Deb's back.

Deb's voice held laughter but kindness too. "It's fine, child. Don't fret so. Oh, that reminds me. I brought you a few goodies." She reached into the still-bulging purple bag and pulled out a few perfect cherry tomatoes and a wine-colored plastic-wrapped loaf. "The first of my Tiny Tim crop and a red velvet cake. Light and tasty as a dream. I'll give you Grandma's recipe next time I come."

Julie's eyes stung. "Thank you."

"What is it, child?"

"I can't bake. I can barely cut firewood. Gardening...I can't do *anything* people do around here. I think I better sell the cabin and move back to the city."

Deb snugged down her tasseled wool cap and shoved her ceremonial items back in her bag. "Nonsense. You just carry on carrying on and everything will work out. Besides, the settling ceremony will soon make things right again."

That night, alone in the cabin, Julie held one of Deb's cherry tomatoes to her nose, inhaling the heady scent of sunshine. The plump promise of rich flavor, the firm solidity that was a tomato—a true marvel. The little yellow seed had known what it was all along, trusted in itself, and flourished. She popped the scarlet orb between her teeth, bit gently on the sweet contents, and let the juice run down her throat.

Then, curled on the sofa, she had a good long cry.

At first, she resisted going over the last time she had seen Tim and the hurtful things he'd said. Finally, she allowed herself tread the familiar path. She relived his shouts, his childish toss of their framed wedding photo, recalling the streak of sunlight that had glared off the picture's broken glass after he had slammed their door.

Everyone had said that they were made for each other. He was a lawyer, she was a paralegal; they had grown up in the same city, liked the same movies, and could finish each other's sentences. His nasty streak had been well hidden.

This time in memory lane, it didn't hurt quite so badly. She actually smiled when she remembered Tim's distaste for tomatoes and arguments over shared pizza toppings. Maybe her heart was getting stronger. After all, like her sore biceps and abdominals, the heart was just another muscle.

She didn't particularly miss the noise and dirt of the city or doing eight hours of paperwork each day. Clerking at Harry's store would pay for her groceries.

The flames in the woodstove flickered and died as she mulled over her options. Maybe she *could* make it here. Finally, she fell asleep, her mind replaying Deb's pep talk over and over—*carry on carrying on*.

Julie carefully measured out the powdered fertilizer and added it to her watering can, stirring it exactly fifty times. It had been six weeks since the big storm and, between shifts at the hardware store, she had thrown herself into gardening chores.

Daily fertilizing in small doses added an extra task but if it helped grow the new batch of tomatoes, she was willing to put in the effort. She carried the watering can from the tap to the rebuilt greenhouse, no longer straining to lift the full can. She opened the door with her foot, glad she had hung the hinges properly this time around.

She paused for a moment to admire the green rows of tomato plants. Their warm musky smell filled the greenhouse as she watered the first container, a foot-

high crop of dwarf Tumblers heading into flower set. The gardening website said that, for this latitude and zone, early August was unusually late to reach that stage but her ministrations seemed to be helping.

The next summertime chore was to open the greenhouse vent, an old casement window, by propping it up with a broom handle. Funny, there was condensation all over the inside walls. She reached out a finger and drew a line on a blurry pane. Last night had been a couple of degrees colder than the night before and the wind was a little brisk today. She seemed to remember the gardening website mentioning that condensation on the windows indicated it was cooler outside than in. Maybe she should keep the window closed to protect her crop even though the day was already beginning to heat up and the weather prediction was for sunshine.

She stood a moment in indecision. It seemed wrong not to open the window given the bright blue sky but she had better trust the website—what did she know about gardening? She finished the watering in a hurry, not wanting to be late for her shift.

The sun was dipping behind the far-off mountain range when she returned. After hours of serving customers, it had been a major effort to stop half-way along her driveway for firewood; however, once she got into the swing of the axe, splitting the logs she had cut last week, she had enjoyed it. Her shoulders would feel the workout tomorrow but the full load of wood in the pickup would keep her warm this winter.

She parked and went to say goodnight to the tomato plants as the shadows lengthened. The glass walls were still blurry and the tall green rows of plants were somehow shorter than this morning. She stopped short in the doorway.

The tomato plants were all shriveled. Bugs? She didn't

see any. The windows ran with moisture and the air was stifling.

Suddenly it all made sense. The excessive heat had been unable to dissipate and the plants had fried. Just to be sure, she checked the gardening website on her phone. Yup, she'd remembered it wrong this morning. Condensation on the *outside* of the glass was a sign that the window was to be left closed. Water droplets on the *inside* were just the result of the greenhouse's overnight heat retention this time of year. She should have noticed that there was no morning dew on her truck's windshield. She should have believed her first instinct and opened the window.

When would she learn to trust herself?

In a sudden fit of anger, she picked up a trowel and hurled it hard over the woodshed, watching it glint as it tumbled end over end. She'd have no tomatoes this fall, other than the pink mealy ones at the grocery store. She might as well give up, just shrivel up like these tomato plants, dry of emotion and ambition.

That's what everyone—Tim, her old boss, her mother— expected her to do. Everyone.

Except Deb.

Except...herself. She squared her shoulders, feeling her muscles tighten against her flannel shirt. Her new muscles. If biceps could build, if a heart could strengthen, then maybe trust in herself was a muscle too.

It was too late for tomatoes but maybe she could grow some quick herbs, like dill or basil, and trade them for tomatoes from Harry's or Deb's crops. She would need that trowel.

A robin trilled a goodnight song as she picked her way down the slope behind the woodshed. The trowel was wedged in a rotten log, next to red globes that glowed as if they had a light of their own. The discarded tomato plants!

The ones that had landed upright had sprouted new leaves and new fruit, surviving on infrequent cold rains and the sunlight that threaded between the fir trees.

The tomato plants had settled in and trusted in themselves.

She stripped off her flannel shirt, shivering in her T-shirt, laying the ripe tomatoes gently on her makeshift carry bag.

Julie smiled at Deb's closing chatter and said goodbye, hanging up the phone just as the oven timer dinged. The homemade tomato paste, a refined essence of all that was good about tomatoes, had thickened up and browned nicely at the edges. She breathed in the rich smell. Deb's recipe had said to dry the tomato pulp in the oven for four hours but it looked done now at the three-and-a-half hour point.

Julie would trust in herself.

She set the pan on the counter, next to this morning's effort: a sunken and pale version of a red velvet cake. She hadn't yet mastered Deb's recipe. In fact, it seemed likely that Deb's hasty scrawl was missing some crucial ingredient that made it so rich and moist.

Julie poked the anemic-looking cake with a finger. She would try again, and again, until she got it right, or made it even better than Deb's version.

She scrawled some notes to herself, reminders of what to try next, and laid down the pen. After a moment, she added a scribble as she realized she could guess the missing ingredient.

Tomato Heirloom
Ann Hart

When I was a child
I ate like a child.
every fish stick, chicken nugget and French fry
covered in tomatoes pureed smooth,
mixed with sugar,
and forced into a squeezable bottle.

When I was a child
I watched as my grandmother
sliced beef steak tomatoes,
fresh from her garden,
on an old wooden cutting board
and arrange the slices
in neat rows
on her best china plate.

When I was child
I wrinkled my nose in disgust
as I watched my grandfather
eat a salted tomato slice
with a silver knife and fork,
as though it were a costly filet.

The cutting board is now mine,
and tomatoes are sliced,
For soup or salad or sauce,
Or put on a plate and sprinkled with salt
Enjoyed with a knife and a fork
While the catsup bottle stands
forgotten in my refrigerator.

Blessed Tomato Bandit

Sam Matteson

Luther Gnade knelt on the Bermuda-sod-hassock before the black loam altar he had built with his own hands. He removed his straw Panama from his grizzled, age-tonsured head and mopped his brow with his forearm. Gnade gazed heavenward through the green lattice and reached up to caress the nearest tomato with all the tenderness of a father stroking the cheek of his infant child. Luther Gnade smiled.

Glancing to the dog-run and kennel at the corner of the duplex, he commented, "A good start, Leo. The first fruits....I been waiting a long time for these Brandywines to come in."

Leo, a plump dachshund, stared back with watery, uncomprehending but expectant eyes. He dragged his stout middle across the grass as he scampered, yapping, up and down the fence, the way he always did when he greeted any being, human or otherwise.

As Gnade withdrew his outstretched arm through the tomato leaves, an invisible incense drifted upward. His smile broadened.

"You smell that, boy? Perfume!"

"Of course you do, Baby Long Nose!" Luther chuckled, in the falsetto-pitched register reserved to address infants and cherished pets. "It's the secret to real tomatoes. We will have them back now, the ones we almost forgot."

Gnade seized the heavy galvanized watering can

72

and murmured a prayer, "May these seeds bear true." He pushed down hard on the handle and gained his feet with an unconscious groan that could have been mistaken for "amen." Gnade shuffled the length of the foundation bed that paralleled the southern wall of the duplex. When he reached the kennel, he bent at the waist, and tickled Leo under his dewy-whiskered chin. From this doubled over position, Luther noticed a green tomato lying under the last plant in the row.

Gnade picked up the errant fruit and held it up to the morning sunlight to examine it with an experienced eye. "Those look like teeth marks."

"Did you see who did this, Leo? A deer? A rabbit?... No, your unending barking would frighten them away, for sure. You're a worthless hound, at least as a watch dog. You bark at everything....But you're sweet, aren't you, Leo, even if you aren't so smart." Leo yapped contentedly at the mention of his name.

Luther Gnade frowned as he lifted his gaze from the tomato in his open palm to survey the yard next door: a child sliding down her Tiny Tyke slide. A yellow sand box behind her. The woodlot beyond. He muttered to no one in particular, "a 'coon, that's it! Not a deer or rabbit. Probably slinked in last night. I'll get that blessed bandit, just like I got his brother, two years ago."

Gnade felt a buzzing at his right hip. Retrieving his cell phone, he peered at the caller ID with a cupped hand that shielded the screen from the glare of the sun.

"JACOB GNADE," it read.

Gnade double-tapped the sleep/wake button to commit the incoming call to message purgatory.

"Not now, Jake Gnade," he snarled at the screen as it went dark.

"Why did you have to go and behave so shamefully? Even when you knew how much it would hurt your mother

73

and me?"

But Jacob could not hear his father. They did not speak. Gnade shoved the phone deep into his overalls and headed toward the front of the duplex.

"Hello, *Schatzl*," chirped Maria, a diminutive matron clad in a blue house dress and yellow floral print apron. "Something the matter?"

"A raccoon visited the tomatoes last night. I wonder sometimes, what was God thinking when He made that masked villain? He didn't consult me."

"I guess it's true, 'Whatever does not kill us only makes us stronger.'"

"I didn't know that you were a fan of Nietzsche."

"No matter if it's big or small, truth is truth wherever you find it."

"Maybe so, but some things God permits make no sense to me. But I know what to do about a marauding raccoon! ...What's for lunch?"

"Tuna sandwiches."

"I'd rather have BLTs."

"Of course you would! I'll make 'em as soon as you provide me with some proper tomatoes," Maria teased, her gray eyes twinkling. "When will they be ready for picking?"

"In a week or ten days, I guess. That is, if I can keep the varmints from stealing them. I'll get the electric fence out after lunch before the rascal comes back tonight."

"Luther, Jakie called while you were outside. He said that he has been calling you and can't get through."

"That's right. I can't talk to him."

"Can't or won't?" Maria clasped her hands at her waist, her fingers interlaced as in supplication. "Luther, he wants to ask you to forgive him, I think. He can't pay back the debt he owes. But he wants for things to be right between you two. It's not good for you. I wish you could see how this is feud of yours hurts *you*...not to speak of his pain."

"That boy of yours is a prodigal...a...a thief! He has made his bed, and now he can lie in it! He borrowed that money without any intention of repaying us! How can he expect us to condone his deceit? He is lost to me! ...That's the end of it!"

A spark of fire flashed momentarily in Maria's eyes, but she said nothing. "Wash *yourself*, then." Maria continued without palpable emotion. Instead, she thrust her hands into the pockets of her apron. There you could discern—if you were looking very closely—her fingers curl into small fists as she stated flatly, "I'll have your lunch on the table in a minute." She turned and disappeared into the kitchen.

When Luther returned from the washroom, he sat down at the drop leaf table. His gaze fell again, for the thousandth time, on five Hummel figurines on the shelf. "Humble figures" he was fond of teasing his bride, especially the ironic glue-mended porcelain statue of a boy carrying a sheep on his shoulders. The limited edition Hummel, "The Lost Sheep," was one of Maria's most cherished pieces, shattered years earlier by the toddler Jacob.

Maria returned with luncheon plates, glasses of tea and cloth napkins on a pewter tray, engraved with archaic Gothic script: *Gesegnete Mahlzeit.* "Blessed mealtime, indeed," Luther's whisper translated.

"Will you say Table Grace?" Maria asked.

Luther nodded, folded his hands and bowed his head.

"Come, Lord Jesus, be our Guest/ And let thy gracious gifts be blest," he intoned.

Maria responded antiphonally, "O give thanks unto the Lord for He is good," as her family, the Kleins, had done for centuries—first in German, then in English.

"And His mercy endures forever. Amen," Luther replied

automatically.

The pair munched their meal in silence until Luther wiped his lips, got up and headed for the door. "Thank you, *Liebchen*. Delicious as always. I'm going to see what I can do about protecting what's left of the tomatoes."

Maria smiled. "Take some water with you, *Schatzl*. It's hot out there now." ... "Go on," she continued, her voice a quiet dove-like coo. "I'm okay. You know I can't stay upset with you, for long."

"A grace to me....Thank you."

Gnade trudged down the grassy alley between his and the neighboring apartment, dragging behind him the electrical fencing that he had recovered from the darkened tool shed. He halted abruptly. The cables, power supply, and stakes clattered to the ground.

"*Gott im Himmel!*" Gnade sputtered as he removed his Panama to mop the sweat from his eyes. "They're stripped clean!" He looked up and down the row. "Damn!" He lifted a branch. "Damn! ...Damn! Damn! Damn!" He shouted.

"Thief...felon, criminal, brute, miscreant...reprobate, ruffian...hooligan, hoodlum...tomato thug, trespasser, transgressor....Uh...God damn bandit!" He sputtered, winding down like the bell of a spent alarm clock.

Instantly guilt stricken, Gnade looked around, then skyward. "Father, forgive me. You know that I cannot abide a thief! Why did you let them rob me blind?" The sky did not answer. There was no sound but the cooing of a distant mourning dove. Gnade left the fencing where he had dropped it.

Maria, startled, looked up from the colander into which she had been snapping green beans, as her husband entered. "Are you okay, Luther? I heard a noise."

"It was me. I'm okay, I guess. I just received a terrible shock. How could those delinquents do this to me?" he whispered to himself. Looking over his glasses Luther

76

explained, "Somebody stole all our tomatoes, every one. Didn't leave a single one. Not one."

"Oh, Luther! How perfectly awful!"

All afternoon, until dinner, he sat in his recliner holding *The Tennessee Gardener* without really reading. Not even a supper worthy of a Bavarian farm house lifted Luther's spirits. After dinner he returned to his blind perusal of other gardening magazines while Maria read poetry in a warm circle of light.

The doorbell interrupted their mutual solitude with the Westminster chimes.

Luther rose from his recliner with an incoherent syllable, shuffled to the door, and peered through the peep hole. "It's the lady from next door."

"Well, let's don't be rude, *Schatzl*! Open the door."

Luther rotated the knob and swung wide the door. A young woman stood on the stoop in the dawdling light of a mid-summer's eve. Her eyes were downcast. A look of mingled shame, annoyance, and submerged anger played across her face. A small child, who was clad in Oshkosh B'Gosh overall shorts, a striped shirt and floral canvas Mary Jane sneakers, clung with one hand to her mother's. With her other hand the toddler steadied the handle of a plastic sand bucket piled high with green tomatoes!

"Hello. We're your neighbors from next door. Lisa, here, has something to tell you. . . . Lisa?"

"I'm sorry, Mister Neighbor. I didn't mean to take your 'maters. I'm sorry." She grabbed her mother's legs and hid her face, sobbing.

"Lisa, give him back his tomatoes."

"I'm sorry," the toddler repeated as she handed the dumbfounded gardener her sand pail. She lifted it with both hands and a grimace. Luther bent stiffly at the waist and grasped the handle. Lisa retreated to the sanctuary of her mother's skirt.

Luther stood holding the bucket in one hand, still slightly bent, inspecting the two foot tall penitent. He said nothing. He only stared, trying to comprehend what was transpiring on his stoop.

Maria stood on tiptoe behind Luther, her face floating near his cheek like a shoulder angel.

Maria spoke absolution. "Don't cry, honey. You didn't mean any harm."

Marie turned to Luther, "See how sorry she is. And doesn't she remind you of Jakie when he was a toddler? Look at that hair! Looks just like a halo even if it's a little askew." Maria addressed the sinner, "Run along, honey. You're forgiven."

"Thank you," was all Lisa's mother could manage as she shepherded her daughter down the steps to the grass-filled no-man's land that separated their apartments.

Luther nodded without a word. Luther closed the door and looked dejectedly at the bucket.

"Come now, Luther! Your precious tomatoes won't go to waste. I can whip up some Spaghetti Pomodori Verdi or green tomato salsa or maybe some fried green tomatoes sandwiches like Oma used to make."

"I guess you're right. I could force-ripen them in a banana sack." He looked up, sighed and continued, "You *are* right. I know you don't hear me say that much, but you *are* right....That tyke does remind me of Jakie, thirty years ago.

"You remember when he did the very same thing?"

"Exactly! I never understood why, though. Jacob never liked tomatoes like me. "

"But you were a grown man before you got the tomato bug. Remember that Big Boy you planted by the back door in our first apartment. It was so hot that summer. But the harvest was a beautiful thing. It was almost worth the misery of no air conditioning. After that you were hooked."

"Yes, but Jakie didn't think much of my tomatoes. I remember him sitting in his high chair dressed only in his diaper. It was so hot! I gave him a piece of tomato that he spit into the box fan and polka dotted the whole kitchen with tomato juice."

"Luther," she continued, "it hurts my heart so much to see you at odds with our only son. Can't you at least talk to him? He so wants to be reconciled with his father.'

"I'll think on it. That's as far as I can go....I once told Pastor Clausen that, in my house, my conscience wears a yellow apron. It's still true." Luther smiled wanly and kissed his wife on the forehead. "I love you, *Liebchen*."

"So that tiny scoundrel was my tomato bandit? I would never have guessed. She looked so innocent. I had hoped to propagate those heirlooms, not just eat them. I suppose that's impossible, now. They are lost."

"I'm so sorry, *Schatzl*."

"Let's turn in. I'm worn out."

Placing her hand on his arm Maria cooed, "I love you, husband. Maybe you'll feel better after a good sleep."

The morning dawned bright and humid. It was going to be another hot day. Luther ambled to the kitchen to cook the coffee, a ritual of devotion he had performed every day since their honeymoon.

Over coffee and small hard rolls of "first breakfast", Maria inquired, "How did you sleep, *Schatzl*?"

"Terrible. I had the worst dream. You remember the Trinity Church that we visited three years ago?"

"The one near Heidelberg . . . with the gorgeous altar?"

"Exactly! In my dream a crowd plucked tomatoes that grew somehow in the nave. They started throwing them at me. I dodged for a while but they finally hit me. It made me so mad that I picked a huge, red one and threw it. But I missed the mark and it mashed into the cross above the altar. The juice oozed down like Christ's blood. Then Jesus looked at me with such sad eyes. It was so real. I felt awful. I was so ashamed."

"It was only a dream, Luther. Sometimes a dream is only a dream...."

"Maybe you're right but I don't know....I don't know," her husband muttered. After a moment he continued, "Maybe I'll go out and water what's left of the heirlooms. It will be hot soon."

"The fresh air will do you good."

Gnade opened the door to greet the yellow light of early morning. He picked up the watering can and opened the door to step out, but then repented and returned to grab the empty sand pale. He descended the stairs, one step at a time. Stopping at the spigot on the corner of the house to fill the can, he proceeded to the sun-lit side yard. Moments later Lisa wandered over from the sand box.

"Hello doggie." The toddler sang in a sweet soprano.

Leo barked, ran around in a circle, and barked again. Lisa giggled.

"His name is Leo. I think he likes you."

The visitor turned toward the green vines that rose beside the house and with a pink finger pointed, "Pretty flower!" She spoke with a mock stern voice and held up her open palm like a policeman stopping traffic, "We don't pick Mister's flowers....No!...No picking!" Luther Gnade heard the echo of a toddler's exasperated mother.

A single Gabriel-horn flower, indeed, graced a distal Jesse-shoot. It stirred in a gentle breeze as if it were preparing to proclaim a second coming. "Why dearie, you are right! If we take good care of it, that pretty flower may grow up to be a juicy tomato and make other tomatoes."

"You like tomatoes?...I bet you do." Luther chuckled. "Would you like to help me water them?"

Lisa ran up and placed a tiny, tender hand on the handle of the watering can beside the wrinkled, sun-spotted grasp of the master gardener. Luther Gnade smiled at his blessed tomato bandit.

Glancing upward, Luther commented as if the toddler could understand, "Maybe we can all start over, even if we miss the mark and can't pay back our debts. Maybe that flower says so....When I finally see God, I must ask Him," he added like a verbal memorandum to himself.

"That's enough water on that plant, honey."

"Here, dearie. Here is your sand pail. Why don't you go play in your sandbox?...Bye-bye." Luther Gnade smiled again as Lisa skipped across the yard and turned her head to wave a benediction just before she rounded the corner.

Arising, Luther Gnade retrieved his phone from his hip pocket and tapped out a number. "Hello, Jacob. This is your Dad. I'm sorry that we haven't talked. I've had a lot on my mind. Is it a good time to talk now?" Luther said, as he too turned and started off again in the opposite direction.

Tomato Paella

Heidi Morrell

1 cup cut up, cooked chicken thighs
3 medium cooked & sliced spicy sausage, (use spicy turkey if counting calories)
2 to 3 tablespoon olive oil
1 big Bermuda onion chopped
2 to 3 stalks celery chopped
4 to 5 cloves fresh garlic
16 small (or 10 large) uncooked cleaned shrimp
1/2 cup white cooking wine
2 cups chopped vine ripe tomatoes (with or without seeds)
2/3 cup white raisins (optional)

3-4 cups cooked rice (1 cup uncooked), use brown if possible, or whatever suits.

(In rice water use 2 chicken bullion cubes or half broth to make the rice richer, more flavorful.)

Spices:
1 teaspoon cumin
1/2 teaspoon fresh or ground rosemary
2 pinches of saffron
1 1/2 teaspoon mild chili powder
Salt & pepper to taste
Hot chili flakes (optional)

1. In a large skillet (iron preferably), cook the spicy sausages and drain.

2. Using the same skillet, heat olive oil over medium/high heat, for 2 min.

3. Add chopped onion, celery, garlic. Sauté & stir for 3–4 min. or until soft.

4. Add shrimp, cutting the big ones into thirds.

5. Heat a couple minutes, add wine and spices. Stir & toss this, don't mush.

6. Lower heat to medium/low.

7. Add sausage, chicken, tossing gently, then add tomatoes. Should smell pretty good by now!

8. Stir as you heat through.

9. If adding raisins, add them to skillet and toss all, right before serving.

Serve over a shelf of rice on a handsome platter with lemon wedges. Add a green salad, white pinot and voila!

The Aztec Thief

Sarah Susanna Wood

The dark black rows are planted with maize. It is not yet germinating. Neither are the arrowheads. Standing in one row, I breathe in the pungent smell of the upturned soil that fills my nostrils. I am looking for arrowheads, advised by a boy I know, that arrowheads are always in recently plowed fields, at least in the South. And he is very Southern. I haven't found any and have been at it all morning. The silver Aztec medallion which I never take off is swinging aimlessly from my neck. That boy is on my mind, the one who tells me how he stops his car to search a plowed field and comes up with a handful of arrowheads. My brow furrows in consternation.

Maize is a regular crop in this field, right next to my grandmother's butter yellow house and its pristine white picket fence. Here in the field, with the light breeze on my face, I am engulfed by the smell of the freshly turned soil. Loose, fragrant, and covering the occasional pink earthworm.

Then, I look at my feet and they feel different to me. Peering down, they seem smaller and browner, toes gripping the loosened blackness. I am standing in a field of maize but it is not the same one; rather, it is on a hill. Holding a handful of round yellow tomatoes, I look across the field of maize that surrounds me, back at the plot of tomatoes I have just come from, scanning for anyone who might have seen me. No one is there. The sky is a beautiful amethyst wash. The sun has just come up this second. It only takes a second or two. The golden orb radiates a bright yellow aura that comforts me. I love to be awake to see it. No one has seen me this morning—I usually come just before light. I hide in the tall maize, my little hands maybe five years old. This is breakfast. I pop a tomato in my mouth and feel it burst between my small teeth. No one appears on the horizon. Then I see two brown figures in the valley below, their dark heads bent over a crop. I feel alone, so I sit with my prizes, watching the antlike people as they work. It's a long way I have walked, worried about my hurt foot. I have never owned shoes. Listening for a while to the whisper of the maize calms me down—the sound caresses my ears with a promise of what I don't know—something, something good. I plop the saved tomatoes into a pocket I have sewn on the inside of my thick huipil, which I am determined not to overload. The four ears of maize I have gathered will be ground into corn meal later. My mother would have been proud of me. I feel important to someone. He is all I have, my little brother.

Next to my grandmother's house, I stand looking at the fence. It wants to shelter us from the world. I touch my medallion with one hand, reflexively, and in the other I hold an arrowhead, a caramel-colored triangle, with chipped and filed edges, and feel the anchoring, to this land, to the Earth, to its people.

Note: The word "tomato" is from Nahuatl, the language of the Aztecs of Mexico and Mesoamerica, and was incorporated into Spanish and then other languages around the world. Today 1.5 million people speak Nahuatl, mostly in the mountains of the central states of Mexico.

Tomato High Priestess

Violet Nesdoly

She had her tomato liturgy memorized
knew by heart all the articles of faith
how you seeded them indoors
six weeks before the last frost
moved the neophytes into the garden
when soil was warm, sunlight glorious.

She watered them religiously
from the bottom
and had her own ideology
of pruning and tying
sprawling and caging.
Her credo of cutworm collars
assured them all salvation.

In the evening they had sweet communion.
As she picked plum, grape, and cherry
their leaves and stems anointed
her hands and arms with their incense.
She fingered the fruits like rosary beads
before popping them into her mouth.

Already in August her kitchen
was font and altar
for tomatoes and toast
tomatoes and cheese
tomato salad, tomato soup.

And how those nightshade fruits
those luscious love apples
answered the prayers
of an empty pantry
filling it with jars of canned tomatoes
bottles of ketchup, jugs of relish
stocking its freezer full of tomato sauce.

My mother was a superior
tomato high priestess
though she never did
convert me to the faith.
I remain agnostic
after several heartbreaking
summers of tomato blight.

Sun-Kissed Tomatoes
Katie Irish

My father taught me how to garden in our tiny 4 x 12 backyard garden, nestled next to the concrete foundation of our 1891 Victorian home. Each spring, as he'd prepare the lawn for a new season, clearing out broken pieces of bark and tree limbs, he also use a metal rake and comb through the stony 4 x 12 patch preparing the soil for a new season.

"Come on, Kates," he'd say "It's time to plant the garden. Remember to wear some old sneakers."

I have no recollection of ever telling my dad I wanted to garden. Surely I admired all of Granny and Boppa's immense, beautifully manicured and varied gardens, loved and tended to by Gram, Boppa and Aunt Helen. Helen would plant flowers (some geraniums, some pansies, come fall some marigolds), but all I remember in Helen's small corner garden was that haunting statue of St. Francis. St. Francis seemed to stare at me all the time, as I danced through the backyard in pigtails and a swimsuit or swang on the tire swing.

The strawberries in Granny's strawberry garden were the sweetest, most delicate, delicious strawberries I ever tasted. She also tended to the large flower garden, positioned diagonally across from St. Francis. This garden was made complete with the shiny, green garden globe proudly situated in the center of the large white rectangular quartz stones built around the garden.

Out of the three, Boppa was the true gardener. He would grow gorgeous begonias from seeds, caring for them as a mother cares for her infant baby. Once they had grown from seedlings into an exquisite flower, large enough to plant, he would nestle each comfortably into baskets that would hang and sway on the front porch for all to admire. When driving from the suburbs, as the coolness of the country air washed over our suburban skin (my mother would open the window, air conditioner on or not and say, "Smell that fresh country air", then close her eyes and sigh), Boppa could be spotted on his front porch immersing his delicate begonias with the long nozzle of his spray watering can.

Then there was his vegetable garden. Peas, lettuce, eggplant, squash, corn, peppers, pumpkins and anything else he could plant in that large sun-soaked piece of land across from the raspberry bushes. I remember the richness of the soil, how dark and moist it was and how *good* it smelt (yes, this was dirt that actually smelled *good*). On Sundays, after the family surrounded the antique dining room table, extended by the large piece of plywood when the entire family gathered, and after filling ourselves with one of Gram's extravagant meals she effortlessly made in the smallest kitchen ever with no dishwasher, Boppa would take us out to admire his garden.

So when my father told me it was time to plant the garden, I obliged. He would purchase seedlings from Leon, the local gardening guru of Woodland Gardens, along with some flowers to plant in front of his parents' grave. I accompanied him on these melancholy trips to the cemetery. I felt I had to be respectful, bow my head, remember all the words to whatever prayer dad decided to say in front of the grave (usually Hail Mary), and console him when he began to cry, as often he did. After the flowers were planted and a prayer was said, we were off to plant our garden.

We started with tomatoes. Beefsteak, Big Boy, some cherry, some plum. Nothing too exotic, just a basic tomato garden so dad could enjoy the ripeness of this summer fruit from his own backyard. These early summer weekend morning, usually just before Memorial Day and always a Saturday, were enchanting in their own right with the coolness of fresh summer air against our skin, sounds of birds flying tree-to-tree as the sun shone down, and was made to feel even better planting tomatoes with my dad.

Our whole process never took more than twenty minutes or so, the two of us working opposite sides of the small garden, tilling the soil and planting the seedling. I remember how dad use to pour water in with the seedling as the earth was peeled back, just to tightly pack dirt around it. He would do that for each plant until we were done.

"That's it?" I would ask.

"Yup. That's all there is to it," was always the reply.

As the summer weeks stretched on, I would regularly check in on the tomato garden. I would weed and would bang thick wooden stakes next to each plant when they had grown tall enough and were in need of assistance staying straight. I would carefully, using old towels cut into ruler-length, slim pieces, tie the green stem close to the stake with the cut towel slices to ensure the plant would not fall and would stay straight. The payoff was always worth the effort. I would be tickled to find small white flowers with yellow centers burst into a tiny green bud, then stretch its way into a delicacy, changing from a small green grape to a bright red globe. I would tenderly grasp each fruit, knowing it was truly ripe when it would fall into my hand without a struggle. Proudly, I would harvest these precious gems, slice into thick red pieces, pair them with wedges of fresh mozzarella and pieces of basil to share as a side-dish with my family at dinner. "Are these garden tomatoes?" dad would ask with a mouthful of meatloaf still dissolving in his mouth. "They sure are!" I would reply, arching my back to sit up even straighter and smiling, proudly.

As years went on, the gardens of my summer days changed. I expanded in that small garden behind my childhood home from just tomatoes to tomatoes, peppers and herbs, always basil and oregano and mint or dill or a little something. I found I loved tending the soil, the peace and quiet of the yard, sun at my back as I would tuck each plant tightly into the soil, as dad had showed me.

When I lived in upstate NY, I had the largest garden I've ever had. There was lettuce, eggplant, peppers, corn and the ever-present tomatoes. This time I knew I wanted to grow different varieties of tomatoes: yellow, heirloom, plum, grape. The tomatoes did well, as did the rest of the garden (minus one or two corn plants that were divulged by a nighttime critter).

I remember when a dear friend from high school, visited from CA for a weekend. We harvested several tomatoes along with a healthy amount of basil and oregano, and we made a delicious sauce straight from the garden, the freshest sauce I ever had. Pouring it over pasta and enjoying some red wine, I knew we made a sauce both our Italian grandmothers would have been proud of. When I lived in a studio in a small city, I had no space to garden and thought of renting a plot. Instead I realized my boyfriend had a lovely porch with a tremendous amount of sunlight pouring in on three sides. I saw incredible potential. One afternoon on my hands and knees, I cleaned the porch with soap and warm water, swept the floor and scrubbed the windowsills. Next I needed flower boxes. That weekend, we went out and purchased four dark wood flower boxes. I thought they were lovely. Our own little greenhouse. I opted to go only with herbs, as I had space limitations, and chose lavender, sage, patchouli, dill, thyme and of course basil and oregano. In a last minute decision, I purchased a fifth wooden flower box and added strawberries, the needed rubicund to my tiny green porch garden. I would get concerned when my Siamese would saunter towards the porch and nestle herself in the corner between two flower boxes, but never did she so much as sniff an herb (uninteresting to her, as was the rest of the world).

The garden did well. Late spring, I harvested all my basil (I had been growing it for weeks knowing how hardy basil is) and made a delicious pesto that I stretched to last two meals (I could eat pesto by the spoonful). I still felt a bit at a loss not growing tomatoes. Farm stands in the city are few and far between, but when I found one, I would hover over the round red jewels deciding which one to touch. I typically chose a slightly firmer fruit so I could watch it ripen before my eyes.

The succulent smell and luscious feel of a sun-warmed tomatoes continues to bring back memories for me. From wandering through Granny and Boppa's garden to sitting under the moonlit sky in NY feeling the energy of my own garden amidst the darkness, and of course the tender, cherished memories of gardening with dad. It is wonderful to stroll through the gardens in one's life on any day.

A Report on the Church's Canned Food Drive, That Box in the Corner by the Plastic Tree
John Pierce

God-given light
of the sun,

tomatoes
diced with a pique
of oregano,

14.5 ounces
of blessing.

This can,
faith like
a mustard seed...

no more spinach,
please.

Heirloom

Karin Britt Gall

Ray Strawser ran his fingers through his greasy hair and patted at his wrinkled jeans and red wool shirt. He shivered in the cold early spring morning. He'd had a coat once but someone had stolen it. The thief had been a transient that the rest of the group had driven out of the encampment. They might be homeless, but there was a code of honor.

Ray folded the blankets from his bed and stored them in the huge plastic bag that he had scored from a Lowe's garbage bin. He scooted to the far end of the makeshift lean-to he'd fashioned from a royal blue tarp. It covered a couple of large cardboard boxes which had once held refrigerators. The entire thing was attached to an old abandoned building in the homeless quarter. The building helped cut the wind, but it was still freezing.

Using a manual can opener he'd kept from the kitchen of his last apartment, he opened his last can of pork and beans. Not much of a breakfast, but it was nourishing and would last until he got something at the soup kitchen at lunch. Sometimes he wondered how the heck he'd gotten into this situation and how he could get out. Everything had gone well until he'd lost his job and ran out of unemployment and 401K. After the bank had foreclosed on the house, his wife Anna had thrown up her hands in disgust and left him. "I'm not supporting you," she'd said. Luckily they'd had no children.

He'd looked hard for a job. He didn't have a college education, but he was clever with his hands. He fixed the machinery and refrigeration units at a packing plant for 20 years and was proud that he'd kept them in working order. The foreman had tears in his eyes when he'd laid him off. "The plant's going to close," he said. "Those new owners have won."

"Maybe we could get a job with them," Ray said.

"Not likely," the foreman said. "They're located in Texas, and they have all that cheap labor there."

In a haze, Ray had signed paperwork for his last check to be deposited to his account and cleaned out his locker.

He'd thought about going to see his grandfather, but the old man was barely making it on his own. Ray refused to be a burden to anyone. He was able-bodied and intelligent. Surely someone would hire him. He wasn't an extremely religious man, but had seen his grandfather pray every day. Grandpa had prayed over the crops in the small farm that he owned and over every meal. Now, that Ray was homeless, prayer had become more important in his life too.

Ray had half the can of beans eaten, when someone voiced a "Knock knock. Hey, you in there, Ray?"

Since none of the makeshift enclosures had doors most of the inhabitants of the camp had devised a verbal code so that they didn't step on each other's privacy.

"Come on in, Hal," Ray said recognizing the voice. The front flap of the enclosure moved aside and a gray-haired man, with long lanky hair and bloodshot eyes bent over to enter. His eyes lit on Ray's food and with an embarrassed laugh he said, "Oh, you're eating. Lucky you. I'll come back later."

"No, Hal, here, I've had plenty. You eat the rest. I've got another spoon here somewhere."

"No, no way."

95

"Please, I'll be okay. You've shared with me in the past. Helped me out." Ray scooted over to the corner of the enclosure and grabbed a spoon. He handed the spoon and unfinished can of beans to his friend who took it with shaking hands.

"Thanks, man."

Ray looked away and re-straightened his pile of blankets in their plastic container while Hal ate the beans with a gusto born of a man who probably hadn't eaten since the previous day.

"I came to tell you to grab your cup. Fred's making some coffee. He found half a can of it in a garbage can."

"Aw, thanks." Ray grabbed his cup and followed the other man out of the tent. The coffee was probably as weak as tea, but Ray was grateful for the sharing attitude that some of the old timers practiced. In the past year, Ray had found that some of the most spiritual people in the world could be found among the homeless.

At lunchtime, Ray walked quickly up Fourth Street to the soup kitchen at St. Cecilia's. He waited in line, slapping his arms moving to and fro in an attempt to keep himself warm. Some of the others with coats did the same sort of jog and dance.

As soon as he got to the serving table Jane greeted him warmly. "Ray, boy am I glad to see you."

"Glad to be here," Ray said with a smile watching Jane put food on his plate.

"Don't leave after you eat. I've got something for you," she said.

"That old refrigerator giving you trouble again?" Ray asked. He'd fixed it for her a couple of weeks ago. He'd told

her what part it had needed. Then, he'd installed it after the part had arrived. Ray had been glad to be useful, and the church had let him hang around out of the cold longer than normal.

"Nothing like that. Something else," she said insistently, slapping mashed potatoes and green beans on the plate of the man behind him. "It's important, I think."

"Okay," he nodded, then joined a group of men at a long table in the corner of the church basement and slowly ate and savored his lunch. From the rest of the group, he learned that a nearby thrift shop had announced a coat give away to the poor.

"Summer's coming, got to get them shorts and t-shirts out," the man said, with a toothless grin.

Ray got up from the long wooden table and thanked the man, intending to walk to the thrift shop and stand in line so he could grab something warm. He took a deep breath before heading through the door out into the cold.

"Ray, don't go," Jane called. "I have something for you."

"Hey, what about me?" a couple of guys said, catcalling good-naturedly.

Ray turned just in time to see Jane blush to the roots of her fading blonde hair.

"What can I do for you?" Ray asked, anxious to get in line for the coats.

"A man came in here a couple of weeks ago, right before I left on vacation. He asked if you ever came here. I said, yes, hope that was okay." She rushed on. "He said he knew your grandfather, and that it was very important that you call him."

Ray glanced at the card. It said, 'Sherman Lake, Attorney at Law.'

"I thought it might be important."

He shrugged. "I doubt it. I'll call whenever I can.

Probably another bill collector."

"Look, you can use our phone."

"Thanks, but gotta go. They're giving away coats."

She nodded. "Remember what I said. See you tomorrow, Ray."

"Yeah, okay. Thanks," he mumbled. He moved away from her and shoved the card into his pants pocket. He really needed to get one of those coats. At the moment, nothing was more important than staying warm. Then he could go stand on a corner with his sign and offer to work for money or a meal. Very few people took him up on either, but it salvaged his pride to offer. Most people just gave him some change or a dollar, which he appreciated, but what he really needed was a job. He'd tried to get welfare, but that had been a joke. Unless you had kids, it was almost hopeless. You needed a permanent address. Well, if he had a permanent address he wouldn't be homeless, would he? The lady had a snotty attitude, and halfway through the process he'd gotten mad and walked out.

A couple of days later, Ray arrived at the soup kitchen for lunch as usual. He'd taken Jane up on her offer to use the church's phone to call the attorney. They'd played phone tag. The attorney had been in court. Finally, Ray left a message advising the lawyer that he'd be at the soup kitchen during a certain time period if he wanted to see him. Ray knew without a doubt the guy wouldn't lower himself to come there. He stood in line for his food, thankful for his new coat. It was warm in the basement, but he wasn't going to take it off for any reason.

After lunch, he went to the men's room and took an old hand towel he'd snagged from the thrift shop out of his coat pocket. He dampened the towel in the sink, splashed some of the liquid soap on it, and without taking off his clothes washed himself as best as he could. Man, what he wouldn't give for a shower or a bath in a real bathtub. He grabbed some paper towels from the dispenser and rinsed and dried himself off. His clothes stunk, but at least he knew he was partly clean.

Someone pounded on the door. "Did you die in there or what?"

"Be right out." He shoved the damp towel in his coat pocket, and ran his fingers through his beard. It was full grown now. It kept him warmer in the winter. Besides who was going to care? It wasn't like he had a job interview.

As soon as he walked out of the bathroom, Ray knew the man had arrived. He had on an expensive suit and his shoes were shiny. He was talking to Jane.

"He was just here a minute ago," Jane said, a worried tone to her voice. "He's very nice."

"I'll wait for him," the man said, patience in his voice.

"There he is now," Jane said, her finger pointing at Ray.

Ray raised his eyebrows and walked toward the man. "You're a long way from uptown," he said by way of greeting. "If you're a bill collector, I'm a little short at the moment," Ray said, laughing at his own joke.

The man nodded as he took in Ray's appearance. When the man's eyes met Ray's they were kind instead of judgmental. "I can see that. Do you have a minute to talk?"

"I've got nothing but time," Ray said, pointing to a table in the corner of the room. It was late and most people had left since the soup kitchen would be closing soon.

After they sat down on the metal folding chairs the church provided, the man got to the point.

"Ray, I am, was, your grandfather's attorney. It's been a while since I've seen you. You were a teenager when we last met. But, I'd know you anywhere. You have Dave's blue eyes, and you look a lot like him with that beard."

Ray stared. He didn't remember ever meeting this man. Then it hit him "What do you mean you were my grandfather's attorney? Did he fire you or something?"

"No, I'm sorry, but your grandfather passed away." The attorney's eyes glazed over for a moment threatening tears.

"What? How?"

"His heart. He was pretty old, you know."

"I meant to see him when I got on my feet again," Ray said. "I didn't want to bother him with my problems."

The attorney nodded. "Well, he figured it out. I promised him I would find you no matter what. I've been looking for you for several months."

Ray hung his head.

"He had a nice funeral. Lots of friends and a couple of cousins showed up. I know your parents are dead too. I'm sorry."

Ray nodded. He'd had no one but his grandfather since his parents had died. They'd both smoked and died of emphysema. The little money that had been left from the sale of the house after their death had gone to pay off their debts.

"Dave's eyesight wasn't very good at the end, so he dictated this letter and wanted you to have it. I'd appreciate it if you'd read it now," he said, laying an envelope on the table.

Ray grabbed the envelope, removed the letter, and scanned it. His grandfather's letter got right to the point.

Dear Ray,

I know you've fallen on hard times. I'm sorry you didn't come to me, but you're just like your daddy. Stubborn to the core. I've left you the farm

*and something to go along with it. Please take care
of it like I taught you.*

Love,
Grandpa

Ray looked at the lawyer, tears falling. Then, he snorted and laughed. "Well, I appreciate it, but I could never pay the taxes on that place. I'm homeless. I don't have a job. My life is a mess."

"Your grandpa believed in you. Said you were the only one that ever helped him on the farm."

"I spent all my summers with him when I was a kid. My father hated farming, but I didn't mind it."

"When your grandfather sold 30 of the 40 acres, I advised him to invest the money. It wasn't much, but the proceeds pay the taxes on the 10 acres that he kept." Every year, the money is sent directly to the county to pay the taxes."

"I didn't know that."

The lawyer opened his briefcase and handed Ray a large manila envelope. "Dave said you'd know what to do with these."

Ray shook the envelope and looked at the attorney. He peered inside and removed a half sheet of paper. The words on it were written with a shaky hand.

These seeds are your future. Take care of them.
P.S. These are called "Mortgage Lifter."
Grandpa

Ray sniffled and held the paper close to him. Then he ran his fingers through the contents of the envelope. There were hundreds of heirloom tomato seeds inside. His grandfather had loved his heirloom tomatoes.

"I took the liberty of withdrawing a little extra from the investment account. I thought maybe you could use an advance. If you like, I can drive you out to the farm."

"Why are you doing this?" Ray asked, awed at the lawyer's compassion and perseverance.

"Your grandfather wasn't just a client. He was a good friend."

Sherman dropped Ray off at the farm, his farm now; he'd left the advance and some papers for Ray to look over and sign so that the estate could be settled. Ray used the key the lawyer had given him to enter the old house. It looked the same as it had when his grandmother had been alive but smelled a little musty from disuse.

Sherman had explained that one of the neighbors had kept an eye on the place until Ray could be located. A widow named Megan Dunn. "I'll let her know you're here so she won't shoot you. She's nice but feisty," Sherman said, laughing.

The first thing Ray did after saying a prayer and thanking his grandfather was to look for some clean clothes. He wanted to take a good soak in the tub before throwing out his old ones. Nothing was going to take the smell of the streets out of them. Fortunately, his grandfather had been about the same size.

After that, he'd have to figure out how he was going to pay for food and utilities and other things the farm needed. Sherman had said that the investment was just enough to pay the small farm's taxes each year. He knew his grandfather loved growing tomatoes, but tomatoes wouldn't pay the overhead. He soaked in the bathtub for over an hour and dressed in some pajamas that he'd found

in his grandfather's dresser.

Oh, how'd he'd loved his grandfather. He'd admired his steadfastness and tenacity and the time he'd taken to teach a boy how to become a young man. They'd kept in touch over the years, but his wife hadn't liked the country, and he hadn't visited the farm as often as he would have liked.

For the first time in over a year, Ray slept soundly in his grandfather's feather bed. In his dreams that evening he was sure he'd glimpsed the old man smiling with pride. Ray wasn't sure why he'd be proud. He'd screwed up his life, and he hadn't even been there when Grandpa died.

The next morning Megan arrived on his doorstep with cinnamon rolls in hand. Her auburn hair and green eyes warned Ray not to take a step out of line. She looked to be in her early forties. She had on bib overalls and a cute white blouse.

"I hope you don't mind my showing up early like this, but your grandpa was always an early riser."

"You knew him well then?"

"Oh yes, we were good friends. We both loved heirloom tomatoes."

"I'd offer you coffee, but I'm not sure if I have any."

"Oh, I'll get it." She blushed. "If you don't mind. I used to help your grandpa."

Megan showed Ray where the coffee was located and then bustled around the kitchen.

"So, I gather you're not from around here, then?" Megan stated, after taking a sip of coffee and a bite of her roll.

Ray wondered how much Sherman had told her.

Probably not much. Lawyers had to keep their client's affairs private, didn't they?

"No, I moved away. Grandpa and I lost touch in the last couple of years or so," Ray said.

Megan nodded and smiled. "Well, I know he loved you. He talked about you all the time, and I just loved his stories. He taught me how to make do during hard times. I learned a lot from him."

Ray started to get steamed. Who did this woman think she was? Had she been trying to take advantage of his grandfather? "Well, I'm glad he had someone to talk to," Ray said. "Do I owe you anything for looking after the place?" Ray asked, wondering how he would pay her.

"Of course not. I was glad to help out a friend. Your grandpa would have done the same for me," Megan said.

Ray felt ashamed. He'd forgotten how generous country folk were.

Megan finished her coffee. "Well, I have to go. I have to transplant my seedlings into plastic pots. Get them going so they'll be ready to put in the ground in May. Your grandpa and I used to exchange seeds. Help each other plant and all."

"My grandfather still planted tomatoes? You mean he didn't hire someone to do it for him? He was in his late 80's." Ray was stunned.

"Oh, no, he loved to plant. Of course, we helped him."
"We?"

"The Heirloom Tomato Club. He was a member for years. Pretty much ran it. He'll really be missed. You know his father originally cultivated 'The Mortgage Lifter' heirloom. He's known all over the country for his seeds and tomatoes.

"Yeah, he was a great guy. Tomatoes were always his hobby."

Megan gave Ray a strange look then said, "Well, let me

know when you want to start your tomatoes. You still have time."

"I'm not sure."

"Think about it," she said, before disappearing.

After Megan left, Ray started cleaning the dusty house. His grandfather had always been orderly, but it was obvious that he hadn't been able to keep up with the place the last couple of years of his life. When Ray finally got to the old fruitwood desk with the inlaid leather top that his grandfather had loved, he hesitated at first then dug into the piles of papers.

Ray found some utility and grocery bills that were marked paid. The writing was not his grandfather's. Had Megan also helped his grandfather with bills? Ray again wondered if the woman had an agenda, and also where his grandfather had gotten the money to pay the bills. The utility bills were higher than he'd paid in his own house. Ray wondered if the greenhouse still functioned. He went out to the barn and saw his grandfather's old truck with the keys in the ignition. It groaned but eventually started. Good. Then he exited the back of the old barn through another set of double doors and spied the greenhouse. He entered the doors and took a sniff. Nothing was growing, but the heat was on low. Hundreds of peat pots were laid out in a row filled with soil, ready to be planted. His grandfather was nothing if not orderly.

Expensive hobby, Ray thought. What he needed was a real job and a real income. He knew his grandfather's social security check wouldn't come close to paying for the heat on the greenhouse. How had he paid for it?

His stomach started growling. He'd have to buy some groceries with the advance Sherman had given him. Then, he heard some cackling. Hens! Grandpa had always kept hens.

"You'll never starve if you have chickens," his grandpa

had said. "You can eat and sell the eggs," he said.

Ray hadn't been too impressed with chickens back then. Now, they never looked so good. It appeared that Megan had been feeding the hens and collecting the eggs. That was okay. It was the least he could do since she'd looked after the place. He thought he saw some feed in the barn and went back to get it. He fed the chickens and walked back toward the house. He'd collect the eggs later.

He ate another cinnamon roll, drank more coffee, and then went back to his grandfather's desk. He searched through all the drawers. Folders for utilities, grain, chickens and the like were all neatly marked. The receipts for each were contained within each folder, but there was no sign of a checking account. Everyone had some kind of an account. Surely his grandfather hadn't paid cash for everything.

Then he saw it. In the bottom drawer sat another manila envelope, and it simply said "Ray." Within it lay an old-fashioned black accounts book. It listed several years of credit entries for feed, peat pots, tomato plants, and the like. It also had entries for all of the sales his grandfather had made each year. There were entries for tomato plants, packets of heirloom seeds, canned tomatoes, and profits from his little roadside stand. The amount was staggering. His grandfather made enough money from the heirloom tomatoes to run the entire 10 acre farm for the year with a little left over for comfort.

If so, where was the left over money, and where were the canned tomatoes? Canned tomatoes lasted for about five years. He remembered his grandfather preaching about it because they had always made a process of culling out the old jars and using them first before they spoiled.

"You have to replenish the stock, Ray," his grandfather had said.

The root cellar. That's where they were. He went down to the root cellar and looked around with a smile. Hundreds

of glass canning jars full of heirloom tomatoes spanned the cellar shelves from top to bottom. He could sell them and have enough money to pay the bills for this year, but how could he pay the electricity for the greenhouse next year if he sold them? Sherman had made it clear that the investment trust was set up so that only so much could be withdrawn each year for taxes. And how had his grandfather canned all of these tomatoes by himself? Ray had an idea about that.

On the way to get groceries, Ray stopped at Megan's neat little yellow bungalow. Her land was once part of the original farm. His grandfather had sold the land to a developer and insisted that it be divided up into five acre tracts.

He knocked, and she came to the door covered in dirt.

"I hope you don't mind my dropping by. I have some questions."

"Sure, come on in. I'm working in the greenhouse. Nothing as fancy as yours, but I love it."

He followed her and sat on a stool in the corner and watched her work.

"So, I figured out how you knew so much about the kitchen. You helped Grandpa can all those tomatoes I saw in the root cellar didn't you?"

"Well, not just me. There were others in the club that helped. We tend to help each other when it's needed."

"But there are hundreds of jars."

"Your grandfather's tomatoes were legendary throughout the state. Those seeds are over 60 years old. People depended on him. There's an almost fanatic following for heirloom tomatoes."

"I saw the chickens. Thanks for feeding and taking care of them."

"Oh, no problem. I sold the eggs. I have the money for

you in the other room."

"No, you did all the work. Please keep it."

She started to say something, looked worried, and then bit her lip.

"Look, I'm on my way to the grocery store to pick up a few things. If you're not busy, how about I make us some dinner? I think I remember how to make pasta and a salad. It won't be anything fancy."

Her face glowed. "I'd love to."

"And maybe you could explain what I should do with all those peat pots in the greenhouse."

"Sure."

When he got back from town, Ray cleaned the rest of the house and made sure it looked presentable. He even went into his old room and looked around a bit. He picked up his old Star Wars toys and action figures and sighed. His grandfather had kept them all. Even his posters were still on the walls. He eyed them and frowned. Maybe those posters would bring a few bucks. They were probably collector items by now.

He wondered what was in his old hiding spot. Underneath the iron bed, there was a chink in the baseboard that opened to a hollowed out spot in the plaster wall. It was probably an old comic book—maybe a valuable one. He shoved the bed aside and carefully removed the baseboard. He started to put his hand inside and then thought better of it. He got a flashlight from the kitchen and stared into the hole. He withdrew a brown plastic pouch. He didn't remember putting anything like this there. He opened the pouch and gasped. Inside, in neat bundles, were 20, 50, and 100 dollar bills. Enough to finance this season's crop of tomato plants. There was a note in the bottom of the last bundle. It simply said, "Replenish Fund."

Ray put the money back in the pouch and carefully

fit it back into the hole and replaced the baseboard. He moved the bed back into place.

He glanced at the clock and smiled. It was time to start the sauce for dinner. He was looking forward to an evening with Megan. It looked like all the hard work his grandfather had taught him was going to pay off in his new life.

In May, the Heirloom Tomato Club helped Ray get his plants into the ground. Ray worked long hours watering and fertilizing them with chicken manure. He used the same organic techniques his grandfather had taught him. Ray also found other seed envelopes marked with names like Gardener's Delight, Lollypop, and Big Rainbow which he dutifully planted. The cream of the crop though, seemed to be Grandpa's Mortgage Lifters. They were big, red, beefsteak tomatoes. Some of them weighed as much as four pounds.

Saturdays and Sundays were spent manning the little roadside farm market that his grandfather had built at the edge of the property. Ray spent early mornings hauling fresh tomatoes and arranging them nicely in the baskets. He also brought dozens of canned jars of tomatoes to the stand to sell to customers that wanted to save them for winter. Many days, Megan would drop by with lemonade and keep him company. They seemed to rub along comfortably with each other, and when they weren't planting, tending, or selling tomatoes, they canned them.

Dave also made a trip to the soup kitchen each week, dropping off fresh tomatoes on a regular basis. When Jane echoed her thanks, Dave waved her away. "I remember all the times I was hungry and you fed me. It's the least I can do."

Soon, word spread throughout the Heirloom community that Ray was continuing Grandpa Dave Strawser's Heirloom Tomato business. Envelopes with orders for seeds arrived in the mail from all over the country. Megan showed him how to dry the seeds. Ray carefully counted 50 seeds into a package. He then put the seed packages into small bubble packs carefully marking "Hand Cancel" on each. These seeds would be used in next year's gardens.

One day, Ray and Megan reviewed Dave's Heirloom Tomato accounts. Ray learned that Megan had been an accountant before she'd married and moved to the country. "You know, you're going to need to hire help next year. Business is booming," she grinned.

"Thanks to you and Grandpa," Ray said, giving her a squeeze and peck on the cheek. "You know, I think I know just where to hire some folks. I'd like for you to meet my friend, Hal," he said. "It's time I explain a little about where I was when Grandpa died."

Country Style Tomatoes

Catherine Moore

1 clove garlic, minced
1/4 cup parsley, minced
1/8 teaspoon salt
1 (8 oz) package of cream cheese softened
1 teaspoon fresh basil, chopped
4 large tomatoes
1/2 cup all-purpose flour
1 egg, beaten
2/3 cup dry breadcrumbs
3 tablespoons butter
3 tablespoons oil
Fresh basil or parsley (optional)

1. Cream together garlic, parsley, salt, and cream cheese; add basil if desired.

2. Cut each tomato into 3 even slices, about 1/2 inch thick, for 12 slices total.

3. Spread 6 slices with about 2 tablespoons of mixture; top with remaining slices to make 6 sandwiches.

4. Dip each tomato sandwich into flour, then egg and breadcrumbs.

5. In a skillet fry over medium heat in mixture of butter and oil until brown, turning once.

6. Garnish with fresh basil or parsley.

Yield: 6 Servings.

111

Tomato Blemish

Lora Keller

Choose a deep red one
with a green blemish
small
as the hole
a needle makes
through Pima.

The spot should be near the stem
so that each morning
as you pour your cream
you can watch this dust dot
bloom,
the genesis of decay.

Ringed in wrinkled green-black skin,
soft blue-white mold will mound.
Good Housekeeping warns
mold has legs.
Shave the fuzz and you'll leave
roots tangled in juice and yellow seeds.

Better to let this spooky shadow grow.
Let it ooze like a sore,
tiny fissures erupting.
Your kitchen a dim garden,
dark theater,
rot drama.

Eccentricity

J.M. Prescott

We live in a zero-lot-line townhouse. The yard is so small, my husband Charles can cut the grass in five minutes; this includes starting the temperamental mower. Sunlight is almost non-existent, as the hickory trees fight to spread their branches and shade the entire backyard except for two spots in which I try to squeeze all my herbs and flowers.

This spring, I have decided to plant tomatoes. Their little seeds tucked in dirt pods, sit on my windowsill facing west, soaking up as much afternoon sun as they can get. I label all *eleven* varieties, so there won't be any surprises.

I purchase seven five-gallon buckets and five huge bags of dirt. My husband drills drainage holes in the bottoms, while warning me that there isn't enough sunlight in the backyard to grow tomatoes. I explain to him my plan of making it a mobile garden, by moving them as the sun moves.

"I'll only have to move these seven buckets, as four tomatoes will be in the planter in the front yard." I say, feeling justified with my idea, I place coffee liners over the drilled holes and fill the buckets with dirt.

My husband smiles and shakes his head. "They'll be too heavy to lug around." Charles knows I'm stubborn, so he doesn't say anything else.

It's been a couple of days and the tomato seeds should be sprouting. Deciding they could use some air,

I proceed to open the window, when a gust blows the growing container on the floor, dumping out the dirt pods and plant markers. After my temporary paralysis and a few tears, I decide I like surprises. There is nothing I can do about it anyway. Who cries over spilt dirt?

A few weeks later, my little tomato plants are about three inches tall and taking on jagged leaves, strongly smelling of tomatoes. I set them outside today, as it is a nice spring day and the article I read said they have to adjust to the outdoors. I will bring them back inside at night. This I will do for about a week, until I plant them.

A week later, I make my way to the Oriental Market to buy fish heads, because I read an article in a gardening magazine, that placing a fish head in the bottom of a hole before planting a tomato will guarantee they are prolific. Everybody wants their tomatoes to be large, juicy, and produce loads of fruit; right?

The fishmonger's brows draw together as I enthusiastically explain why I need exactly eleven fish heads. He goes off mumbling to himself in a language I can't understand and returns with a plastic bag of disgusting fish heads; their eyes look at me accusingly. I wonder if I can ask him to close their eyes. Since he is letting me have them free, perhaps I should just ask him to put them in an opaque plastic bag, before my suddenly overworked gag reflex has its way!

Today is the day I've been waiting for. I'm going to plant my lovely little tomatoes in their respective buckets. I dig a hole for the slimy fish head and with a plastic glove reach in the bag and grab hold of one. Once again, I have to use great control not to throw up. Head in hole, handful of Epsom salts, more dirt, and a lovely little tomato plant.

"Whatcha doin'?" I recognize the voice without turning around.

Duh…as if she can't see what I'm doing. "Planting my tomatoes."

My neighbor from across the street stands behind me looking over my shoulder. Does she keep an eye on my house? She seems to show up when I'm doing something outside. Daisy always dresses a bit strange. Today she is dressed in a dirndl skirt with a peasant blouse reminiscent of the 60's and on her feet sit sparkly ruby slippers. I wonder if she took them from Dorothy.

"Oh God, that's just disgustin'! What is that smell?" I turn to face her as she holds her nose and makes the most hideous face.

Something in me rejoices just a little, as I bring forth the bag of fish heads and shove them at her. I resist smiling and with my most innocent voice proceed to tell her how I am planting my tomatoes.

"Aren't you afraid they'll taste like fish?" she asks, her voice hitting that octave that makes me cringe.

"Nope."

She shakes her head. "You are certainly eccentric." I'm surprised she knows that word.

"I'm eccentric?" I ask, wondering why she would label me that way.

"Come on," she laughs. "You are the only one I know who puts aluminum foil on her storm door and windows. You built an oven out of mud and bake your bread in it."

"That isn't being eccentric. That's being wise and economical. It saves on electricity." I look at her to gauge her response. "The sun is so hot, I can't even touch my doorknob without getting a second degree burn… especially in August and the outside oven keeps the air conditioning from running." Eccentric? When I think of eccentric, I think of someone who constantly acts weird and dresses strange. I think of Daisy.

She stands and watches as I fill every bucket with a

tomato plant and water them. Moving to the front yard, she follows as I hand her the bag of fish heads and I drag a big bag of dirt. My neighbor squeals and holds the bag of fish heads out in front of her as I did before I finally got used them.

"Do you need so many tomatoes?" She drops the fish head bag on the ground, her face still drawn up into a sneer.

"There are eleven different heirloom varieties. I have grape tomatoes and tiny little currant tomatoes. There are red ones, plumbs, striped, yellow, purple, orange, and black tomatoes." I explain, dumping the dirt into the planter.

"How will you know which is which? Didn't you think to label them?" She snickers.

I blow out a breath, count to ten, and swallow my pride. "I did have them labeled, but they accidently blew off the sill when I opened the window and lost their labels."

"Hmmm." She walks to the other side of the planter. "Well, I better go. I have things to do also." She states.

I nod. "Bye then."

It rains on the weekend and I worry that the wind will be too much for my tomatoes. Taking every umbrella I own, I tie them down over the tomato buckets. My husband just laughs at me. "Eccentric." My head nudges my conscious. "Nope, just cautious." I tell it, looking around to make sure my neighbor isn't watching me. I think I saw her curtain fall on one side.

Several more weeks pass, and the time has come to stake my tomatoes. I find some nice bamboo stakes and secure the stocks with cable ties. It is hard to contain my excitement as I see a few of the plants have small white flowers, which I know will turn into tomatoes. However, they not only have flowers, I can see aphids, tiny bugs that suck the life-force right out of a plant. I run to the house and quickly Google tomato pests.

Oh, my God! Besides aphids, there are tomato blights, cankers, huge horned worms, and some tomatoes, deficient of nutrients, just fall off the plants before they fully develop. Why didn't I read this before? My poor tomatoes! How will they survive? Okay, I tell myself, you only have to do something about the aphids today. I can wash them off, or I can look to see if there are any tiny wasps hanging around my plants. If so, they will kill the aphids and I won't have to do anything.

A sigh of relief sets my anxious heart back to beating normally. Some plants do have wasps hanging around. However, to some, I take a spray bottle of water mixed with a drop of dish soap and wash them away. There…I'm doing right by my plants! I'm a good tomato mama! "Eccentric." That dreaded label sneaks back into my head. "No, just a vigilant Gardner." I tell myself.

My tomato plants continue growing and more and more little green tomatoes appear. Today, I'm looking for aphids again. From the corner of my eye, I see something move, but don't see anything when I turn and look in that direction. It must have been a leaf. Then I notice several leaves at the top of the plant have stubs coming off the stock where there should be new leaves. I look closer and see a green "Jabba the Hutt" with horns. It is as long as my pointer finger and just as big around with wrinkles and hairs sticking out at all angles. "Yech!"

My neighbor crosses the road. "What are you starin' at?" Attired today in a dress that looks like it lost its way several decades ago and flip-flops that have plastic flowers glued to them, she carries a canteen around her shoulder. Who's eccentric?

"My tomato has a worm eating it." I point to the ugly fat green blob.

She is so close, her nose is almost touching it.

"Back up. It might sting or something." I warn her, pushing slightly.

"How are you going to get rid of it?"

I shrug my shoulders. "I think I can just pick it off and step on it."

Her face screws up in disgust. "Better you than me."

I reach over and pick it up between my pointer finger and thumb and as it squiggles, I scream and toss it on the driveway. My foot makes quick work as I squash it. Guess eating only chlorophyll turns you into green goop. I walk over to the grass and clean the bottom of my shoe.

My neighbor looks at me. "Do you think all this is worth a few tomatoes? Couldn't you just go to the farmer's market and buy some, cheaper than all this?"

"Yeah, but it wouldn't be homegrown. Buying them at the market means their DNA could be mixed with lizards or snakes." I explain.

"You're weird," she states. "Go to one of those organic markets, then."

"I want to grow them myself," I state emphatically, stomping my foot. Whoa, where did that come from?

"I see you lugging those heavy buckets into the driveway every afternoon to make sure they get sunshine. You're going to injure something." Daisy stretches her back. "How high is your water bill? You water them twice a day in this heat." She takes a drink of water from the canteen and offers me some.

I shake my head. "No thanks." Who is eccentric? Not me, I'm tenacious.

She helps me look for more worms.

This is the hottest summer in twenty years. With daily care over the next month, my plants grow to great heights and with another length of bamboo lashed to the first they are almost nine feet tall and filled with green tomatoes. However, none of them seems to ripen.

Back to Google. "How to ripen tomatoes…"

"Whatcha doin' that for?" Daisy appears in her fluffy slippers, some type of striped bloomers, and a bikini top. My eyes can't believe it!

"I read on the internet that tomatoes get jealous if they see red and will ripen."

She laughs heartily slapping her hand to her knees. "You believe that? You *actually* believe tomatoes have feelings?" Tears are running out of her eyes and her nose is snotting, while she continues to insult me.

Placing a red ball in the next bucket, I ignore her. "That's what I read. They don't exactly get jealous, but somehow they can interpret the color and will try to mimic it. These tomatoes need to ripen."

"You are so eccentric!" Wagging her head in amazement, she leaves me to my project.

Eccentric? No, scientific!

Three more days and the nights are as hot as the days. No red tomatoes! The article says that tomatoes need a change in temperature of fifteen to twenty degrees to jumpstart the ripening process.

I finagle my husband into helping me with my next project. It wasn't easy. After he stopped laughing and realized I was serious, he felt guilty and reluctantly agreed to help. This evening, we are attaching sandwich bags full of ice to the branches of the tomato plants. I figure this will help lower the temperature enough to start the ripening process.

Oh, no. I see Daisy making her way across the street. Decked out in a muumuu and her plastic flowered flip-flops, she has her hair pulled on top of her head with the ends cascading like a spouting whale, held by an entire bouquet of plastic fruit. In her hand is a tall glass with several paper umbrellas.

"Brace yourself." My husband chuckles and moves to

the buckets in the driveway.

"Whatcha doin' now?" She bends over looking at the sandwich bags filled with melting ice. "What the hell is that?" Her laughter infuriates me. "They're so jealous you want to throw them a party?"

A smile shows up on my face. How did that happen? "No. We are trying to help the tomatoes to ripen, by lowering the temperature."

"You let her talk you into doin' this?" Daisy asks Charles. He shrugs smiling. "You could just pick them green and take them in the house. They will ripen there." I hate it when she is logical.

"Vine ripened tomatoes are best." I counter.

She shakes her head. "You are really eccentric, but you keep things interesting."

Eccentric? No, practical and a little bit daring.

In the morning, I remove the bags of melted ice before anyone in the neighborhood can see me. My fingers brush against the tomato leaves, releasing their pungent odor. I'm a little bit downhearted this morning. I've worked so hard to raise these tomatoes from seeds and now they have grown so tall, I have to use a step ladder to reach the top. If only the tomatoes would ripen, I could feel gratified with all the work. Maybe I will have to resort to picking them green, but I decide to give them a few more days.

Late afternoon, I'm checking for pests when Daisy makes her appearance.

"Whatcha doin'?" She is dressed in a sleeveless tank top and stretch shorts. She has cut her hair and she looks reasonable for a change.

"You look nice." I say. "Like the hair cut. Suits you."

She ignores the compliments and stares at a tomato. "Well, looky here. I think this tomato is startin' to change color."

I lean in close and we look at each other and smile. "It

120

worked!" We say together.

"Jinx; you owe me a coke!" She grins.

A few days later, I walk over to Daisy's house with a basket of tomatoes and a bottle of coke. She answers the door in a nice pair of slacks and a dressy top. "Going somewhere?" I hand her the basket. She sees the coke and smiles.

"I start a job today." She says proudly.

"Oh, that's wonderful! Where?" I can't imagine what kind of job she could get, she usually dresses so eccentric. There's that word again.

"I'm going to work at Wal-Mart."

"Good luck!" I smile. "See you later?" She nods. Daisy is a very unique person. She is my neighbor, but she has also become a friend through the years. If she thinks I'm eccentric, I really don't mind.

I am happily justified with the tomatoes I am reaping. Will I do it next year? I don't know. It probably cost me more to grow them than I would have spent buying my tomatoes all summer at the Organic Market. However, the experience of planting the seeds and aiding in their growth is rewarding when I take a bite of a perfectly delightful tomato.

Perhaps my adventure in gardening tomatoes has placed me in the eccentricity category. I probably did things most people wouldn't have tried.

Tomato eccentricity! Yep, that's me!

Caprese Bake

Laura Rushing

2 pints cherry tomatoes (about 1.5 pounds)
1 teaspoon kosher salt
2 teaspoon extra virgin olive oil
2 garlic cloves, minced
1.5 cups spinach, roughly chopped (optional)
Mozzarella cheese, to taste (sliced or grated)
1 3/4 oz container basil leaves, chiffonade

1. Preheat oven to 425 degrees.

2. Sprinkle cherry tomatoes with salt and let sit on a flat surface for 10-15 minutes while you're prepping the other ingredients.

3. Dab tomatoes with a paper towel to remove excess moisture.

4. Halve the tomatoes (or keep whole, at your preference). Add the tomatoes, oil, garlic, and chopped spinach together in an 8 x 8 glass baking dish.

5. Bake for 30-40 minutes, stirring at least twice, until tomatoes are softened.

6. Sprinkle the top with the basil chiffonade and add mozzarella on top of the basil.

7. Broil 30 seconds to 1 minute, or until cheese is melted.

La Cosa Nostra

Robert Iulo

My Aunt Lena, a first-generation Neapolitan-American who grew up in Manhattan's Little Italy, happened to fall in love with a first-generation Sicilian-American. This wasn't quite as tragic as Romeo and Juliet. Really, it was no big deal—except where cooking was concerned.

Shortly after the wedding, Aunt Lena's Sicilian-born mother-in-law, Rose, came to dinner. My aunt put together an extensive menu, including a Neapolitan standard: lasagna. The basic family recipe is broad pasta layered and baked with a garlic based tomato sauce, three cheeses (ricotta, mozzarella, and Parmesan), and meatballs "no bigger than a dime." My mother and aunt could roll these little gems between their palms three at a time. Rose said she loved it, and sometime after that, she invited my aunt to dinner, saying she liked her lasagna so much she thought she'd serve her own version of it—of course, with a Sicilian twist.

In Rose's version, the garlicky sauce was supplemented with chopped onions. In addition to the three traditional cheeses, Rose added a good amount of provolone. And, layered with the strips of pasta, she added sliced hard-boiled eggs and some sopressata. The all-important little meatballs were gone. My aunt politely ate some of Rose's dish and commented on how good it was, all the while hiding her outrage that a family recipe should be so casually bastardized. She hoped she would soon have her

123

chance to avenge this affront to the cuisine of Naples. She didn't have to wait long, as March 19 was coming up. That's the feast day of St. Joseph, when many Sicilian households traditionally serve pasta con sarde. The name means "pasta with sardines," but the dish also includes an elaborate sauce made with chopped fennel leaves, raisins, and pine nuts — all very traditional Sicilian ingredients. (The fennel gives the sauce a greenish hue, and the color is as important as the taste.) The whole thing is served with a sprinkling of toasted breadcrumbs. So my Aunt Lena invited Rose for a St. Joseph's day dinner, and said she wanted to serve pasta con sarde. Like a good daughter-in-law, she asked her for her family recipe, and Rose was happy to supply it. My aunt followed the instructions precisely, but during the simmering of the sauce, she added enough crushed San Marzano plum tomatoes (imported from Naples, of course) to turn Rose's green sauce red. Rose, in turn, controlled her reaction to this wrong-colored sauce, and said it was all delicious. My aunt's honor was satisfied. The unexpected twist was that this new tomato-based version of pasta con sarde was actually very good, and my aunt's Sicilian husband and his Sicilian friends preferred it to the green version. The new recipe was so highly praised that the women in my family, right down to my daughter, still make it with San Marzano tomatoes.

This all happened more than ten years before I was born, but throughout my childhood, I heard my mother and aunt talk about it with great pride. The Napolitani had won that battle, but the war never really ended. I was twelve when I ate lunch at a friend's home, where his grandmother served us delicious sandwiches made with breaded flounder fillets. When I got home, I made two mistakes.

First, in my blithe innocence, I asked my mother and aunt, "How come your fillets aren't as tasty as the ones

Vinnie's grandmother makes?" Second, I forgot that Vinnie's grandmother was Sicilian. My mother and aunt always treated me like a little prince who could do no wrong, but this time I really made them angry.

"If you like Vinnie's grandmother's cooking so much," my mother huffed, "you should eat there from now on." And she wouldn't talk to me after that. I knew she didn't mean it, but I also knew she was very upset. When I sat at my family's dinner table that evening, hoping the afternoon's conversation had been forgotten, I discovered that I wasn't allowed to have any of the pasta lenticchie and pork chops with vinegar peppers everyone else was eating.

"Since you don't appreciate the way we cook," announced my aunt, "this is what you'll eat from now on."

And she and my mother made a big show of serving me a baloney sandwich on Wonder Bread. When I'd finished the sandwich my penance was complete. They forgave me, and gave me my real dinner. And I was very careful to watch what I said about their cooking after that.

My sisters were much more aware of, and loyal to, the Neapolitan cooking tradition than I was. One of them, like my aunt, married a Sicilian. His mother told her she would teach her how to cook some of her son's favorite dishes. But my sister's response was, essentially, "Thanks, but no thanks. I already know how to cook." I'm sure this same sort of conversation also took place between Sicilian daughters-in-law and Neapolitan mothers-in-law.

Both Sicily and Naples each have access to abundant seafood and rich volcanic soil. Before the unification of Italy, both areas were under the rule of many different countries that influenced their cuisines. Past Arab domination of Sicily left a legacy of using fruits and sweet spices in savory dishes. In Naples, occupying rulers added tastes of Aragon and France to the existing Greco-Roman based cuisine. The rivalry may not have mattered much back in the old country, where the kitchens of these two regions were separated by hundreds of miles. But in Little Italy, the Sicilian immigrants tended to settle on Elizabeth Street, while the Neapolitans lived on Mott Street—just one block apart. At this distance, there was sure to be some culinary conflict, and it was a strictly female conflict. The males ate both cuisines with equal gusto. Boys played together and men worked and socialized with one another; they had common interests outside the kitchen. But the women, who took pride in their cooking, couldn't overcome this underlying cultural friction. Not being able to talk about food, or exchange recipes, or even go grocery shopping together without some subtle eye-rolling, made it difficult for the Neapolitan and Sicilian housewives of my childhood to become close friends. But they did have at least one thing that bound them together: They all looked down their noses at the Toscana housewives from the north who cooked with butter instead of good southern olive oil.

Poison Apple Soup

Scáth Beorh

3 large cans(12-16oz each) fire roasted tomatoes
1 large yellow onion
1 cup new wine
6 cloves garlic, minced
6 cups broth (meat or vegetarian)
1/2 bunch green onions, minced
1/4 cup olive oil
Salt
Black pepper

1. Mince yellow onion. Sauté in the olive oil on medium heat until it caramelizes.

2. Add minced fire roasted tomatoes, minced garlic, minced green onions, and new wine.

3. Add the broth, and add salt and black pepper to taste.

4. Simmer on low heat for 45 minutes.

5. Top with shredded mild cheese if desired.

Serve with bread or crackers in a bowl or bread bowl.

Note: New wine is unfermented grape juice, red suggested for this recipe.

Ned and the Tomatoes

H. David Blalock

Ned was allergic to tomatoes.

He discovered this fact as a youngster, working in a grocery on Main Street in the tiny town of Crow's Nest, Arkansas, population 102.

He had decided to try to earn some money to buy a bicycle but for someone of the tender age of eight there were very few employment options available. The local newspaper route was already taken by Freddie Simpson and Arnie Cox did the lawn mowing or snow shoveling. He thought about doing car washes until he found out that the three cars in town were all owned by one person, the mayor. And the mayor and his dad didn't get along because his dad was the only person who didn't vote for him.

Ned's uncle Jack told him that the Safeway in Barton Creek, about three miles away, was hiring stock boys. He worked there in the meat department as a butcher's assistant and said he would talk to the manager if Ned was interested. Of course, he said yes and soon found himself riding along with Uncle Jack to work every day.

Until that fateful Monday he was supposed to help restock the vegetable refrigerator.

There's something in tomatoes that he reacted violently to. The doctors couldn't figure it out. The EMTs that responded to the 911 call when he went into anaphylactic shock went through the motions efficiently

and probably saved his life but they, too, said they'd never heard of anybody being allergic to tomatoes.

Ned found out later that the allergy is extremely rare. He had to stop eating pizza, spaghetti, and anything with sauce on it. Whenever he'd eaten pizza before he hadn't had anything worse than a bad itch. The doctors told him it was probably some kind of internal trigger that caused the allergy to suddenly manifest so fiercely. Not uncommon, they said, but that didn't make him feel any better.

His life suddenly became an obstacle course filled with tomatoes. Tomato sauce, boiled tomatoes, cherry tomatoes, roma tomatoes, plum tomatoes, golden sweet tomatoes, jersey devil tomatoes, diced tomatoes, tomato paste, ketchup, tomato puree; they seemed to be everywhere and in everything. Salads, entrees, even desserts. Like its cousin the nightshade, it had become poisonous to him, but unlike the other food he was supposed to avoid (and didn't), it seemed to be following him around.

He would be playing baseball and somehow a tomato would come out of the crowd and hit him squarely in the face.

He would be riding his bicycle to the store and a tomato would roll in front of him, get squashed under the wheels and splash juice on his bare ankle.

He would be standing at the bus stop and a person walking by with a grocery bag would stumble, throwing tomatoes at him.

He had to leave his job at the grocery because when he went back to work and was walking down the vegetable aisle, the tomatoes suddenly spilled out of their display and hit him so hard he fell over.

His parents kept telling him it was all coincidence. Right up until he ran away from home at twelve. He ran until he thought he couldn't run anymore, then he ran some more. He found himself at last looking out of the window of a bus at a sign that said "Welcome to Arizona."

Maybe he could be safe from tomatoes if he went and lived in the desert. Surely, there wouldn't be any of the cursed things there. The arid nature of the place would certainly protect him from them.

Little did he know the tomato lurked even in the driest of places.

As he was trekking through the desert, tired, thirsty, and famished, he stumbled across a bush with red berries. Desperate for nourishment, he picked a handful of them and popped them in his mouth before noticing the welts coming up in his palms.

They were fruit of the *Lycium andersonii*, known by some as the desert tomato.

Confused by the situation and not understanding why he was having such a reaction, Ned stumbled hurriedly along until by chance he found a road just before falling unconscious.

Troublesome dreams haunted his delirium. He was chased by tomatoes wanting to smash his head in. They gibbered and screeched as they pursued him. He fled headlong, little knowing or caring where he was headed. His one desire was to escape, to reach that one place in the world where he could be free of the damned fruit.

He awoke in a hospital bed, a saline bag hanging at his side and a nurse, who had probably been born shortly before Nimrod started the Tower, fussing over his IV.

"Where am I?" he struggled to ask, managing only a croak.

The nurse peered at him, pushing back her horn-rimmed glasses. "You rest, dearie. You're dehydrated and weak from exposure. They found you on the road almost dead. Anaphylaxis, they said. You were very lucky. Another few minutes and it might have been too late. The doctors

say it's important we find out as soon as possible what happened because the next time could be the last. So, what are you allergic to, honey?"

He coughed and cleared his throat. "Tomato," he wanted to say, but it came out "Dunno."

"Well, never mind, my dear," the nurse said, patting his arm and smiling through million-year-old teeth. "We'll find out when you're a little better." She walked to a serving table nearby. "Meanwhile you need to rehydrate. I have some nice tomato soup for you. Now, open wide..."

Ned could only manage a squeak.

Adolescence

Violet Nesdoly

Five tomatoes ripening
on my window ledge
four are green and hard and small
the fifth is on the edge.

A Rebel in My Salad

Samantha Memi

I was eating my salad, enjoying the peppers and olives, but every time I tried to pick up a slice of tomato with my fork it jumped out of the way. I tried another but it did the same. All the tomato slices avoided my fork; I had to chase them across the plate and the more I jabbed at them the more they jumped about. Pieces of tomato were jumping off the plate and landing on the carpet.

"Samantha, don't play with your food," said my mother.

"I'm not. My tomato won't stay on my fork."

She reached over with her fork and jabbed at a slice of tomato. It jumped out of the way. She tried to get other slices but the result was the same. One piece jumped so high it hit her in the face.

"Samantha, have you been teaching your tomatoes to mutiny against authority?"

"No, mum."

"Then why are they being so disobedient?"

"I don't know."

"I think you do. Just you wait till your father hears about this. This tomato didn't grow on a plant just for you to teach it to be a communist."

"How can it be a communist?"

"If it won't obey authority, it's communist."

"No, mum, communists follow authority."

"Don't you dare argue with me. Whatever's happening

to you. Pushing your salad into rebellion. Disagreeing with your mother. It's all those Lemony Snicket books you've been reading, isn't it. Isn't it!"

At that moment my dad came home and realized from the tense atmosphere that something was wrong.

"What's wrong?" he asked.

"Your daughter is teaching her salad revolutionary terrorism."

Dad looked at me meanly. "Samantha, will you never learn. I don't know what's got into you. That's not what you do with your food."

"It was my tomato. It didn't want to be eaten."

"Oh, I see, it's the tomato's fault. Of course, you're never to blame for anything. I suppose the farmer teaches his vegetables guerrilla warfare."

"She got her tomato to jump up and hit me in the face."

"That's it, young lady. I'm phoning your psychiatrist. You obviously need treatment."

My psychiatrist was old but had probably been pretty when young. Her office was clean and efficient and cold. I sat rigid, gripping the sides of the chair.

"So you want to be a communist," she said.

"No."

"According to your parents you want to create a new world of communism, and will do anything to achieve it."

"That's not true."

"Why would they say that if it isn't true?"

"I don't know."

"You seem to be in denial."

"I had difficulty eating a tomato, and my mum thought I'd trained it to be rebellious."

"Had you?"

"No."

"Then why would she think you had?"

"I don't know."

"Your mother isn't given to flights of fancy, is she?"

"No."

"She seems a very down-to-earth person, wouldn't you say?"

"Yes."

"So why would you train a tomato in revolutionary activities?"

"I didn't."

"But your mother says you did, and by your own admission your mother speaks the truth, whereas you, it would seem, prefer to hide behind a smokescreen of lies and deceit."

The psychiatrist looked smug behind her face powder and pale pink lipstick. She took a breath.

"How many tomatoes have you trained in guerrilla tactics?"

"None."

She sneered, or seemed to.

"I'm going to recommend you be held for observation, and that your food be strictly checked. You're young. Have you ever considered how food feels when you teach it to do things it knows are morally wrong?"

I learned my observation would consist of my having to cross the Grand Canyon on a tight rope on a monocycle.

An observer explained, "You will be closely monitored; if any revolutionary symptoms reveal themselves we will know about it."

I was nervous. Both my parents had come to watch. Even my grandma. A hot dog van. An ice cream seller. Crowds of onlookers, hoping to see an accident, viewing me as an unruly child.

The psychiatrist said, "You just need to believe in

135

yourself and everything will go well. But if you've lied the tightrope will know and *twang!* down you'll go."

I practiced on the monocycle but fell off repeatedly.

The day for the observation was bright and sunny; soft clouds waltzed languidly over the pale blue ceiling high above

I began my ride. The cheers and boos of the crowd were silenced as I ventured out over the canyon. Halfway across I wobbled, but a sunbeam broke through the clouds and shone down to give me the confidence to continue. I had only a few yards to go when I slipped and the cycle fell away, whistling into the canyon. As I fell I grabbed the tightrope and clung on for dear life. Slowly, hand by hand, I moved along the wire, mercifully managing to reach the other side with only a few minor scratches.

The crowd cheered. My crossing was acknowledged a success and I was declared innocent of all injurious charges. TV reporters rushed to interview me. My parents were delighted and told me they forgave me all I had done to hurt them.

"Samantha," said my mother, "we're so proud of you."

"Don't you know what you've put me through? You never believed anything I said."

"But darling, everything we did we did for you."

"If it wasn't for a sunbeam, willpower and luck I'd be at the bottom of the Grand Canyon."

"Oh Samantha, don't be bitter. We did our best. "

I asked Child Services to find me other parents.

"It's not that easy," they said.

"I don't want to live with people who think I train salads to rebel against society."

I was placed with an elderly couple. They both smiled a lot and looked weak and pliable. They hadn't seen my

Grand Canyon exploit and seemed to like me for who I was. I felt certain they would be less critical of my eating habits. Their home was simple and my bedroom was small. I unpacked my meager possessions and looked out the window at the green fields and blue sky. I was happy.

In the evening my new mother called me down for supper. They were seated at the table; a floral cotton tablecloth; three white plates. A steaming pie, mashed potatoes, peas and carrots.

"I forgot to ask you," she said. "Is there any food you particularly don't like?"

"I'm not fond of tomatoes," I said.

"Neither am I," she stated philosophically. "If you ask me it's a damned rebellious vegetable. Shouldn't be allowed on decent folks' plates."

And she laughed, and nudged her husband, "This old boy, on the other hand, trains 'em to catch rabbits. You like rabbit pie?"

"Mmm, love it," I said.

"With gravy," she snorted and winked as she cut me a slice.

I knew then I would be happy with these peaceful, sympathetic folks, who understood the dangers of vicious vegetables and knew how to use nature to benefit the dinner table.

"Tomato Fangirl"
Nicole Lim

Tomatoes

Lucas Olson

It was pure September, green in the middle but laced on the edges with red and gold, hinting at a coming cold with the color of fire. There, on the boundaries of weather, the seasons seemed to change from day to day, each checking to make sure everything was still all right. Summer was not quite gone but not quite there either, still holding on tightly with a single hand. Some days you had to wear a scarf, other days you could only wear shorts. The last good days for swimming were in the past (at least until next year), but it was still warm enough to sit on the beach with a warm drink and watch the ocean murmur its way through the tides. School had begun for some but was not yet tiresome. It was still new, names still pinned to the bulletin board on construction paper cut-outs of autumn leaves. The daytime smelled like new plastic pencil holders and mulch.

It was a pure September day and Maisie was sitting with her mother in the kitchen. Her mother was chopping things: cucumbers, broccoli, two different kinds of lettuce. Each thing she chopped she would dump into a bowl and mix with a couple of wooden spoons (they did not have salad tongs). Maisie's mother stood still for a moment, after pouring in a cutting board full of shredded carrots. She had one hand on her cocked hip, and with a finger of the other she tapped her chin, trying to think.

"Maisie?" she said.

Maisie perked up from the out of date Chinese food

141

menu she was drawing on with orange crayon. She had been waiting around to be useful and felt an overwhelming sense that this was her moment. Her mother's finger lay still on her chin.

"Will you run out and grab some tomatoes?"

Maisie frowned (tomatoes did not feel like "her moment"). But nonetheless, she asked, "How many?", because 'no' was not an available answer to her mother's question anyway, and even if Maisie had been disinclined to fetch anything, it was a reason to go outside, which was enough.

Maisie's mother looked at the wicker basket of garden vegetables, which she had never felt was quite full enough.

"Three," she said, certain. She uncocked her hip, removed her finger, and resumed her chopping, now moving on to bell peppers. It would be a very full salad with little dressing, which was how she liked it.

Maisie stuffed her crayon into one of her pockets, hopped off the stool she'd been kneeling on and, confidently barefoot, strode outside. She took with her a pilfered carrot, already mostly in her mouth before she was even out the door.

Thirty minutes later Maisie came back in, grimier, her hair messy and loose, her hands in her pockets, her clothes a little frayed at the edges, and altogether without tomatoes. She was still grinning. As there were no uncut carrots left to take, she picked a piece of one out of the big bowl of salad and put it carefully in her mouth.

Her mother sighed. With the same breath as the sigh, she said, "Maisie."

"What?" Maisie asked. She recognized the sound of disappointment and knew the different routes it could take.

"Tomatoes?" her mother asked.

"Oh," Maisie said, as if her mother had just explained something incredibly complicated to her. "I forgot to get some more."

"You forgot to pick *any*, Maisie."

"No, I got them," she said. "But I lost them."

Her mother turned around to look out the kitchen window. She saw the straight route from the kitchen door to the garden, which looked green and undisturbed.

"How did you lose them, exactly?" Maisie's mother asked.

Maisie hesitated. She sensed a potential bargain.

"Are you mad?" she asked.

"You were gone for twenty minutes, Maisie. We could have eaten by now." Which, of course, meant yes.

"If I tell you how I lost the tomatoes, will you not be mad?"

Her mother re-cocked her hip, now adding a raised eyebrow. Her eyebrows were often sharp and pointy, trimmed around the edges so they were all straight lines. Maisie loved her mother but she did not like her eyebrows as much as her father's, which were bushy and looked like brown caterpillars.

"That depends on the story, I suppose," her mother said.

Maisie nodded, because that was what she expected. She climbed back up onto the stool, getting comfortable, and took a deep breath.

"So when I got to the garden..."

So when I got to the garden the tomatoes were gone. I looked all around—behind the pepper plants, under the pumpkin and squash leaves, in the fronds of the basil bush you let go to seed—and all of them were gone. I checked

all three of the tomato vines and each one was empty. I did find one tomato, but it was green and in the dirt and half rotten and covered in bugs so I didn't think you wanted that one (and I didn't really want to touch it anyway).

Then I heard rustling in a bush nearby, and when I looked up, I saw a little man standing there, trying to hide behind the leaves. At least, I think he was a man. He was also a bunny. He had the floppy ears and the legs and a lot of the fur and he also had wispy brown hair coming off his cheeks that looked like whiskers. He was standing completely still, staring at me with big, wide, dark-brown eyes.

He was holding all of our tomatoes in his arms.

"Hey!" I said. "Those are our tomatoes!"

Then the rabbit man ran. I followed him though, my bare feet kicking up a cloud of dirt when I bolted out of the garden (I might have squished a basil plant I'm sorry).

We ran all through the yard: around the big bush, under the low tree, over the big red wheelbarrow, through a tire swing (well, he jumped through the tire swing; I just went around it). Then he hopped over the rose bushes into Mrs. Applebaum's yard.

I knew the short cut though and we went over Mrs. Applebaum's car (he dented it with his foot, but I slid over it so the dent is his fault), ran circles around her clothesline when he tried to hide in her hanging bedsheets. When I was distracted with the sheets he ran over the bushes on the other side of Mrs. Applebaum's yard.

Now I know you told me never to go in there

'cause "the house is abandoned and I bet it's haunted too" and "it'll probably fall like a Jenga tower the next time there's a strong wind" and "Maisie, if you go in there you WILL step on a nail and you WILL get tetanus and they'll give you a great big shot right in your BUTT and so help me I WILL tell your father," but the bunny man had stolen all of our tomatoes so you know that I had to.

So I followed him (but I had to take a running jump to get over the rose bushes). When I landed on the other side he was just standing there breathing heavily and looking satisfied with himself. I don't think he had expected me to follow him. He was still holding all the tomatoes and he hadn't dropped a single one the whole time he was running.

"Jeez, girlie," the bunny man said. "Leave me alone."

"Well," I said. "Give me back my tomatoes." Then he groaned and ran through the overgrown grass (it was as high as my butt and tickled when I ran through it) right into the abandoned house. The door was just hanging open so he didn't even need to stop to open it.

So, even though the house was scary and probably haunted and was leaning to one side like an uneven picture frame, I followed him in anyway. I didn't even step on a nail or anything, even though the floorboards inside were all gray and splintery.

I followed the bunny man all through the house, turning from one room to the next to a hallway to the kitchen back to the front room then back into the hallway. Then he took a sharp turn, kicked open a really weird looking door with some carvings on it, and started running down stairs into the basement.

The stairs went on for a long time, and eventually both of us were jumping down two steps at a time to try and outrun the other. I was right behind him by the time we got to the bottom (or I think I was; it was pretty dark down there). And I chased him all the way across the big empty cobwebby damp stone basement, until he ran up a couple steps and knocked open the slanted cellar doors that went back into the yard. He looked down when he got outside and blew a raspberry at me, so I followed him right upstairs back into the yard.

Except when I got up the stairs and outside, I wasn't in the old abandoned yard with the tall yellow grass and the family of raccoons. I was somewhere else. I was in the greenest place I've ever been. Even greener than the butterfly house at the zoo, and that was all just thick sugary plants and flapping wings. This place was different. If the air could have been green, it would have been.

I was in the woods, but really big woods, with trees as tall as skyscrapers and as thick as lighthouses. Their branches were so high and so heavy that there was no sky except the leaves. Clouds hovered beneath them, bending around the trunk of the trees as they went. In some places—I only saw a few—the leaves had turned color, gone yellow likes suns or red like grapefruit. In a few other places the leaves had fallen down, and there was no blue behind the hole they left in the sky, just gray the color of slush. But the rest of the woods were still wet and green like summer. The ground was covered in moss and grass, like walking on a blanket. And the birds, mom! There were so many that when they flew together they looked like a river flying in between the branches of big trees. All of them seemed to be flying off in one direction.

The cellar doors closed behind me when I got outside, and I turned around when I heard the noise of them shutting and a heavy metal sound like pieces clicking together. Instead of being old red wooden doors on the side of a house, they were nestled in the roots of a great big tree.

But I couldn't stay and look at it too long 'cause the bunny man was off and running again. He'd run into a big, big, huge crowd of animals that were all moving in one direction. They were all sorts of animals—deer, birds, foxes the size of horses with more tails than I could count, horses even bigger than the foxes with eight legs like spiders, spiders even bigger than the horses (they just had the normal eight legs though), gophers and giraffes and groundhogs and a bunch of things that were almost like people like the bunny man. I could see where the bunny man was going because the animals would yell when he bumped into them. So I followed right after him bumping my way through the crowd (some of the animals yelled at me too). I was worried the bunny man was gonna get away, because he was going through the crowd faster than I was, but then his foot caught on a tree branch and he tripped.

He fell right face first into the ground and

squashed the whole armful of tomatoes against the ground. Almost all of the tomatoes got smushed, but I saw a few roll away from him when he fell, so I jumped right over him and grabbed them before he could move.

"Ha!" I said, holding them up in the air, and then I blew a raspberry at him.

He looked up at me, kinda sad-like and with his face all covered in tomato. "Are thems all what's left?" he asked.

"Uh-huh, and they're *mine* so buzz off."

"Like hell they is, girlie. I found them fair and even, so I did!" He got up off the ground, waggling one of his fingers at me while he tried to wipe as much squished tomato of himself as possible.

"Pfft." He reached for the tomatoes but I jumped back away from him. "Stole them you mean. These are my family's tomatoes, we grew them."

"Oh that so? You grew them up yourselves? You water them all the time?"

"Well," I said. "It rained a lot this summer, so we didn't have to."

"And you gave them all the minerals?"

"Those were in the dirt already! I learned that in school last week."

"Well," the rabbit man said. "Sounds like they grew themselves then. Just 'cause you been pickin 'em don't make 'em yours. Now gimme!" He reached again; I jumped again. This time, to make sure he didn't get them, I stuck one tomato in each of my cargo pockets (I *told* you they were good for something mom) and then just held the third one tightly in my hands.

"No way," I said. "They aren't for you!"

"No, they aren't," he said. Suddenly he looked really sad and his ears flopped down. "They're for the Queen."

"The Queen?" I always had wanted to see a queen. They get to wear those big clothes and the big golden crowns and tell people what to do from awesome chairs. I think I'd like to be a queen, or at least give it a try. (Not a princess though, they never *do* anything, they just kinda hang around and wait for boys or frogs or other gross things to kiss). "Queen of what?"

"You don't even know what's on, do ya? Don't even know what you're doing with that fruit?"

"Well," I said. "I was gonna eat it later. You know, in a salad."

"It's equinox, girlie. The Winter Queen's calling court. We're supposed to be paying tribute, asking for boons."

"Best get in line too," said a passing turtle as big as a bumper car. His voice sounded like a tuba.

"Well, that's neat," I said. "But I gotta get these tomatoes home or my mom is gonna be real mad." I started to walk away but then the bunny man just laughed at me.

"Where you think you're off to, girl?" he asked.

"Well the door is over there, so..."

"That door locks behind your type. You're stuck here." Then his smiled at me with big buckteeth.

I frowned at him and ran back through the crowd the way I'd come, bumping into a bunch more animals (and running underneath a house that walked on chicken legs). The bunny man laughed at me the whole way, walking along behind me. At first I thought the door had disappeared, like happens sometimes in the story books, but it was still there—bright red and buried in the roots of a tree. I almost screamed I was so happy that I found it. Still holding the tomato in one hand, I grabbed the rusty metal handle on the door and pulled.

And pulled.

And pulled some more.

And still it wouldn't budge. All the while the bunny man was laughing at me.

"What you think, girlie? You'd just run in here for your groceries and scoot on back home?"

"I can't be stuck here," I told him. "I need to be home for dinner."

He danced around on his little furry feet, hopping beside me in circles. "Oh no, little girl. You ain't making it home for dinner. Not for breakfast neither. I hope you like The Wilderness 'cause like as not you'll be staying..."

I frowned at him (and I definitely, definitely wasn't crying not even a little bit at all) and he smiled like he had been waiting for it.

"Unless..." he said.

"Unless?"

"Might be there is a way," he said. I went to grab him and he hopped out of reach. "But why should I tell you for nothing?"

So this is where I lost the first tomato, you know, 'cause I *had* to give it to him or else I wouldn't have been able to get back home and we wouldn't have gotten any tomatoes. (Yeah, I *know* we don't have any tomatoes right now but

I didn't know that then, jeez.) So I reached into one of my pockets and gave the bunny man one of my tomatoes. He hopped around real excited when he got it, holding it up in the air like that scene at the beginning of the Lion King.

"So?" I asked him, after he'd been jumping around for a while.

"Huh?" he said.

"So how do I get home, stupid?"

"Oh, you just gotta ask the Queen for it as your boon. It'll cost ya though."

"I don't have any money."

"Queen don't take money, girlie. And you'd best get in line if you wanna get home before sunset." He pointed at the crowd of animals we'd been running through. They had straightened out and formed a long line running deeper into the forest. Every few seconds the animals would all step forward. "And trust me, you wanna get home by sunset. Nighttime in here ain't a good place for your type folks." Then the bunny man ran off, still holding the tomato up like a trophy.

Not sure what else to do, I just wandered into line behind a dog with two different colored eyes and a man that looked like he was made out of plants. I had to stand right behind him. He smelled like low tide and used a walking stick taller than he was.

I just looked at the tomato in my hand while I waited. I don't know why the bunny man wanted the tomatoes so bad. I know they taste good but the one I was holding looked kinda weird and lumpy. It was still all covered in tomato juice from when the man had tripped and it looked like it was all bloody.

As the line moved up, I started to notice animals coming back from the front. Some of them looked really happy, some of them looked really sad, and other ones were hurt. Sometimes there would be a few minutes and no animals would show up at all. (I hope those animals just went back a different way, instead of... whatever else).

"What's the queen look like?" I asked the toad in line behind me, but he didn't say anything.

"Is she nice?" I asked a big cat with antelope horns as he was walking back from the front of the line.

"What's she queen of, anyway?" I asked no one in particular. Nobody answered at all. Then we took another step forward, a big elephant at the front of the line moved out of the way, and I saw her.

Her throne was real, real tall, and it looked like a bunch of sticks and vines had gotten twisted up in a tornado, except at the top where it spread out into a giant thornbush with red flowers. The throne had to be really tall, I think, 'cause the Queen was the tallest thing I'd ever seen. I couldn't tell you how tall in inches or centimeters or miles or anything 'cause I don't think you can measure her that way. She just looked long and stretched out and her fingers were as long as my arm. She was beautiful too, I guess, in the same way that a sword can be beautiful. She was really sharp too, just like a sword. It looked like she could cut something open just by touching it. She didn't look like she had eyeballs. It looked like she had trapped ice behind her eyelids instead.

I couldn't take my eyes away from her the whole time the line was moving. I didn't even realize the line *was* moving, until someone by the throne called "NEXT" and the stinky green man stepped forward. Which meant I was next after him. (I was nervous, but I tried not to squeeze the tomato too hard because then you wouldn't be able to cut it up for the salad).

"Your Majesty," he said, after taking a deep bow. "I come for a boon."

She gestured for him to continue with a wave of her finger.

"I would like to..." he swallowed. If he wasn't made of plants I would think he was sweating. "I would like to..."

"Speak, leave, or be burned. I don't have time for mumbling oafs." The Queen's voice sounded like a blizzard.

"I would like to be freed from service, my Lady."

"And what do you offer in exchange?" the Queen asked.

"Noth—nothing to offer, my lady, but I have given you loyal service since the day you—" The man didn't finish. The Queen gestured with a different finger, and two men emerged from the woods. They had really long pointy ears and skin so pale it was almost white. They were naked except for angry-looking wooden masks they wore around their faces. They grabbed the plant man by the arms and dragged him off into the woods. He didn't make a sound as he went. He just stared at the Queen and looked heartbroken.

"NEXT," a voice called, so I stepped up.

"Um," I said. "Um."

The Queen's long fingers rapped against the arms of her chair. I bowed like the man had and said: "Your Majesty, I come for a boon."

"And what does a child want that I can give her?"

"I want to go home," I said. And then, because I thought it might be important. "You know, in time for dinner and stuff."

"Passage from my kingdom is not cheap, little girl. I hope you have more to offer than the green man did."

"Uh, well. What do you want?"

The Queen smiled down at me. I didn't like it at all. Her teeth looked like shark teeth. "An apt question." She brushed her long fingers against her sharp chin, like she was thinking. She thought for a while, and towards the end I was getting kind of bored so I was hopping from foot to foot.

"Part of you must stay here," the Queen said. "Your heart."

"I'm using it though! I need it to move my blood and stuff."

"You don't seem to be using it girl, you seem to be holding it."

I looked down at the tomato in my hands.

Lumpy. Red. Wet with tomato juice. If she couldn't see the seeds then I guess it looked kind of like a heart. So you see, mom, I *had* to give it to her or I wouldn't have been able to come home not even at all. So I said:

"Okay."

And two more masked men came out of the woods on either side, each one carrying a box. The one on the right held his open, so I

154

put the tomato inside. He snapped the lid shut and sank back into the trees. The one on my left then opened his box and there was a big iron key inside it. I picked it up and frowned.

"There's not a lock on the cellar door though."

"There are many kinds of locks, girl. Take it and be gone."

So I shrugged and grabbed the key and left, walking back down along the line. I skipped most of the way, even though on the dirt that kind of hurt my bare feet. Way down at the end of the line I saw the bunny man, holding the tomato I had given him.

"I see you got your key, girlie," he said. "What did she want?"

"My heart. I gave her a tomato instead."

The bunny man looked down at the tomato in his hands and suddenly looked very scared. "The Winter Queen don't like it when people get tricksy. You sure that was wise?"

I shrugged.

"You best get out of here fast, girl."

"Okee doke," I said, and went back to skipping.

The cellar doors opened up easy as anything when I was holding the key. I went down the steps and I was back in the old house. I rushed out of the basement (it had only gotten darker), but I was careful on the stairs and the floor of the old house 'cause I didn't want to hit any nails. I pulled the carved door to the basement shut behind me when I came up the stairs and took a closer look at the carving. It looked like the queen, holding something up in her hands. She looked angry in the carving. I left quick.

I did stop on the porch though. I know the house was empty, but it seemed rude to just leave the door open, so I pulled it shut behind me. I was still holding the key in one hand, and I was curious, so I stuck it in the lock of the closed door and twisted it. There was a heavy metal sound and then the door didn't move anymore. Then I walked off the porch, crawled through the bushes, and I came home!

In the time it had taken Maisie to tell her story, her mother had finished making dinner, her father had come home (and been caught up), and dinner had been completely eaten. They were sitting now in a darkening dining room, each with an empty bowl of salad (that Maisie's mother had already decided was okay without tomatoes).

Maisie's mother nodded, dabbed at her mouth with her napkin and then said:

"Maisie, go to your room."

"What?" Maisie said. "Why?"

"Because fibbers go to their room, especially big fibbers."

"Well, I think she did a great job on that story," Maisie's father said.

"Quiet, Scott," her mother said, then she turned back to Maisie. "That story didn't make any sense, Maisie. There is no such thing as rabbit people, or Winter Queens, or magical cellar doors. You didn't even count right at the end. You *should* have another tomato in your pocket."

Maisie tapped her chin thoughtfully. "Oh yeah, I forgot about that one."

"Yes," her mother said. "You did. Clean your place and go to your room. No TV tonight, and no desert, and

no books either. And we'll talk about you playing in that deathtrap of a house later."

"But, mom!"

"No buts! Clean your place and then your father will bring you to your room."

Maisie and her dad both grumbled as they stood up from the dining table. They stacked their dishes by the kitchen sink, and then Maisie's father slowly lead her up to the attic room where she kept her bed and her books and where she hung all of the pictures she drew of the things she swore she saw.

"I thought you did a great job on that story, dear," her father said.

"It's not a *story*, dad; it's *real*."

Her father smiled. "Well, either way, good job." Then he kissed her on the forehead and gently pushed her into her room, pulling the door shut behind him as he left. Maisie heard him walk quietly back down the stairs and then start washing the dishes.

"Whatever," Maisie said. She stuck her hands into her pockets and came out with two things: first a heavy metal key, which she twirled on her finger, and secondly a tomato (which she had indeed forgot about). She took a bite, squirting tomato juice onto her cheeks, and thought it tasted pretty good. It might even have gone well with the salad.

Tomato, The Red Menace

John Grey

You look out from your box
at a green, green world,
unduly pressured by the likes
of cauliflower, cabbage,
broccoli and Brussel sprouts
into being ashamed of
your shiny red skin.

Your résumé reads
planting, pollinating,
ripening and picking,
but this means nothing
to the poking, prodding finger,
the fat squeezing hands -
as if you've ever been anything
but fresh.

Lettuce and the like
get tossed into shopping baskets
quick as an outlaw
drawing a six-shooter
but no one takes on
your juicy plumpness
without this thorough
interrogation.

It's as if they're somehow
subconsciously cognizant
of your early reputation—
the toxic nightshade nemesis,
the insidious love apple.

You're as crimson as blood,
maybe that's the problem.
You're never just eaten,
you're spilled.

The Harvest

John Vicary

A hand hovered before reaching down to make the final selection. Tomato held still and silent; its patience was rewarded as it was lifted free of its brethren and placed in the sack after a cursory examination for flaws.

"Ow!" The sack was dark, but Tomato could tell by the muffled exclamation that it'd been placed upon a legume's body, possibly a head. It shifted in subtle apology and felt the whole bag of what could only be more root vegetables move to accommodate its movement. Tomato felt itself slide towards the bottom.

"Pardon me, but could you roll to the side? You're crushing me against Potato," Radish said.

"Oh, of course," Tomato said. It wedged itself against Ginger root and then blushed at the unintentional intimacy.

"Where are we going?" Yam wailed from the top of the sack.

"Duh," Beet said. "Duh. Duh."

"No one knows!" Onion started to cry. "We've been kidnapped!"

Radish cleared its throat. "Friends! We must find the last measure of our courage in these trying times and resolve not to panic."

"Who died and made you King Weed of the Produce Patch?" Parsnip sneered.

Potato rocked back and forth. "Radish is right; fighting

160

isn't the answer! We should hug it out. Anyone?"

"Right here, Idaho," Ginger purred.

"What else would you expect from a rhizome?" Parsnip spat.

"Duh. Duhduhduh," Beet said.

Tomato looked at Beet. "Is it okay? Why does it keep saying that?"

Yam glanced down from where it was wedged against Rutabaga, who appeared to be sleeping. "Beet was dropped," it whispered. "It just keeps making that noise now."

"Oh." Tomato nodded. Maybe it was for the best. "So, no one knows where we're going?"

"We're all fricking geniuses, Tomato," Parsnip griped. "If you haven't noticed."

Ginger shook her root, a movement that drew the eyes of all the tubers. "I heard we were going to start a farm."

"It makes sense," Radish said. "We were chosen, don't you see? For our superior qualities. We are going to part of something bigger than ourselves, something better than any of us has the power to imagine!"

Yam trembled. "But we were taken! Just…picked! My mom was right there, and I'll never see her again! Why me?"

"Why? Why any of us?" Onion asked, breaking down into fresh sobs.

"You're in the blush of youth! The vigor of your cells is evident in your vibrant coloring. Perhaps Ginger is correct and it is to be a new collective, a radical and fresh harvest where we begin the seed our vaunted progeny!" Radish twiddled his stems. "Can you imagine the importance for our prospective gene pools? It's a new frontier, friends! Excellence has been recognized and rewarded!"

"Duh," Beet said. It drooled a little.

"Totally! Give me five, bro. Great speech." Potato

grinned, but Tomato directed its gaze away, unsure of the eye in which to look.

The gentle swaying they'd all grown accustomed to ceased, and they were jostled against each other as the sack was thrown onto a hard surface. "Excuse me," Radish mumbled, pulling its face from Parsnip's leaf cluster, when the sack opened and Yam was whisked away.

"Not Yam!" Onion cried. "It was so young!"

Rutabaga yawned itself awake. "Whazzup, bitches?"

"Fear not for Yam—"

Chop

Radish paused. "Yam is but the first of us to experience the brave new frontier—"

Chop Chop Chop

"What's that?" Ginger asked.

Radish frowned. "The doorway to our freedom. Nothing more."

A hand reached in, and Parsnip was the next to go.

"Fear not, friends, for the—"

Chop

Radish raised its voice to be heard over the rhythmic cleaving. "All is well. Preparations are merely underway for our arrival in the fresh hearth."

Onion was the next to be selected, and the hacking heralded an overwhelming odor. Potato's many eyes watered.

"Let us embrace our dawning genesis."

One by one, the bag was emptied of its contents until only Radish and Tomato were left. "I shall see you on the other side, old chap," Radish said as pair of fingers grasped its stalk and it was lifted free. "Oh! That isn't what—"

"What is it? What do you see?" Tomato tried to shout to Radish, but it was too late. It was gone.

Tomato listened to the steady *chop* and tried not to be nervous. It was just as Radish had promised; the foundation

was being laid and some furrows being dug. Its new home must be ready. It was Tomato's turn next.

When the hand reached for Tomato, it was glad. Fingers tightened around it, and it was ready for its future. The sack opened, and Tomato opened its eyes to see glory awaiting.

Tania's Parmesan Chicken

Tania Simcock

4 boneless chicken breasts
1 large white onion
2 large eggs
1/8 – 1/4 cup of milk
1 to 1.5 cups fine dry bread crumbs
1 to 1.5 cups Parmesan cheese
1/4 cup olive oil
1 cup grape tomatoes
1 cup Mozzarella cheese, grated (more or less to taste)

Herbs/Seasonings – recommended
Rosemary
Garlic
Italian style

1. Preheat oven to 350°F

2. Slice onion into large pedals and place in a single layer on the bottom of a casserole dish.

3. Mix eggs and small amount of milk to create an egg wash, pour onto a large plate or keep in shallow bowl, set aside.

4. Mix breadcrumbs and Parmesan cheese at a 50/50 ratio, add small amount of rosemary or other herbs.

5. One piece at a time coat the chicken breast with the egg wash, then roll into the bread and cheese mixture until covered. Place on top of the onion bed in the casserole dish.

6. Once all chicken breasts are in the casserole dish drizzle the olive oil over each piece.

7. Cover the casserole dish and place in the oven for 40 minutes.

8. While the chicken is cooking: Using an electric mixer, blend the grape tomatoes but not to the point where they are completely pureed, chunks are acceptable. Mix in preferred seasonings/herbs (if adding rosemary use small amount).

9. After the 40 minutes remove chicken from the oven, spoon the tomato mixture evenly over each chicken breast. Cover the casserole dish and cook for another 20 minutes.

10. After the 20 minutes remove from the oven and spread mozzarella cheese over the tomato mixture. Return to oven, uncovered, for about 10 minutes or until the cheese is melted.

Serve and enjoy!

The Little Red Pumpkin (of Doom!)

Richard Leavesley

Thomas Richard Toah was, as his name might suggest, a tomato. He wasn't cut out to be in fact cut out and lit up as a child's party favor; though his original destiny as one of the world's favorite sandwich fillings was exactly a fun prospect either. Compared to his current situation though he believed that being chopped up and squashed between two slices of bread and butter with a strange slice of cheese somehow seemed more dignified and honorable.

He had a "face" carved into him, badly, by a small child whose father had told her that she was too little to carve anything big, and that he didn't want her to cut herself, so he'd supplied her with a small plastic picnic knife to complete what was clearly her first attempt. With this she had roughly gouged two hugely mismatched "eyes" and jagged diagonal slash that Thomas assumed to be a "mouth". After that he had been placed on the porch step with the others, struggling through that cold October evening, crying seeds onto the concrete. At least he was too small to have his guts ripped out and replaced with a hot candle. Instead they had placed a tea-candle behind him, to light up his "face", which constantly roasted what would have to be his "bottom".

But worse than all of this was the company he was forced to keep: three huge pumpkins sat there with him. Now, as everybody knows, pumpkins are the rudest and most thuggish of vegetables, particularly when they're all

dressed up for Halloween, and these three were determined to make tonight Hell for him!

"We're going to Ketchuperize you!" whispered their leader, who imaginatively called himself Skull because of his expertly carved creepy skull face. The smallest of the three, Kiss (due to her pouting lips and half closed slatted eyes) kept giggling annoyingly after every remark, whilst the largest, a bloated thug who called himself Smiley kept awkwardly trying to nudge him off the porch step. He had the grimmest face of all—kind of warped and lopsided— but was probably too stupid to realize that he was anything but smiley.

"Yeah," Kiss tittered, "We're gonna puree you!"

"Yeah," Smiley chipped in, "We a gonna, like, uh, chop ya up 'n' stuff!"

"Leave me alone!" Thomas sighed for the umpteenth time that night.

"Tough!" Skull grinned, "Nobody ain't going nowhere!"

"So where are you going?" Thomas asked.

"What?" Skull frowned.

"Well, if nobody isn't going nowhere then you must be going somewhere!"

"SHUT UP!" Skull roared, "When it turns midnight everything comes alive and you're going to be dead! When we get the life spark I'm going crush you to paste!"

"Yeah," Smiley chipped in, "We a gonna, like, uh, chop ya up 'n' stuff!"

"You already said that, ya spud!" Skull hissed at him so frighteningly that the bigger pumpkin rocked back a little.

"What's the life spark?" Thomas asked.

"You don't know nothing!" it was Kiss that answered (and Thomas refrained from making another joke at the expense of poor grammar, which would have been wasted

on this audience anyway) "Everyone knows that at the last moment of Halloween, all living things that have been marked as tributes to The Old Gods, like what we have, get an extra spark of life!"

"And we get to tear up this town," Skull added, "Starting with you."

Thomas found that a little disturbing, and also very interesting. Very interesting indeed "What's your problem with me anyway?"

"We hate your lot," Skull sneered, "Coming here from your fancy supermarkets, hogging all our fridge space, stealing our jobs!"

Again, very interesting, "So you don't come from the supermarket?"

"No," Smiley mumbled, "We was growd in yonder garden, like proper vegetables is meant to be."

I'm not a vegetable, Thomas thought about telling them, but he knew that facts were wasted on the ignorant. More importantly, he'd learned something very interesting and useful about them. He would've grinned if he wasn't already permanently grinning.

"So, is there any way we can forget about all of that and just be friends?"

The pumpkins just laughed at this.

"Ok. So, just so you know, when the time comes I will fight back."

They laughed even harder.

If Thomas could've shrugged he would've. Fair warning.

The rest of the night went surprisingly quickly. Humans came by in their masks and costumes, carrying bags and buckets of bad food. Occasionally they would stop and laugh at the messy little red "pumpkin" and his well-carved "friends". The real pumpkins continued to goad him, but he blissfully ignored them. Eventually the visitors stopped

168

visiting and all became quiet.

Finally the clock above the town hall chimed midnight. The witching hour.

Thomas felt a burst of energy flowing into him. He felt alive and could move in a way he never could before. No wind or plucking human hands required. He spun swiftly on his axis, knocking the tea light, which had long since gone out, away from him.

The pumpkins loomed over him, looking cruel and wickedly alive, drooling juice and candle wax onto the step.

But Thomas simply grinned his crooked grin and pounced. He was just a red blur smashing into and through them like tissue paper. Given voice for the first time in their lives, screams of surprise and pain were the first and last sounds they made.

In a mere five seconds Thomas stood alone on the cold porch step, surrounded by a mess of orange pulp. His grin was bigger than possible. Sometimes, he told himself, there really were advantages to being a genetically modified fruit!

La Tomatina

Robyn Groth

He
threw
the first
tomato.
It was friendly fire.
In fact, the whole war was civil.

Market Feud

Herika R Raymer

If there was ever evidence God had a twisted sense of humor, Rena was experiencing it now. Rena stood between two kiosks at the Hot Springs Farmer's Market, and was uncertain which way she could turn. It appeared that either way she went, it would start a terrible fight. Not over her, thank goodness, but over what she was considering buying. She was not sure whether she should laugh at the absurdity of the situation, or be annoyed at the inexplicable stubbornness of people. At the moment, she chose the wisdom of silence while she quickly tried to think of a resolution.

Rena was here with her brother Clyde, who was job hunting in a town mere hours away from their hometown of Atkins. She wandered the streets as she waited to hear about the interview's outcome and could not help but feel as if she were a world away from home. The buildings here were beautiful if not crowded, though there was a tension in the air she could not quite pinpoint. From some snippets of conversations she had heard in the cafes, apparently there was a federal crackdown going on over illegal gambling. Nothing surprising there really, but it seemed locals were concerned about how the negative attention might affect the growth of the town. Even with the recent construction of the freeways, which helped bring tourists in, the local town folk apparently had internal concerns that might affect local economics. Rena did not think the residents had anything to worry about. She had enjoyed

walking the shops of Bathhouse Row and sampling the culture around her. Her favorite thus far was enjoying one of the few thermal water spas, which were still open due to many of the downtown bathhouses being closed. Well, that and the horseback riding. Warmed naturally by geothermal heat, the baths here were delightful. She was spoiling herself, she knew. Still, there was nothing wrong with a little pampering, right?

Then she saw the Farmer's Market.

It was off one of the roads leading out of Bathhouse Row, and it was beautiful. It was not exactly like the one in Atkins, but it was familiar. The kiosks lined up with various goods being offered, while farmers, artists, and craftsman enticed passersby to examine what they had on display and, even better, purchase one. Walking among the attendees, she felt better. The bit of homesickness subsided the more she moved among the other bodies in the crowd. A band set up at one end of the market, delighting the people with some traditional tunes. A few people even paired off and danced modestly. She smiled as she watched. It surprised her a bit when a young man approached and made a slight bow, holding his hand out in invitation. It was a slight shock when she accepted the offered hand. The dance was invigorating, and she was laughing by the time it ended. Hungry and thirsty, too. Thanking her dance partner, she returned to the kiosks to find something appetizing.

Everything looked good, but nothing in particular she was hungry for. Then she noticed two kiosks, directly across from one another. One had an array of fruits, freshly picked was what the man was saying. The other had a selection of vegetables, grown in the best soil boasted the farmer behind the stand. They talked simultaneously, loud but not yelling. It was as though they were trying to draw people to their particular stands.

"Try our delicious fruits!" the one to her left invited.

"Freshest vegetables you will ever eat!" the one to her right countered.

People stopped at the booths and looked over what was being offered. She did the same. First she stopped at the fruit kiosk, recognizing some and curious about others. They did look tempting, but she was not sure if it was what she was hungry for. Although, she might consider picking up a few for later. After all, there was no telling when her sweet tooth would announce itself. It would be nice not to have to share. Best not to buy on impulse, though. Her father was always rather particular about that.

Rubbing her hands together, she had turned to the booth across from the fruit kiosk. There, an array of vegetables beckoned. They looked firm and fresh, and she prudently placed her hands behind her back to keep from touching any of the produce. 'Look with your eyes, not your hands,' she could hear her mother saying. Still, the cucumbers looked especially tempting, as did the okra. Too bad she was unable to fry them. Although, she could buy some and take it back. It would possibly save one trip to the grocery store. She spied a particularly luscious array of tomatoes.

Her favorite!

Looking at them made her mouth water.

She began to think of all the recipes she could make with them, or just eating them by themselves. After she took mental stock of her funds, she realized she could afford a few items, and decided on getting some vegetables and fruit. So, mentally putting tomatoes at the top of the list, she put together a short list of what she would like to purchase. After getting a generic quote, she then turned to the fruit kiosk to see what she could afford from there. It was then that she noticed it.

There were tomatoes at the fruit stand as well.

Looking back at the vegetable kiosk, she saw the selection there, and turning back to the array before her she realized they were just as appetizing here as well. Looking ripe and juicy, she could just picture herself picking up one of them and biting in. Relishing the taste. Still, it bothered her that there was a selection at both kiosks. Impulsively, she asked the question.

"You sell tomatoes?"

The fruit teller stood straighter and a strange glint came to his eyes. He looked proud, but also challenging. Rena felt intimidated at that moment, wondering what she had said wrong.

"Tomatoes are a great fruit," he declared pointedly.

"Really?" to be honest, the idea had never occurred to her.

"Grown off a vine and containing seeds," he went on as he gestured to the red spheres. "Tasty on their own, these wonderful fruit are available for your eating delight."

"Excuse me!" a new voice interrupted.

She turned, startled by the interruption. Not only her, but also some of the other passers-by also stopped and glanced between the two kiosks across from one another. The man behind the vegetable display gestured to his selection of tomatoes.

"Tomatoes are great *vegetables* used in savory cooking as well as among other *vegetables* in salads," he explained tersely.

Rena noticed his attention was not so much on her as it was on the man opposite him.

Involuntarily, she stepped back, out of line of 'fire'. The animosity between the two men was almost palatable. Her hands fidgeted until she clasped them together. She looked between the duo as they continued their heated discussion.

"These *fruits* are a wonderful addition to any meal,

174

being able to be eaten alone and enjoyed without the addition of condiments or other flavoring," the man smiled. "Although the addition of such can enhance the taste."

"As a *vegetable* it compliments not only other *vegetables* but also adds flavor to various stews and soups. Last I heard, no *fruit* was added to stews."

"*Fruits* have been added to salads, however."

The man glowered, and then sneered. "The courts disagree with you."

The pregnant silence which followed made Rena aware that she was not the only spectator to this altercation between the two men. Looking around, she noticed there was a circle of people watching the terrible scene. Even worse, she was at the center of the viewers and between the two kiosks.

"Courts?" she squeaked.

The vegetable teller grinned. "The courts decided that tomatoes are *vegetables*, not *fruit*."

The fruit teller scoffed. "Only for money," he said dismissively. "Everyone knows tomatoes are *fruit*. That fact cannot be changed because the government wanted to make more money."

The vegetable peddler crossed his arms and gave a mocking look. "I suppose you displaying your 'fruit' is just for show?"

The fruit peddler glowered and crossed his arms as well. "You 'vegetable' folk managed to get a *fruit* declared a *vegetable* simply because you were jealous of having to pay a tax we *fruit growers* did not have to."

His opponent's face darkened. "A vegetable is a vegetable."

The man shrugged. "Except when it is a fruit."

Okay, Rena thought, *this disagreement has obviously been going on for longer than I have been here. I wonder if I can just sneak away without sparking any more arguments.*

All I wanted was to pick something fresh up to eat.

She attempted to back away from being between the two combatants. Except when she took just one step, both men focused on her. The intangible weight of their gazes froze her in place. She could feel her cheeks flush with embarrassment, and could almost predict what was going to be suggested next.

"Let's let the lady decide," the vegetable seller invited.

She almost groaned aloud. Her interest in the tomato at the vegetable stand had not been missed, and the man knew he had a sale. Only now her favorite food was being used to try and give more evidence in an ongoing feud that she had no desire to be a part of, even obscurely. Thing was, up until this point she had not really thought about the tomato as a fruit or a vegetable. Mainly because she enjoyed it both by itself and with other food. Little cherry tomatoes were her preferred snack when possible. She had also been known to be reluctant to eat any type of salad that did not have at least a few slices of tomato in it, to her it just did not seem complete. Her favorite soups and stews had tomato juice in them. In addition, even though it was a bit strange, occasionally she even liked to drink tomato juice by itself - just as she did orange juice or even grapefruit juice.

So, in effect, Rena had enjoyed the tomato as both a vegetable and a fruit.

Now she was being placed in the position where she had to choose. Worse, her choice was going to be used as evidence towards one opinion of the disposition of the food. How in the world had she gotten herself into this position?

She tightened her clasped hands, wanting terribly just to walk away. Except that she was encircled and was the focus of this uncomfortable confrontation. Swallowing dryly, she looked back and forth between the two kiosks.

176

There had to be a way to get out of this situation without causing more discord. The impression that more hostility between these two men was not a good outcome overcame her. She was sure there was a way out of this; she just had to think of it.

The obvious thing was to buy something from both booths.

Problem was, she was sure whichever one she bought from first would boast a 'win'.

Was it wrong that she still wanted her tomatoes?

So the dilemma was, how could she get what she wanted without giving one or other of the antagonistic men what they wanted.

Not moving from where she stood, she shifted her gaze from the men to the produce in front of them. She knew they were not going to give her much time, but she was thinking rapidly. Her stomach was tight, belying any previous hunger pains. However, she knew that once all this was over the hunger would make itself known once more. Though she doubted she would be able to look at tomatoes the same way again.

An idea surfaced, allowing her to relax. She just hoped it worked.

"Gentleman," she squeaked and grimaced. She cleared her throat before speaking again. "Would you please bring me one of your best so that I might compare them?"

The men looked dubious but complied. It was not unusual for someone to examine a piece of produce more closely, even going so far as to test the firmness as a testament of its edibility. Each took great care to scan their selections, making sure to pick up the piece they thought the most tempting. Rena noted each man had an assistant, who also took time to glare at each other from across the concrete path separating their booths.

What an odd variation of the Hatfields and McCoys, she

thought.

Eventually the men approached, each carrying a few tomatoes they deemed the best. They tried to stand out of arm's reach, showing her their products from that distance. She gave them a sidelong look.

"I cannot properly examine them that way," she admonished them gently. "Please bring them closer."

With expressions of distrust, they inched closer. She motioned them to continue to do so until she could see the red food clearly. The silence around them was broken by some mutters and whispers. This did not help her feeling of being pressured. From her peripheral vision, she could see that some of the onlookers had left - obviously bored with the local drama. Those who remained, however, appeared keen to know how it would end. Either that, or some of them felt slightly protective of her and wanted to be sure she would be okay. She determined the latter by the way a few of the men eyed the two men holding out the tomatoes. One of them was her dance partner. His calm blue eyes met hers, and he gave her an encouraging smile. Too bad he could not come over and rescue her.

The men were beginning to shift their weight from one foot to another, indicating their mounting impatience. She could not postpone them any longer and could only hope that her solution was accepted by both men. Only one way to find out.

"These look delightful!" she declared as she reached out both hands and, simultaneously, plucked a tomato from each man's hand.

They objected loudly.

Rena spoke again, attempting to ignore them. "I believe I will snack on this delightful fruit while using this luscious looking vegetable in a salad at home," she went on.

They paused, and then looked rather upset. She had

not given one or the other what they wanted. They had wanted her to choose one or the other, positioning her in such a way so that whichever way she turned could be used as her answer. Even if she had gotten both. This way, she had brought them both to her and still managed to get one from each of them at the same time. The men were not happy, but as the crowd approached they unwillingly backed away. It would not help either of their sales if they continued to make a scene. She made sure to pay them, shaking as she did so. She could feel their glares following her as she left. There was no doubt that she would not be returning to this Farmer's Market.

After the unpleasantness, the warmth of a heated water spa was welcome. Unfortunately, it did not relax her completely. She was very glad to see her brother when he arrived at the hotel room that afternoon. He was grinning— the interview had gone well and he was expecting to get a call.

Their drive home was bittersweet for her. The delights of the bathhouses, horseback riding, and cultural displays would always be with her. However, they would always be overshadowed by the Market Feud over whether or not a tomato was a fruit or vegetable.

Tomato Perugu Pachady [Or Tomato Yogurt Pickle]

Rao Vandana Parankusam

Preparation Time – 10 to 15 minutes

3 fresh ripe tomatoes, diced
3 tablespoons refined oil
1 1/2 teaspoons salt
200 grams (approx. 7oz) yogurt

Spices:
1 teaspoon split Bengal gram
1 teaspoon split black gram
1 teaspoon cumin seeds
1 teaspoon mustard seeds
8 seeds fenugreek seeds
2 whole red chili broken into two pieces each
Pinch of asafetida powder
Pinch of turmeric powder
Pinch of red chilli powder (optional)

1. Heat a shallow pan slightly and then pour oil in it. Let the oil heat on low flame for a minute.

2. Now add split Bengal gram and split black gram.

3. After half a minute add cumin seeds and mustard seeds and fenugreek seeds.

4. After half a minute add red chili pieces.

5. Let the ingredients fry evenly, until the mustard seeds start popping.

6. Add the tomato pieces, salt, chili powder, asafetida powder and turmeric powder. Mix the ingredients well.

8. Cover and let the tomatoes cook till soft on medium flame.

9. Remove from flame and let the mixture cool.

10. Place yogurt in a mixing bowl. After the mixture has cooled, add it to the yogurt and mix well.

Yield: 2 servings

Serving Suggestions:

Served with rice. When mixed and eaten with rice, it is not very spicy.

Served as a side dish with oily foods or for Biryani.

Variations:

Fresh coriander leaves can be added as topping while serving.

This dish can be prepared with tomato puree if fresh tomatoes are not available. In this case, cook till the oil separates from the mixture.

you show you love me…
chocolate-covered tomatoes
on Valentine's Day

- Tracy Davidson

My Darling Governor

E. M. Eastick

Maybe it was my dad's rise to corporate power that drove me to join the Young Socialists, or maybe it was some innate sense of justice, but when I met the governor for the first time, her black eyes couched in those luscious lashes smiling at me with an inner secret that I could only dream of discovering, the cause became my everything. *She* became my everything.

I knew about the stories when I signed up. A disloyal maid had blabbed about a Ouija board she had found in Claudia's office, which fuelled accusations of Claudia harboring a sinister interest in the supernatural, but to me, she was a goddess. If she engaged in pagan rituals every night, I couldn't have cared less.

"Nigel?"

I snapped out of my daydream of Claudia and I dancing round a candle naked and stared at the large red-haired woman who screeched at me often, seemingly for no reason at all. Ethel was the self-appointed slave driver in the campaign office, but as far as I knew, she held no greater rank than the rest of us volunteers.

"Did you pick up those flyers from the printers? Claudia will be here soon. She'll want to see them."

Her name, even when spoken by a whiney old dragon, sent shivers down my spine. "I was just leaving." When I glanced at the wall clock, I realized I'd been just leaving for an hour. Had I really been idly sitting at my desk

daydreaming about the most alluring woman in my life for an hour?

"Well, what are you waiting for?" The screech had assumed a nasty nasally tone.

"Gone already." I shoved the wooden chair back hoping to clip the ugly toes spilling out of the Bohemian sandal, but Ethel whipped her foot sideways in an impressive show of foresight and clicked her tongue in obvious annoyance.

"No detours," Ethel called after me as I pushed through the glass door into the street. "And no daydreaming...."

I scooted down the side of the campaign office and stopped on the corner to light a cigarette. If only I could deal directly with Claudia without Ethel poking her knobbly nose in. Long nights in the campaign office, alone with Claudia after everyone else had gone home; we would prod and pull at the heart of our tender society and devise ways of ensuring equality for all: that was my dream. Or at least the prelude to it.

The rumble and creak of a roller door tore through the hum of the traffic. It was the delivery bay to the campaign office. As much as I wanted to be back by the time Claudia arrived, preferably as the first to present her with her new campaign flyers, I had no urge to return too quickly should Ethel claim the flyers for her own glory, tearing my throat out in the process. And so I dragged on my cigarette and watched two trim deliverymen of Latino appearance unload a small lorry, which had deftly backed up to the open roller door.

A string of Spanish dribbled from one man to the other, prompting the second man to scuttle into the back of the truck. He came out with a stack of plastic chairs precariously perched on a hand trolley. I felt my shoulders slump. More furniture meant more campaign workers. Where were they going to fit? Already the office was packed to capacity, maybe even to the point of violating fire safety regulations. How would it look if the re-elected governor was found negligent in her duty to provide safe working conditions for her staff and volunteers? I refused to think of Claudia being harassed and bullied by media and law enforcement officers. Maybe the extra chairs were for a speech in the park. I flicked ash from the end of my cigarette.

As the deliveryman disappeared into the building with the chairs, the other man, the one who seemed in charge judging by their relative verbosity, emerged from the lorry with a white polystyrene box. The visible side showed a picture of vine-ripe tomatoes, four of them tethered together with vibrant green stems. I thought of the Italians working in the office, Mario Giuseppe and Frank Munz. Technically, Frank was German, but I knew his stepmother was from Sicily and made fantastic marinara. Was one of them planning to cook us all dinner? Now that would be something new.

I watched for other ingredients, but the box of tomatoes was the only hint of food items to emerge from the truck. The first deliveryman carted reams of paper and a new laser printer, a welcome addition to the piece of junk we had, a habitual jammer and paper eater. The second delivery man carried three pallets of bottled water, unnecessary, I thought, considering we had a filtered water dispenser, but useful when leaving the office to solicit votes.

That seemed to be all the deliveries for one day. The two men wasted no time in securing their lorry and driving away, just as I was finishing my cigarette.

The three blocks to the printing office offered nothing in the way of stimulation. The light industrial area attracted none of the glitz or style of downtown, nor any of the grime and weirdness. I planted my hands in the pockets of my jeans and allowed myself to slip into another daydream featuring my beautiful boss. I'd signed up as a volunteer at the insistence of my then girlfriend, the daughter of one of my dad's cronies. Sara's motives were similar to my own, which drew us together until both of us realized we had nothing in common besides cowardly spite towards our fathers. Sara met Tom, an older man and a whole lot of trouble as far as I could see, and when neither of them turned up at the office a week after meeting, I guessed she'd left me. As distraught as I should have been, I welcomed the diminished sense of guilt whenever I thought about Claudia.

Although I'd dealt with Simon's Printing a few times previously, an Indian man I'd never seen before handed me a sample of the new flyers and grinned crazily as he ran the credit card, and I checked the information. A full-length shot of Claudia with her arms crossed and her back against her slogan, *Stand Tall for All*, didn't captivate me like the real thing, but I nodded my approval, nevertheless. It would do. Seemingly thrilled by the transaction, the Indian guy shoved the box into my arms and waved me goodbye. He *waved* me goodbye, which I thought was a little over the top for a printing shop.

I dawdled back to the office. When I saw Claudia's Lexus parked illegally on the street, I quickened my step and arrived covered in a thin film of sweat. I noticed the rich floral scent of perfume first, and then I saw the long raven hair spilling down the back of a burgundy suit jacket. She turned and smiled at me, those dark eyes beckoning me forward. My fingers tightened round the box so I wouldn't drop it, and I stepped up to meet her.

"It's about time." Ethel's shriek drilled into my brain, but I refused to shift my eyes from the vision before me. "Give those to me." I clutched the box tighter as Ethel tried to pry it from my fingers.

"Let him show me." The deep, honey voice cut off any further thoughts Ethel may have harbored of stealing the moment.

I ducked round the dowdy woman with red hair and continued on my path to Claudia, the box held forward like an offering to a deity.

"I'm sorry, I don't remember your name." Claudia extended perfect hands to accept the box.

"Um, Nigel," I stammered.

She smiled again, and I melted like an idiot. Clearing my throat, I helped her set the box on the nearest desk and watched her open the lid and extract a single page. Seemingly satisfied, she replaced the paper in the box and focused back on me.

"Will you be attending the debate in the park tomorrow?"

There was a debate in the park? How could I have not known that? At least it explained the chairs. "Of course," I said. "I've been looking forward to it."

Her face assumed a contemplative expression, and I thought she must have seen through my ruse, but when she took my hand and squeezed it gently, I didn't care what she saw. In fact, I wanted her to see more of it. She leaned forward and purred, "I have a special job for you tomorrow if you're interested."

"Sure," I replied, perhaps a little too eagerly. "Anything."

She leaned closer and whispered. "Meet me in the back room at eleven. I'll show you what you need to do." Her irises, deep brown with an animalistic sharpness, flickered sideways as if to assess how effective she'd been at secrecy. Judging by the level of bustle and noise I'd come to appreciate from working there, her message had fallen on my ears alone.

When I glanced sideways, I saw Ethel glaring at me with arms crossed. I smiled at her smugly, and then looked back at Claudia. "You can count on me, ma'am."

187

Armed with very little sleep, my brain having been busy throughout the night with romantic scenarios featuring me with Claudia, I drudged through the morning of folding flyers and arranging envelopes. Ethel had so far left me alone, as she was occupied with a new volunteer who appeared more clueless than the average newcomer. The beanstalk of a man nodded beneath his beard whenever Ethel spoke, but seemed not to pick up the tasks requested of him.

At five to eleven, I silently cheered for the challenge the new guy was presenting to Ethel and edged to the back of the room. I stopped at the door that led to the restroom and storeroom, and noting that I hadn't attracted any attention, least of all from Ethel, I slipped away from the bedlam.

Claudia was smoking, and sat with one long leg crossed over the other, her navy skirt resting just above her knee. I drank in the shapely calves and four-inch heels and delayed drawing attention to myself as long as possible. When the door hushed closed behind me, she looked up, smiled, and stubbed her cigarette in an ashtray printed with the *Stand Tall for All* slogan.

"Nigel, you're right on time." She stood and strode toward me, her hips swaying widely and rhythmically, perhaps suggesting something more than they should have. "Now this is what I want you to do."

Before I could offer the customary 'hello,' or 'how are you?' or 'my dear governor, you look ravishing as usual,' she had taken my hand and led me to the corner of the storeroom. My fantasies roared inside me, but instead of taking off her jacket, she bent over the polystyrene box I'd

seen delivered the day before. As she slid off the lid, the smell of musty earth and wet lawn clippings rose from a huddle of dark fruit amid graying leaves and stems.

"When you arrive at the debate, I'd like you to take these." She offered me two large tomatoes, deeply red with white and gray fuzz where the stems had been.

Doubtfully, I accepted the fruit. They were soft in my hand and carried the sour smell of a discarded orchard. "Tomatoes?"

"Manzoni is a capitalist pig who talks rubbish," she said, one hand on her hip and the other waving through the air like a conductor's baton. "When I nod to you, throw one of these at him." She smiled as if she'd asked me to pick up milk from the store. "If you can, throw both."

"You want me to throw overripe tomatoes at Manzoni?"

Her eyebrows lifted in what looked like sympathy. "We need to get the message across."

"By throwing tomatoes at our opponents?" I couldn't believe such a sophisticated woman would resort to such primitive tactics. But then again, it wasn't her who would be doing the throwing.

"The police will be there, so you need to be sneaky about it."

"How exactly does one throw a tomato sneakily?"

She tilted her head back and laughed like I'd said the most hilarious thing ever. When she finally stopped laughing, she patted me on the arm. "You're young. You look fit. If they come after you, just run."

"And what if they catch me?"

"Then you may pledge your loyalty to the cause, but you are absolutely not to tell them you're on my campaign team, do you understand?" A long fingernail hovered in front of my nose.

I figured if I got arrested, my dad would bail me out.

"Okay," I said sheepishly. "I've always thought Manzoni was a bit too smug, anyway."

Claudia glanced at her watch, a silver, no-nonsense Seiko, and adjusted her suit. "The park should be set up by now. I'd better get going." She headed for the small tradesman's door beside the roller door, and I wondered why she didn't go through the campaign room, to at least draw energy from her supporters. Before I could ask, she turned and waggled a finger at me and spoke in a singsong voice. "Don't be late." And then she was gone.

Ethel stood beside me in the shade of a large and leafy beech tree. I'd tried to edge away from her, but when four more volunteers joined us, one being the bearded reedman, each agreeing with Ethel that the chairs should be reserved for potential converts, I found myself trapped.

A podium set with four plastic chairs and a single lectern cast an official air over the breezy location. I don't know what Claudia did between leaving me and arriving at the park, but somehow she was the last candidate to step onto the platform and take her seat. If her goal was to draw attention to her style and elegance by being late, she succeeded. From the rows of chairs to the grass and trees, every eye watched her in deferential silence.

It was a warm day out. A jacket would have been handy for hiding the tomatoes, but collapsing from heat exhaustion was not an appealing side effect, so I had gently placed the squishy fruit in a recycled plastic bag and knotted the handles. I clutched the bag to my thigh and wondered how I could ever pull off the stunt Claudia had assigned to me.

On the podium, Tony Manzoni appeared relaxed. Even with his large belly, he sat straight and still, his fingers entwined and resting on his chest like a university professor. His olive skin added a youthfulness to the wrinkles around his eyes, which gleamed with a hidden humor as he waited.

The event facilitator, a woman whose political reports I'd seen on T.V., stepped up to the lectern and deftly introduced the candidates. When Claudia's name rang through the P.A. system, Claudia smiled in that mysterious way she has and swept her eyes over the audience. When her eyes locked onto mine, she winked.

"What's in the bag?" Ethel hissed in my ear.

Annoyed, I blinked away the start of another fantasy. "What?"

"I said, 'What's in the bag?'"

I turned my head to look at her sternly. "What business is it of yours?"

I recognized the smooth voice in the background as Claudia's. She had begun speaking, and Ethel wasn't even listening.

"Don't do it, Nigel. You'll regret it."

Was the tomato stunt a test? Was I the victim of an office prank? I doubted Ethel had any interest in protecting me from either scenario. "Don't do what?"

"I'm serious. If you throw those tomatoes, your life will never be the same."

As much as I tried to focus on Claudia's address, Ethel's words shook me more than I cared to admit. "We need to get the message across." In my voice, Claudia's words sounded pathetic, even to me. I pushed between bodies, wrinkling my nose to a whiff of body odor, and settled three people away from Ethel. From the corner of my eye, I could see her shaking her head and looking at the ground.

Claudia settled back into her allotted chair, and I could

see she was watching me. Tony Manzoni approached the lectern, and my gut tightened. Would Claudia really go through with this? The bag rustled as I undid the knot and looped one handle over two fingers, ready to reach in with the other hand should Claudia signal.

When Manzoni waved an invisible wand over the sacredness of opposite sex marriage, Claudia looked at me and nodded. She could have been agreeing with her opponent's sentiments if not for the storm that raged in her eyes.

With a deep breath, I pulled a tomato from the plastic bag, stepped forward from the crowd, and hurled the tomato at the face above the lectern. The microphone split the tomato in a splatter of pieces and sent mush showering over Manzoni's tie. Dots of red speckled his white shirt and dribbled down the shoulders of his jacket. Gasps and giggles rose from the audience.

Manzoni paused mid-word and searched the crowd with his eyes, calmly, evenly, but I'd sunk back into the socialist fold and his eyes fell on stoic bodies, protective, not because of me, but because of the cause. Frowning, he flicked bits of tomato from his clothes and continued to speak. "That's why I never became an actor," he said with a smile. The crowd laughed with him and listened more intently.

A single police officer, a man my own age but two inches taller, approached the crowd under the tree and quietly asked who'd thrown the tomato. He was met with shoulder shrugs and mumbles of ignorance. Any decent police officer would have noticed the plastic bag, now with only one rotten tomato inside, but the officer was either sympathetic to our cause or not very bright, and he continued with his surreptitious investigation, quizzing those standing behind the last row of chairs, glancing in my direction but taking no action.

I had to give Manzoni credit for his resilience. He continued speaking as if nothing had happened, as if he hadn't been attacked by a tomato, as if his shirt wasn't dotted with pink and red stains. When he insinuated a holiness behind his worldviews, this time in defense of individual rights regardless of his earlier remarks, I saw Claudia nod for a second time. Did she really want me to throw the second tomato? Incredulously, I lifted the bag and lifted my eyebrows. She nodded in response, her own eyebrows, finely penciled like modern art, raised in confirmation.

Swallowing hard, I dipped my hand into the bag and withdrew the second tomato. With a quick step and lunge, I shot the missile to the stage. This time, the tomato soared past the microphone and clipped Manzoni's left ear before exploding into fragments and raining onto the grass behind the podium. It was impossible to escape the police officer's attention a second time. Following Claudia's advice, I ran, but the officer was fit and nimble and managed to tackle me to the ground a hundred yards from the beech tree.

The holding cell smelled of piss and vomit and a brave attempt at drowning the odor in disinfectant. Surprisingly, Ethel was the first to visit me. "I should have told you," she said. "Claudia's a great leader and a wonderful woman, but she's not mentally stable."

Nursing my head in my hands, I looked up with minimal effort. "You think?"

"I tried to warn you."

"You said my 'life would never be the same,'" I replied with air quotes. "Bit of an exaggeration, wasn't it?"

Ethel stared at me through the bars, as if bursting to say something she couldn't.

"I'm not the first person to be arrested for political protesting." A glimmer of pride, knowledge that I'd done something daring and radical, warmed my aching head.

"I wasn't talking about your arrest."

Before she could explain, I heard a rattle of keys and saw the officer who had secured me in the cell earlier appear from around the corner. Beside him walked my dad, trim and dashing in a three-piece suit, the mauve tie straight and impeccable, his auburn hair, dotted with gray, slick and neat.

"Throwing tomatoes?" he said with calm amusement. "Really?" He shook his head, a tiny smile playing on his lips, while the police officer clanged open the cell door. "You're getting more like your mother every day," he mumbled. "Let's go." He glanced at Ethel before deciding she wasn't worth an introduction, and took me by the arm.

"You might want to stay away from the office for a few days, Nigel," said Ethel as we left her by the holding cell. "Claudia shouldn't be linked to what you did."

She was right, of course, but as my father dragged me from the police station, I burned to know what Claudia thought of my actions. I'd done what she'd asked, and we'd gotten away with it, as a team, just the two of us. My thoughts swam in images of intimate celebration: the sparkle of approval in her eyes; our elbows locked as we sipped champagne like honeymooners, the sea of laughter and congratulatory touches as we recounted the look on Manzoni's face, not once, but twice. As I reached for my cigarette packet, I knew not even wild horses with straitjackets could keep me away from the campaign office, from Claudia, from my destiny.

The next morning Ethel met me on the street, at the door of the campaign office, before I even had a chance to glimpse inside.

"Go home, Nigel. And if you have any sense, you won't come back."

"What happened to just staying away for a while. Now you want me to quit? For good?"

"I'm trying to help you."

As laid-back as I considered myself, Ethel was seriously testing my tolerance. Instead of losing my cool, I crossed my arms and smirked. "You're jealous, aren't you?"

Ethel sighed. "I'm not jealous, Nigel." Her voice was softer than I'd ever heard it, but still annoying.

"Then get out of my way."

"I beg you, Nigel, do not go in there." She flicked her eyes in the direction of her right shoulder, at the office behind her. Through the window I could see the activity, the jerk of bodies moving like bees in a hive, industrious, dedicated, devoted to their mentally unstable queen.

"Is Claudia here?" I hadn't seen her Lexus, but nor did I pass the delivery bay on my walk from home, so her vehicle could have been hidden out of sight.

Ethel paused at the question, the same unsure and pleading expression stamped on her face as when she'd spoken to me at the police station. "She's waiting for you—in the back room."

Defeated, she allowed me to push past her and followed me inside. The other volunteers turned to watch me, and with smiles and cheers, began applauding. My spirit soared. I smiled and nodded like a champion as I weaved my way to the back of the room and waited for the noise and activity levels to return to a dull rustle and

murmur before opening the back door.

Ignoring Ethel's glower from across the room, I stepped across the threshold. Claudia was poised in the same position in the same chair as when I'd met her the day before. This time, though, she sprang to her feet, an admirable accomplishment judging by the height of her heels, and flew at me with open arms. Her heels clicked on the concrete like a hyperactive cricket. By her zeal, I expected a warm, tight, bear hug and perhaps a few kisses, but when she reached me, she held me firmly by the shoulders and offered the type of air kiss you give to relatives.

"Bravo, my dear boy." She smiled broadly as she stood back and released me from her mechanical embrace. "I am so proud of you." Her hands joined in front of her breasts, and then dropped to her side.

"He didn't seem too worried about the whole thing," I said, attempting modesty.

"Don't be too sure. He may have appeared unruffled on the outside, but inside he was probably crying like a baby."

Manzoni didn't strike me as the type to cry like a baby, inside or out. "My aim wasn't very good."

"Oh, you were wonderful, Nigel. Thank you."

I let the praise wash over me in silence. Claudia turned sharply and walked to the small table hunched in between the edge of the roller door and the brick wall. "Now let's celebrate." I saw the two opaque green cups—more suited to a children's birthday party than a political party—just as she swept them up in her long fingers and turned back to me. It wasn't quite the champagne-drinking ritual I had imagined, but I accepted the cup regardless.

"Here's to us," she said, raising her cup.

Us? I liked the sound of that. "To *us*," I concurred, the grin on my face impossible to tame. A pungent weedy

smell shot up my nostrils before I could drink. Instinctively, I yanked the cup away. "Um...what is this, Claudia?" It was the first time I'd called her by her given name, and I waited for her reaction, both to the address and to the question.

"It's a health tonic. It's what keeps me young. I only share it with special people." She winked. "Drink up, it's good for you."

I eyed the drink suspiciously. "I'm still pretty young. I'm not sure I need a health tonic yet." In the colored cup, it was impossible to see what color the tonic was, but it was dark and smelled awful. Wondering how I could sustain the celebration without offending Claudia, my brain flashed with an idea. "Why don't I head down to McNally's and grab us a bottle of champagne or sparkling wine or something? Nothing too expensive."

When Claudia dropped her chin and peered at me through her lashes, a tiny smile on her lips and her fingers slowly unbuttoning her jacket, I knew I wouldn't be heading down to McNally's for any kind of alcoholic beverage. She peeled off her jacket, revealing a creamy satin blouse with the top button undone and the promise of more sensual things beneath, and laid it over the back of the wooden chair. "Do you really think I asked you in here just for a drink?"

My whole being flooded with fear and excitement, all meshed into a dangerous desire I couldn't have controlled, even if I'd wanted to.

The syrupy voice dribbled over me. "Do you think you can keep up with me?"

"Um..." I balked at the challenge. *Could* I keep up with her?

Her fingers rested under the plastic green cup I'd forgotten I was holding. "Drink this, and I *know* you'll be able to keep up with me."

Dumbly, I let her guide the cup to my lips and

swallowed back an impulse to gag.

"Come on now, darling." Claudia's other hand circled my waist. I opened my mouth, held my breath, and swallowed down a mouthful of the repugnant concoction.

My eyes began to water, and my stomach cramped.

"Leave him alone!" I hadn't heard the door open, but I recognized Ethel's screechy voice.

Claudia slid her hand from my waist and took the cup from me. Abruptly, she turned away, laid both cups on the table and retrieved her jacket. "You're too late, Ethel. It's done."

"Wha'?" My eyelids felt heavy, and my vision blurred to a smoky haze. Disoriented, I stumbled sideways and landed in strong but flabby arms.

Ethel's voice rattled like metal filings in my ears. "Don't you worry, Nigel, we'll get you to the hospital."

"He doesn't need a hospital." Claudia's voice sounded like a distant waterfall. "He's one of us, now."

"Wun-a...?" My tongue refused to function. "Clord...?" And then my world went black.

I awoke in hospital. I could tell by the chlorine smell long before my eyes could focus on the beige walls and baby blue curtain surrounding my bed.

"You're going to be fine, Nigel." Ethel stood by the door. She wore a floral pink muumuu and the same sandals she wore to the office. I wanted to be angry at her for haranguing me, for intruding on my life, but that sense of justice I prided myself on told me that Ethel may have saved my life.

"What happened?" My voice was broken and craggy.

"I tried to tell you Claudia was sick."

"Sick? She tried to poison me!"

"That's not how she sees it."

I wondered what Claudia was doing at that moment, but I couldn't place her. Was she remorseful, disappointed, more determined than ever to finish the job? "What do you mean?"

Ethel scraped a visitor's chair closer to the bed and sat. "I heard her telling you about her so-called health tonic."

I exhaled sharply. "Health tonic, my ass."

"To her, it is. That's what she believes. By giving it to you, she thought it would be good for you, too."

"What was it?"

Ethel sighed. "You might find this hard to swallow, Nigel." She reddened at the pun. "Sorry."

"Tell me."

"It was tomato juice."

Ridiculously, this made sense to me. The liquid was thick and dark and musty smelling. "And what else?"

"Unfortunately, Claudia uses all parts of the tomato plant for her tonic: leaves and stems as well as the fruit."

I nodded my understanding. "All those parts that are poisonous, you mean. So how come Claudia isn't affected?"

Ethel sighed again. "Do you know what the scientific name for a tomato is?" When I looked bored, she continued. "It's *Solanum lycopersicum*. Solanum is from the nightshade family. . ."

"As in *deadly* nightshade," I mumbled.

". . . and lycopersicum means 'wolf peach.' " She stared at me as if I would be hit by the lightning bolt of understanding any second.

"Okay."

"Claudia holds an ancient superstition that tomato greens can turn a person into a werewolf."

199

I was silent with incredulity. I'd heard the rumors, but nothing could have prepared me for Ethel's fanciful claims. I wallowed in despair for a full minute, nursing my breaking heart at news that my darling governor was totally loopy.

"She thought she was giving you eternal life as a werewolf, Nigel. She wasn't trying to poison you."

My dry mouth croaked a final appeal for normalcy. "You can't be serious."

"I am serious, and so is Claudia. I tried to warn you."

"You've known how crazy this woman is for heaven knows how long, and you work for her? Why don't you go to the police?"

"And tell them what? Claudia hasn't done anything illegal."

"She tried to poison me." My voice was higher pitched than usual.

"You can't prove it. It could have been an accident. You were throwing tomatoes after all. And it's not like you're dead."

I felt dead, too dead to argue. As much as justice told me Claudia belonged with the criminally insane, I couldn't fight those dark eyes and that silent allure. "So what do I do now?"

"Like I said before, leave and don't come back."

"But—"

"You're young; your dad's rich. Pack a bag and move to Australia or somewhere."

"But what about Claudia? What if she tries to poison someone else?"

Ethel smiled like a hunter. "You know what they say: keep your friends close and your enemies closer. I've been keeping an eye on Claudia for years now."

I pictured myself on a Sydney beach, watching girls and bronzing my biceps. I could finish off my studies at a local university, maybe work in a pub on the weekends. I'd

heard Australian governors were assigned, not elected, and their roles somehow symbolized the Queen of England. I could file campaign work under past experience and find a new passion.

While I planned a fresh start in a far away country, Ethel rose and patted me on the hand. "You may want to act quickly," she said with a ragged smile. "It's a full moon tonight."

I tried to smile back at the joke, but my eyes dropped in regret. As much as I resented insanity for stealing Claudia, and as much as Ethel grated on my nerves, I would miss them both.

As Ethel pulled her hand away, I noticed a tuft of hair on the back of her knuckles. My stomach tightened as I watched her walk to the door. "By the way," I said, "how did you know about this whole werewolf thing? Did Claudia tell you that stuff?"

Ethel turned and leered a smile. It was the first time I'd seen her smile with her lips apart. The sides of her mouth seemed to bulge with oversized teeth. "Enjoy Australia," she said in her shrieky voice. "And remember: stay true to the cause, won't you? You'll always be one of us." The shuffle of her sandals floated back to me as she walked down the hall and out of my life.

My insides still hurt, like they were twisting out of shape, and I figured the tomato poison lingered as a painful reminder of how lucky I'd been. I thought of buzzing for a nurse, but instead, I laid back and watched the daylight fade to dusk through the window. Closing my eyes, I slipped into a daydream about my new life, without Claudia. But I couldn't shake the feeling that my darling governor would always, somehow, stay with me. My whole body ached with an unfamiliar pull, and when it became constant, like a new and treasured friend, I smiled for the future. Maybe a change was just what I needed.

If Only

Melissa Z. Savlov

If only our biggest fight had been
Whether a tomato is a vegetable or fruit
If only I hadn't thrown the fruit at you
    because, after all, it was the same size as a baseball
      even though I missed;
          I never was a very good pitcher.
If only the juice hadn't stained the wall
    and I hadn't immediately begun picking the seeds
      off the (formerly) white paint
        when you disappeared out the front door
If only we'd shared that love apple
    kissing, with juice on our chins
      instead of bickering
Oh, if only, if only, if only
The point is, it happened
    and now, here I am, bereft

The Tomato Quest

D.G. Driver

Her giggles were like tiny bells, high-pitched and light. "What are you doing, silly?"

"Will you just sit down like I told you to and indulge me for a moment?" I didn't move from my kneeling position, but I pointed at the chair firmly. Lillian faked a pout but did as I asked, plopping down onto the soft cushion of a chair on the front porch of her father's estate. After she smoothed the skirt of her chiffon dress over her legs, I took her left hand into mine.

"Lillian," I began, but she interrupted.

"Oh, Dash! Really? Is this really happening?" Her feet wiggled excitedly, almost kicking me in the shin. "I can't believe it."

"Would you get still?" I asked, barely able to control laughing at her. "You're making this so much harder than it needs to be."

"How about I just say yes, then," she said, leaning forward and kissing me gently on the forehead. "That will make it all easier than it needs to be."

"You're saying yes?" I double-checked. "How do you know I'm not asking you to take a walk with me or a horse ride?"

"On one knee?"

"Is that what gave me away?" I took a breath and calmed the laughter bubbling up inside me. Trying to be as solemn as possible I asked, "Will you marry me?"

No giggles this time. Only the sweetest possible, "You know I always promised I would—if you ever asked me, that is."

"I'm asking now."

Lillian's smile was brighter than the summer sun, making me glad that my words brought her so much happiness. I stood up, still holding her hand. I brought it to my lips as I bowed before her and kissed it gently.

"I promise to put a real ring on this finger one day soon."

"Oh, Dash," she giggled, taking her hand back and gazing at it as if there already was a diamond there. "I know that you will."

"But first, I'll need to talk to your father."

A flicker of worry passed through her countenance and then fled. "Yes. That does have to happen." She stood up moved toward the front door, keeping her chin tucked coyly and her eyes peeking over her shoulder as she walked. I noticed that her cheeks were flushed. "He's inside. I'll fetch him."

"I hope he approves."

"Of course he will," Lillian said, spinning to face me completely, her hands clapping lightly. "He knows how much we love each other." She took my face in her delicate hands and kissed me lightly. Then she giggled again and flew into her home.

I'd known Lillian all my life. Our fathers had been friends from the war when they were young. Mine had saved Sir Barrymore's life at one point. When the war was over, out of gratitude, Sir Barrymore offered my father a job keeping the grounds of his estate. My father was a dutiful worker and possessed an amazing green thumb. He created a magnificent garden that was Sir Barrymore's pride and joy.

Lillian and I grew up running around the small paths

through the shrubs and flowers and picking berries or grapes from the vines. I fell in love with her when she was a silly little girl in ribbons and curls and loved her to this day now that she was a young, beautiful woman. Sir Barrymore hardly owed me anything, but I hoped that out of affection for my father and their long friendship, he would honor my request to marry his daughter.

"Absolutely not."

Sir Barrymore hadn't even allowed me to ask the question as he stepped out his front door. Lillian must have given him an idea of what I was going to say. She had not come outside with him, so I assumed he told her the same answer. I was so flummoxed; I stood there with my mouth agape, desperate to find words. He answered my unspoken question, "You may not marry Lillian. You are not suitable."

"But Sir," I tried. "Lillian and I are in love."

"Of that I have no doubt," Sir Barrymore said. Nothing about his tone was cross or even annoyed. Just matter-of-fact. Almost friendly, albeit condescending. "Walk with me." He put an arm around my shoulder like I was a son and guided me down the wide front steps to his lovely manicured front lawn. We followed a pebbled path around the house to the beautiful garden that stretched for three acres behind his home.

I'd spent my whole life amongst this land, but on a shimmering summer day like this it could still take my breath away. The vegetable garden was off to the left in neat columns of vines and mounds. A fruit tree orchard clustered far to the right. I always loved the way the trees grew in perfect rows and recalled many happy memories of climbing into the branches to pluck apples, plums and peaches. Apricots were Lillian's favorites. Between the practical gardens were the grass and neat shrubs, plants, and flower patches laid out in symmetrical patterns, accented by fountains and statues. Sir Barrymore and his wife had hosted many events here, and I had spent many hours imagining what my wedding on these grounds would look like.

Sir Barrymore removed his arm from my shoulder and spoke. "Your father has created magic with my land. I am grateful to him every day for all that he has done. And I've paid him handsomely so that your family could live in comfort."

"My family is equally grateful to you," I told him.

"I know that your father has taught you his skills with the grounds keeping, and you are planning to take over his work when he reaches the end of his ability."

"It has been discussed," I admitted.

"I can't have my daughter married to a gardener. Especially a gardener who works for me. It's beneath her. You understand, of course."

I did understand, but I have to admit I was taken aback to hear him say it. I knew somewhere deep inside me that society rules could interfere with my hopes and dreams. Any other man of my station wouldn't dream of proposing to the daughter of a man of his high standing. Perhaps I had been naïve to think that the close link between our families would be enough to override such old-fashioned notions.

My voice was low as I tried to force my words through the knot forming in my throat. "Is there anything I can do to change your mind, sir?"

"No, my boy. This is probably my fault. I know that you and Lillian have been playmates since childhood, and I should have seen the affection growing between you. I thought that she would have more sense and that your parents would dissuade you from unrealistic notions. They were apparently as blind as I, or they would have put a stop to it."

He avoided looking at me. He kept his eyes on his garden, but I noticed he winced as he spoke, almost like it hurt him to tell me these things.

This emboldened me enough to say, "Lillian loves me, sir. This'll break her heart."

"It is a first love born of innocence, not real love. She will recover," he said plainly. "I have arranged a meeting with a fine gentleman of good standing. I'm already impressed by his prospects, and he can offer a fine home for Lillian where she can raise a family in comfort."

Sir Barrymore did a curt nod, as if to say that he was done sharing his thoughts. He turned away from me and started for the back doors of his home. A pain I'd never known rushed through me and seized up my muscles. Not only was I not being allowed to be with the woman I loved, but he was going to give her to someone else.

"Please sir!" I forced it out, spinning around to face him. "Give me a chance! Let me find my fortune, and when I return I will prove to you that I have the means to care for Lillian the way you see fit."

He smiled politely at me. "Impossible. You are a groundkeeper's son. What fortune could you possibly find?"

I stood tall and raised my chin. "I don't know, but I *will* find one."

All of the kindness evaporated from the nobleman's countenance. "I am fond of you, Dash, but this is not a game."

A game? What if it was?

"Challenge me," I told him. "Give me a deadline."

"Fine!" His exasperation with me rang clear. He strode past me with determination and went straight to the vegetable garden. He picked a basket off the ground and began plucking tomatoes off of a vine. He filled the basket with a dozen or so full, round, ripe tomatoes. I couldn't

207

imagine what he was doing and stood awkwardly behind him until he finished, waiting for him to say something.

At last he shoved the heavy basket into my arms. "You want a challenge? You have until these tomatoes rot to find your fortune."

"That will only be days," I said. "How could I possibly find my fortune in a few days?"

"Days or years makes no difference," he told me. "That is the point I'm making. You will never be a fit match for my daughter." He waved at me to get out of his way and headed back to his house again. "Now make yourself some soup and stay out of my sight. I have no more patience for you today."

I stood with my basket of tomatoes and stared until Sir Barrymore disappeared into the house. Lillian's beautiful face appeared in the window, and I could tell she'd been crying. I waved at her. She looked over her shoulder and then suddenly backed away out of sight. I knew then that Sir Barrymore would never let me in her presence again.

The basket of tomatoes weighed heavily on my arm. The tomatoes were firm now, not quite ready to eat, but they wouldn't stay that way. I knew Sir Barrymore wasn't issuing a real challenge to me, but I decided right then and there to take it as such anyway. I would return before these tomatoes were rotted and win the hand of my love.

The entire time that I packed, my parents repeatedly called me a fool for proposing to Lillian, and my mother worried incessantly that I had damaged the relationship of Sir Barrymore and my father. I assured her that Sir Barrymore valued his garden too much, and therefore she shouldn't worry. Father gave me some money, and Mother

carefully packed my tomatoes in a box. It was hardly a light load to carry, but the tomatoes would be safer and perhaps last longer this way.

I paid for passage on a merchant ship heading across the sea, hoping that in a new town I might have some luck. On my first afternoon, I took my box of tomatoes down to the hold and put it in the deepest, coldest corner I could find and covered it with some burlap sacks so it wouldn't be found. I hoped that the cool, damp spot would help keep the tomatoes fresher longer.

I mostly kept to myself on the ship, only joining the rest of the travelers at mealtimes, which had consisted mainly of boiled potatoes, bread and salty meat. On the second evening, I smelled a delicious stew being brewed and followed my nose to the main cabin. I sat with the others at a long table and served myself a bowl. The stew brimmed with tomatoes. Although, my mouth watered at the sight of it, my stomach began to churn. I caught the attention of the cook and asked, "Fresh tomatoes are rare on a ship like this, aren't they? Where did you possibly find them?"

The cook beamed. "A happy accident! One of the men was moving things about in the hold and found a box of them. A lucky find, don't you think. We'll have 'em tonight and tomorrow before they go bad."

I wanted to vomit right then and there, but I bit it back. I went into the galley where I found the remaining tomatoes, only six, still in the box. The cook followed me, and I could hear the other men grumbling about me out at the tables. "You're not allowed in here. Get out!"

"These are my tomatoes," I informed him.

"Like hell they are."

"They are." I lifted the box and showed him Sir Barrymore's crest printed on the side. "I work for Sir Barrymore of Grennensvale. Have you ever used supplies

from his gardens in the past?"

"Well, no, but..."

"I hid them in the hold for a reason." Before he had a chance to stop me, I grabbed up the tomatoes and squeezed past him.

"He's stealing the tomatoes!" the cook shouted as I ran past the men eating their stew.

Several men stood as if to chase me, but I was too fast. I rushed to my quarters and stuffed the box deep inside my pack and pushed it far under my bunk to make it difficult for any the other five men who shared the sleeping cabin with me to root through my things. Minutes later the captain of the ship arrived to take me to his office. It took some convincing, but once he finally read through his food orders and saw that there was no record of ordering fresh tomatoes, he finally relented and let me go. The cook was furious and threatened to hurt me if I stepped foot near his galley again. And though I was starving, I stayed away from the dining area. The temptation to eat one of the juicy tomatoes under my cot was high, but I resisted and tried to sleep through the rumbling of my stomach.

The following day our ship made anchor. Although I'd paid for passage to a town much further than this, it seemed safest to disembark. I bought myself a good meal at a local tavern, and while I was eating, a man I recognized from the ship grabbed the chair next to me and sat down. He was in his late twenties, by the look of him, chin-length dark hair and trim beard. His smile was friendly as he clapped my shoulder.

"You escaped, huh?"

"I did," I said. "I feared I would never get to eat again if I stayed."

"At least nothing without a fair amount of the cook's spit in it," he agreed. He held out a hand for me to shake. "Name's Evan. Woodworker seeking fame and fortune."

I took his hand. "Dash. Groundskeeper also in search of fortune."

He raised his eyebrows. "Tough field for finding fortune, Dash."

"Yes, well, I'm on a search for a different way to earn it, I guess."

"You're unlikely to find it here." He leaned back and put his hands on his chest. "Allanon isn't the richest of towns."

"Why are you here then?" I dared to ask.

"This is my home," he said. "Stopping in to drop off some earnings to my wife and pay our debts. I'll make some new inventory then ship out again."

"You're a good man, I think," I told him.

"My father raised me well." He signaled for the barmaid to bring him some ale and gestured for me to have one as well. "So, I don't suppose you're planning to stay here."

"From what you say, this wouldn't be the best stop," I said. "I haven't got time to linger where I can't be successful. I'll take the next ship and move on."

I told him my story. When I finished, Evan leaned forward and rested his elbows on the table. "Do you believe in magic, Dash?"

"Not really, no." Although that wasn't entirely true. When a person works with plants, it's hard not to believe in magic. Watching a seed grow into a plant and then bear fruit, or seeing a flower bud and then open, the mind believes that many things are possible. Perhaps that's why I held the concept that I could have Lillian to wife so deeply in my spirit.

"Well, you should."

Evan proceeded to tell me of a legendary witch who resided in the forest beyond Allanon and that she had a treasure hidden in a cave behind a waterfall. "You could find it and make it yours."

"That hardly sounds like an easy adventure."

"Trying to travel to a distant shore, find a fortune, and get back before your tomatoes rot doesn't sound easy either. If you left this moment, you wouldn't even get to land before you'd be out of time."

"How do you know this treasure is real? And if it is, why don't you get it yourself?"

The barmaid put our steins on the table. Evan gave her a couple coins and then took a large swig. "My father claims to have once seen the treasure and the witch, and he made me promise I would never attempt to see her myself."

"Because she's dangerous?"

"Because the spell she cast for him would be broken."

I cocked my head. "What spell?"

"He never told me."

I took a long drink of my ale and slammed the stein back on the table, out of patience for this nonsense. "You're teasing me. Did the cook put you up to this?"

He shrugged. "There won't be another ship until tomorrow. You have time to find out if I'm lying or not and still make it back to the boat on time." He got up and tipped his hat to me. "Good luck."

Evan's suggestion needled at me. I couldn't sit in the tavern forever, and after checking with the dockworkers, I found out he was right about the next ship arriving. I had time to kill. The town was quite small: one inn, a few shops, public buildings, and homes with a wide stretch of untended fields between them and the forest's edge. I imagined everyone in this town knew each other well, and after some leading questions I got several responses to the quality of Evan's character and that of his family. It didn't appear that he was the kind of man who would trick me.

I sat on a bench and inspected my remaining tomatoes. They had reddened considerably and were already soft enough to leave a dent when I touched them. I decided to brave the journey. If there was no treasure, I'd only wasted time that I would have otherwise spent sitting in a room in the inn. I shouldered my heavy pack and began walking.

The forest was cool and dark. The trees and plants grew close together, making it hard to walk without being constantly slapped in the face by leaves. The din of chirping birds was so loud I didn't hear the rushing water right away. A river was nearby.

I followed the sound until I came to the water's edge. Carefully, I walked along the rocky shore until I came to the base of a small waterfall, maybe thirty feet high. A recent rain had the waterfall flowing strongly. Rocks and boulders wet with spray lined each side. I moved toward them, hoping to find a way to climb up and see if there was a cave opening behind the water.

As I neared the waterfall I heard a loud growl so deep and powerful, I felt it in my chest. I froze in place, hoping the beast that had made the noise wouldn't notice me and would move on its way. Another growl let me know it was closer. One more heartbeat passed, and a giant black bear lurched out of the trees toward the water. It saw me and rose up on its hind legs. The bear was all snarls and growls, teeth as long as my fingers, eyes yellow with rage.

I dropped to the ground and tucked myself under a dense shrub. It stomped toward me, snuffling as it sought me out. Frantically, I opened my pack, trying to find something I could use as a weapon. All I really had was a short paring knife and the box of tomatoes. The box was heavy; I might be able to hit the bear with it, though I hardly thought it would cause any harm.

I opened the box to find my tomatoes snugly layered

inside. I grabbed one, and just as the bear's giant face poked under the shrub to find me, I shoved the tomato at its snout. The bear sniffed it and then opened its maw to grab it from my hand. I snatched my hand back in the nick of time before losing it. The bear swallowed the tomato in one gulp. I grabbed two more tomatoes and tossed them away from me. To my relief, the bear's gaze followed the tomatoes, and he went for them instead of me.

I scrambled out of the shrub and ran toward the waterfall. The bear swung around after eating the two tomatoes and lumbered toward me. I tossed another tomato and began climbing. Now I could see the cave entrance. I only had to get a little bit higher to be safe from the bear. There were only two tomatoes left, but the bear was coming fast. With the choice being the tomato or my foot, the answer was clear. I tossed another tomato as far as I could. While he was distracted, I ducked into the cave.

I had one tomato left. I put it in my pocket as I leaned against the cave wall and caught my breath. It was nearly pitch black in there. How was I to find a treasure in the dark? And how could I leave again with a hungry bear waiting outside for me? Even if I found this supposed treasure, how was I to get out of the cave with it? I was trapped.

My eyes began to adjust to the darkness, and what little daylight filtered in through the waterfall helped me make out the shapes of the walls around me. Keeping a hand on one moist wall, I ventured further into the cave, deeply regretting that I hadn't brought a candle or anything to use for a torch. I could only see a couple feet in front of me, but in the distance I detected a faint glow coming from above. Perhaps there was a hole in the roof of the cave letting in sunlight. Maybe it would be big enough for me to climb out.

The light grew brighter as I neared it, and the walls of the cave opened to a small room. I could see the hole now.

As I moved about the perimeter of the room looking for rocks I could climb, my hands brushed across the top of a wooden board. Hidden behind a boulder, wedged in a curve of the wall was a large wooden box. I attempted to pull it free, but it was lodged in tight. I pried open the lid.

It wasn't much of a treasure, but the box was full of fine things. I saw necklaces, golden cufflinks, a goblet, a porcelain doll, and a pair of tortoiseshell hair clips. There were things of little value like a small painting of a child, and a woven scarf. I even saw a few gold teeth. I shuddered, imagining how those were procured.

I reached into the box to pull out a watch on a chain. No sooner did I feel the weight of the gold in my hand, than it turned to dust. I opened my fingers and let the dust spill back into the box. By itself, the dust gathered into a ball and within moments it had reformed into the watch, whole once again.

"It's magic!" I said. "An enchanted treasure. But how will I be able to take it with me?"

"You can't," came a voice from the darkness, a deep, sultry female voice. Hardly the scratchy, throaty sound I would associate with a witch. I spun around to find a woman walking toward me. She had long, flowing black hair and a gown the color of fine wine. I couldn't place her age, for the shadows of the cave hid the details of her features.

"Are you the…" I struggled to say it, thinking it suddenly seemed rude to ask "…witch?"

"I've been called that," she said. "I've also been called other names." She pointed at the treasure. "Take your hands away from my collection." Her voice was firm, and I didn't doubt there were would be consequences if I disobeyed.

"I apologize for disturbing you. I'm seeking my fortune, and I was told there was a treasure in this cave…"

She put up a hand to stop me. Her fingers were longer

than I've ever seen on a woman. "I know why you're here. The same reason everyone comes here. You have a wish."

"No. I don't have a wish," I tried to tell her. "I am just trying to…"

"Find a fortune in a cave to take back to your home in order to win the hand of your true love."

I gaped at her. "How could you know that?"

"I see it in your heart."

I actually looked down at my chest as though I would be able to see through my flesh and ribcage to the heart that beat rapidly beneath.

"You're running out of time, and I'm the only one who can help you. What will you trade to make your wish come true?"

I rifled through my pockets like a sad beggar. "I have nothing of value. I'm nearly out of money, and all I have left is a tomato." I pulled out the purple and slightly squashed tomato.

"That will do," she told me, putting out her hand.

"I can't return home without the tomato. If I give it to you, I won't be able to fulfill my part of the bargain."

"You weren't going to be able to fulfill it anyway," she said frankly. "It's nearly rotten."

It wasn't like I didn't know before that moment, but the reality of failure knocked the wind out of me. I leaned against the cave wall. My throat tightened, and I squeeze my eyes shut against the tears that threatened to fall.

"You truly love her." The way she said it, like she was charmed by the notion of it, caught me off guard. I looked at her. It was obvious that this witch was a beautiful woman, and yet her beauty didn't entice me. I could think only of Lillian's blonde curls, her lovely smile, her tingling giggle.

"I do."

"Then I will help you, for true love is rare and something I cherish."

216

Once again she put out her hand. I handed the tomato to her, although reluctant to let go of it and curious as to why she would want it. Once in her hand, the tomato glowed for a moment, and when it settled, the tomato was pinkish-red as if freshly picked from the vine.

The witch returned the tomato to me, and I put the now firm and ripe tomato back into my pocket.

"You're letting me go?" I asked.

"Every wish granted here comes in exchange for something. You have nothing to trade but that tomato, and, frankly, I don't want it. Instead, you will trade a favor."

Her long fingers rummaged through the things she had collected in the treasure box. None of them turned to dust in her hands. At long last, she pulled out a small wooden toy, a bunny dressed in a smart jacket, only slightly bigger than her hand. It looked brand new, never played with. She passed the toy to me.

"This was given to me by a poor young man. His wife was with child, but she was sick. He was afraid that she and the child would die. This toy was something he had made for the child, and it was all he had on him. He cried when he gave it to me, certain that the trade would not work, that what he was giving me was not good enough to buy my magic."

She tapped the bunny's nose and smiled at it as if it were alive. "It is my favorite."

"What do you want me to do with it?"

"Take it back to him."

"That's all?" That hardly seemed like much of a trade. "Where do I find him?"

"He lives in Allanon. He won't be hard to find."

I put the bunny in my other jacket pocket. "When I've given the toy back to its owner, what then?"

"Hurry home, of course. I've only bought you a little time with that tomato." She gestured to the opening of the cave.

I started toward it, but I hesitated. "What about the bear?"

"It's gone."

I believed her, even though there was no reason she should know any more about what happened to the bear than I. My next question burst out of my mouth before I could stop it, "Did the man get his wish? Did his wife and child live?"

"She lived long enough, and the child lives still."

I thanked the witch for her kindness and began to walk away again, but one more question burned at me. "Why do the treasures in your box turn to dust?"

"They are broken promises," she said. As she spoke, gray streaks began to fill her hair. Her shoulders slumped, and her body became more fragile. "If I grant a wish, and someone uses it poorly, then their wish is taken away again." She began to look like the witch I had imagined before I arrived. "If you break your promise, your wish will turn to dust as well." She cackled, and the sound of it finally forced me away. I ran through the tunnel and out of the waterfall opening.

It was dark when I arrived back at the town. I headed for the inn, but I didn't have enough money to purchase a room for the night. So, I went to the docks and began to bed down on a pile of rope for the night. In my pitiful efforts to get comfortable, the ears of the wooden bunny jammed into my side. I pulled it out and studied it by the moonlight.

The woodcarver who had made it was quite skilled and had taken his time with this toy. It was smooth in my hands,

and I could see intricate carvings for the bunny's whiskers and hair. I imagined the rabbit could speak. Then, as if words had come out of its mouth, I suddenly remembered something. Evan had said he was a woodcarver. He was a young man and married. Could he be the man the witch had spoken of? I had to find him.

It didn't take long to find out Evan's address, and I was soon at the young man's door. Evan was delighted to see me and introduced me to his lovely young bride, Nancy. I was told they had been married less than a year. There was no child, but one was on the way. This didn't quite make sense to me. The witch had given me the impression that the wish was fulfilled, and Nancy hardly looked sickly. She was the most robust pregnant woman I'd ever seen.

They offered me food and drink and wanted to know everything about my journey to find the witch. At the end of my tale, I showed them the rabbit. Evan snatched it up and studied it. "This is exquisite."

Nancy admired it too. "It looks like something you could have done."

"I'm not as gifted as this," he said, hugging his wife, "but my father, he could have made something like this."

"Your father?" I asked.

"Yes. He was a woodcarver and now is mayor. Would you like to meet him?"

Minutes later the three of us were in the front parlor of the mayor's mansion. Sir Ryson stood with his hands clasped behind his back, wearing a robe over his shirt and pants, for it was late in the evening. While I stammered out too many apologies for bothering him, Evan took the rabbit from me and handed it to his father. Sir Ryson lifted the wooden toy close to his face and turned it around to see every bit of it. He bit his top lip. A tear snuck down his cheek.

"Where did you ever…?"

Evan told him about my journey to visit the witch. I explained that I was to take the rabbit to its owner. "Is it yours?"

"It is," Sir Bryson said weakly. He tossed a glance at his son and then focused on the rabbit once again. Suddenly I understood. Evan was the fulfillment of his wish.

"Your wife?" I asked cautiously.

Sir Bryson put an arm around his son and gave him a squeeze. "She stayed long enough to give me this prize."

"I'm so sorry."

I stayed with Sir Ryson at his invitation to enjoy a glass of wine after Evan and his wife left. He offered me a room for the night, and we spoke again in the morning over breakfast. I told him of my arrangement with Sir Barrymore, and he balked at the ridiculous challenge.

"No man could accomplish what he's asked of you."

"I'm trying anyway," I confessed.

"And I admire you for that, but you will never return before that tomato rots. Nor have you found your fortune."

I dropped my head. "I'm aware."

"Cheer up, lad. I've a proposition for you." I doubted anything he had to say would be helpful, but I raised my head and listened politely. "We have quite a bit of fertile land between the town and forest, as you may have noticed. However, we have no one to farm it, and we are dependent upon imports for our food. If your father has trained you well, I would give you the honored position of farming our land. You would be paid generously, given some land and a home of your own. It isn't a fortune, but it would be a fine living, one fine enough to impress someone like Sir Barrymore."

We shook hands on it, and he wrote a letter to Sir Barrymore explaining the position he was offering me. I tucked my letter in my pocket and made my way to the docks. I got on board the ship that would take me home.

On my first night aboard, I went to the main cabin to have supper, only to find the same cook working on this crew. I kept my head low and my mouth shut, sitting as far from the galley as possible. I prayed that he wouldn't notice me, but I didn't know how to stay undiscovered for three nights. Before leaving the table, I grabbed up as many rolls as I could and snuck them under my shirt when no one was looking. Perhaps I could live off of those for the next couple days. I left the cabin at the same time as three other men, positioning myself between them so I wouldn't be seen as I left.

The following morning, I nibbled on one of my rolls instead of having the hot breakfast being served. By suppertime, my stomach was growling at me. The soft tomato in my pocket beckoned me to eat it, and I feared that I couldn't resist the temptation. Finally, I gave up and went for a meal. I was late arriving, and there was nowhere left to sit but at the end of the table nearest the entrance. I began to turn around and stopped when I heard the cook ask, "Are you coming in, or aren't you?"

I lowered my head, ducking my chin into the collar of my jacket and nodded. I slipped onto the bench, and the cook slammed a bowl down in front of me. I reached for the ladle of the soup in the middle of the table, and just before I got the steamy broth to my bowl, a hand grabbed my wrist.

"Well, look who it is," the cook said. "The fella who stole my tomatoes. The one what got me put off my crew." He yanked the ladle out of my hand and threw my bowl across the room where it slammed against the wall. The

other men at the table cheered and laughed at the show. The cook grabbed the neck of my shirt and pulled me to my feet. "You don't get to eat *my* food on this ship." And with a foot to my backside, I was out the door.

I made my way back to my cot and pulled out another hard roll. I only had to survive one more night after this, and then I'd be home where there was a garden full of food. I fell asleep dreaming of tomatoes, cucumbers and carrots.

The shuffling of shoes and throaty whispers of men entering the cabin later in the evening stirred me from my slumber. I assumed they were my regular bunkmates, and I rolled over on my itchy pallet and tried to go back to sleep.

"That's him!"

The sound of the cook's voice was better than a bang on a brass gong for jolting me to my senses. My eyes popped open, and I sat up as fast as I could. The cook and two other men I recognized earlier in the evening were crowded at the side of my bunk. There was nowhere to go. The cook yanked my arm to get me to my feet. I hadn't steadied myself on them yet when one of the other men punched me in the gut. I doubled over in pain. The cook pulled my hair, raising my face again. Knuckles smashed across my cheek and nose. Hot blood instantly began running over my lips. I groaned, and I was barely able to mutter the words, "Why are you doing this?"

The cook hooked his large hand under my jaw and brought his face close so that his fowl breath made of onions and tobacco rolled over me. "You steal from me? I steal from you." He nodded at his comrades. "Get his bag."

"I don't have anything to steal."

"He's right," the one that punched me said, holding up my pack. "Dirty clothes and a few rolls from the kitchen. That's about it."

The cook took one of the hard rolls from his friend. "Well, look at this. You're at your old tricks, stealing food..."

"The tomatoes were mine!"

"I should turn you in to the captain."

"No! Can't we handle this as gentlemen?" I asked, begged really.

"No," was his answer.

And with that he plunged a knife into my side with enough force to knock me backward into my bunk. My head banged against the wooden post behind me. Through a dizzy haze I heard one of them say, "Now you've done it," and another one add, "Let's get out of here."

"Serves him right," the cook said. He yanked the knife out of me and then fled with the others out the door.

I felt warm liquid spill just below my ribcage, and yet the pain in my head from the bump seemed to outweigh any pain from the stab wound. I wondered if that's how a deathblow was supposed to feel—like nothing at all. There would be no pain once I had bled to death.

Doing my best to lift my head, I felt around where I'd been stabbed to find the wound. I lifted my jacket and shirt, but there was no mark. A squashed tomato rolled out of my pocket onto the pallet. It had been punctured. The tomato had saved my life.

I held the broken fruit in my hands, torn by my feelings. This strange little thing had been the motivation for my quest, it had saved my life, and now it would be my undoing because it was ruined. I closed my fingers around the soft flesh of the tomato and slung my arm back, intending to blast the tomato across the small room and watched it splatter on the opposite wall. But just as I was about to let go, one of my bunkmates entered the cabin. Sheepishly, I tucked the squashed tomato into my pocket before he noticed it.

"You been in a fight, mate?" he asked.

"It shows?" I asked, laughing as much as I could manage.

He climbed up into the bunk above me. "I hope the other guy looks worse."

I held my tongue. I didn't need to tell this man who had attacked me. I only had to survive one more night on the ship, and then I'd be home once again. I stayed in the cabin the following day and night, allowing everyone to think I was too injured to leave my bed. The moment the ship lay anchor, I grabbed my belongings and ran for the deck.

My parents were thrilled to have me home again and smothered me with kisses, hugs and lots of fresh food. I cleaned up, smoothed out my letter from Sir Ryson, put my stabbed and squashed tomato in a small pouch, and strode to the front door of Sir Barrymore's estate. Lillian answered the door. Her eyes were shiny with tears.

"I saw you coming up the walk," she said, reaching out her arms to give me a tight squeeze. Then she pulled back, keeping her hands on my shoulders, and looked me dead in the eyes. "You shouldn't have come back, Dash. Father has promised me to someone else."

"I know he has," I told her. "But he and I had a bargain. Please call him for me."

"No need." Sir Barrymore stepped onto the landing behind his daughter. She took her hands off me at the moment he put a protective hand on her shoulder. "I heard you had left. I didn't expect you to return."

"We had a deal," I reminded him.

"I don't recall striking any deal with you." His brow creased as his irritation rose.

"You told me that if I took the tomatoes and found my fortune before they rotted, I could return and win the hand of your daughter."

Lillian's jaw dropped. "Father! That was a horrible trick to play on Dash. You know he could never make anything like that happen!"

"I didn't think he'd take me seriously," Sir Barrymore said to his daughter. "I assumed he was smart enough to know that was not a realistic challenge."

I took a deep breath and put my hands on my hips with as much confidence as I could muster. "Well, I did take you seriously, sir. And I did set out to find my fortune. As required, I found it before my last tomato rotted." I reached into my pocket and retrieved the letter from Sir Ryson. I handed it to Lillian's father.

He read it carefully, nodded, folded it up and handed it back to me. "It sounds like an honorable position, and you will do well in it. I had hoped that you would take over for your father here when he gets too old…"

"But then I would never be successful enough to marry your daughter," I reminded him.

"No, you would not." He paused and bounced on his heels a couple times, trying to find an argument for me. At last he lifted a finger and spoke, "But what of the tomatoes? Surely they rotted long before this letter of employment was procured. So, I have won the deal fair and square." I lifted the pouch and undid the leather ties. I took out the mushy tomato. Sir Barrymore laughed at me. "Like I was saying…"

"It's squashed, yes," I said, "but it's not quite rotten."

Lillian took the tomato from me in both of her gentle hands; the juice ran between her fingers as she lifted it to her eyes to examine it closely. "It's not rotten, Father. He's right about that. Look." She held the tomato toward her father, but he waved it away.

"This is absurd! This tomato quest was not meant to be a real bargain. I was only teasing, offering false hope. Now, both of you stop being foolish. Lillian will wed whom I see fit."

Lillian cried out, "But Father, I love Dash!"

I took her hands to soothe her. As our hands entwined around the pulpy tomato it began to tremble and then glow. Before our eyes the tomato became solid again, plump, and bright red as though freshly picked from the vine.

"Father, do you see it?" Lillian asked, her voice barely a whisper.

"It's a miracle," the old man said in awe. "How is it possible?"

I told them of the witch who had a fondness for true love and about the magic she had given me. I didn't know it was with me still.

"You two truly love each other? It isn't a childhood fascination after all?" Sir Barrymore asked. Lillian and I nodded, staring into each other's eyes and smiling. Her father sighed and finally smiled too. "Then I give you my blessing."

My parents joined her family for supper that evening so we could begin planning our wedding. The main dish served? Tomato soup, of course. Oh, it wasn't from the magic tomato. We have that to this very day, placed on our mantle, fresh and red as the day it was picked. I think it will always be that way, for Lillian and I will always be in love.

"Tomato Princess"
Betty Rocksteady

The Great Red Spot

Peter Goulding

From Earth, the Great Planet appeared a faint dot
but slowly it broadened, the nearer we got.
Our nerve ends were jangling, our foreheads grew hot,
speculating on what might await us,
but we little suspected the famed Great Red Spot
was ten million square miles of tomatoes.

The readings had said it was some kind of gas,
a poisonous vapor where no-one could pass.
But the Jovians cunningly hid the great mass
of fruit that grew in all the craters.
One of the crew yelled out, "Methane, my ass,
that's a planet-sized field of tomatoes!"

At first, the discovery led to much mirth
and we laughed at the crop around Jupiter's girth,
but though we attempted, for all we were worth,
to switch on our communicators,
we couldn't relate to the folks back on earth
that we'd landed in miles of tomatoes.

The little red men came and took all the crew
to an underground city away from earth's view.
They asked "Are you hungry?" and then, right on cue,
there came seventeen little red waiters,
each carrying bowls of a sweet-smelling stew,
which seemed to contain sweet tomatoes.

We've been here a year now; we're ready to drop—
tomatoes, tomatoes, tomatoes non-stop.
It seems that, on Jupiter, there's but one crop
and our stomachs are starting to hate us.
You wouldn't believe how your spirits can flop
on a mono-food diet of tomatoes.

The Beauty of Being

Robert J. Krog

In the morning, the round, reddening tomato hung quivering on the vine as the wizard, his beard tucked into his belt to keep it out of the way, poured water over it from the glistening spout of his silver can. It quivered still as he spoke gentle words of encouragement to it.

"There you are, so plump and nearly ripe. Such a good tomato, you keep growing and getting red and juicy for one more day, maybe two, then you go into a soup, or maybe I'll just eat you like an apple." He reached down and caressed it, straightened and went on through the garden pouring water over every plant from his inexhaustible can. At the end of one row, he stopped, noting damage to some of his squash.

"Varmints," he stated, deeply disgusted, and stomped into the cottage.

Behind him, in the garden, the ripening tomato trembled on the vine. Inside, he found his apprentice dutifully studying a new spell.

"I have to go into town today," he told the boy. "I won't be back until tomorrow afternoon."

The boy looked up, trying to hide his elation. He said, "I'll take care of things while you're gone."

The wizard merely grunted.

"Really," the boy said, "I'll practice the new spell, and I'll sweep the floor. I'll milk the goat and slop the pig. I'll clean

up after dinner. I'll water the garden."

"I've already watered the garden," said the wizard, "and the garden is what worries me the most."

"I'll water it in the morning. I promise. I won't slack off while you're away."

"Bah!" said the wizard, "Your behavior is my least concern. You'll have pig hooves at the ends of your ankles for a week, if I see fit, that is if I don't just send you home for good."

The boy fell wisely silent and waited for his master to say what was on his mind.

The wizard looked out the window, fuming.

"Varmints," he muttered.

The boy's ears perked up, but he held his tongue. When, after several minutes, his master had said nothing, he went back to his studies, poring over the spell to turn a spider web into a doily.

"Stop what you're doing, boy," ordered the wizard, at last, "I have another task for your meager skills."

Unsure of what was coming, but too wary of his master's wrath at this point to be anything but obedient, he stopped and gave him his attention.

"I have a new spell for you to learn," stated the wizard. He stopped, then said, "No, there's no time for you to master a new spell, but I can put one in a wand and have you discharge it at the appropriate time. Come with me, and I'll show you something new that you'll probably forget by tonight."

The boy nettled on the inside but obediently followed his master over to the wand chest in a corner of the cottage. The wizard drew out a battered, old wand and proceeded to place a spell in it, slowly and carefully. The boy watched, interested in, but largely ignorant of, the proceedings. When he was done, the wizard said, "You have but to point it at the dogwood tree on the edge of the garden at dusk and order the tree to stop anything from eating the vegetables in the garden. The spell will last until dawn, when you arise, and then you can watch for varmints yourself. The spell will give the tree sentience, a reasonable amount of basic knowledge, and mobility. Your thoughts and words will give it its mission and sense of purpose, so be clear in what you are thinking and feeling as well as in what you are saying." He handed the wand to his apprentice.

The boy took it eagerly and brandished it.

"Don't gesture with it just yet, boy; it might go off!"

He stopped and set it down, carefully. "So, I'll say, 'You, tree, protect the garden from varmints that would eat the vegetables. Don't let anything eat the vegetables. Smite them and stomp them if they try.'"

"Yes, well, that might work, but really, try to be concise and clear. Now, back to your lessons." The wizard walked away, grumbling, "I don't know if I can keep that boy, he has no talent and doesn't apply himself." The boy heard him, but went back to his studies.

Out in the garden, the tomato slowly reddened on the vine.

Around noon, the boy hitched the donkey to the cart and brought it around to the front of the cottage. The wizard got in and drove away without a word. He'd already told the boy all he needed to know for that day.

But the boy only waited until the cart was out of sight down the dirt road before running inside and finding the wizard's stash of liquorices and other sweet treats. He was soon sitting on the porch in the rocking chair with his feet propped up, a handful of sweets he was sure the wizard would not miss on the table beside him, a cup of goat's milk beside that, and a novel in his hand. It wasn't often he had time alone, and one just couldn't study and practice every hour of the day. He tried to let the wizard's lack of faith in him roll of his back, but there it was, rankling deep in his mind as he licked the fingers of the hand that was not turning the pages.

It was only an hour later that the sweets were gone, pace them though he tried. The novel took another several hours to finish, but by then he was thirsty. He went to the well and drew water and then wondered, just wondered if he hadn't noticed a bottle of whiskey or two in the wizard's secret stash.

He had. There was one full and one mostly empty. It was like fire when he sipped it, but he sipped it anyway. Strange thoughts and feelings came to his mind then, and he wiled away the fading, sunlit hour singing songs about lost loves and railing against how unfair the wizard was to him.

"What's the use of it all?" he asked, when the first bottle was empty, casting his gaze to the ceiling above which, his drunken mind shrewdly guessed, there might be a sky and, in it, some kind of divinity that knew the answer to his questions. "Why am I studying so hard, if he doesn't appreciate it? What am I to do with myself if he sends me home? They won't want me there, that I can tell you; no sir, they won't. I'd sooner have hooves and stay here than be there. Oh, what am I supposed to do?"

He cast about for some better means of expressing himself, and tried a spell as proof of his competency. It did not work, and he stared long and hard at the goat in the yard, wondering why it had not turned into a radish.

"Still," he said, standing up amid the clatter of his chair falling to the floor behind him and throwing his gaze again at the presumable sky somewhere beyond the ceiling, "I'm learning at my own pace and getting better. I bet I said fifty percent of the words for that spell, and that's, well, that's fifty percent, which is half, which is pretty good for a beginner!"

He reached over and snatched up the wand the wizard had left for him to employ on the dogwood at the edge of the garden.

"This," he said, "this, I cannot mess up. This, I can do, because it's child's play."

He staggered to the door, looked out into the twilight, and shook the wand rather more than was required to get its attention, as only a simple flourish was called for. "You, tree," he said, pointing it at the part of the world in which stood the tree, "patrol and protect the garden from any varmints, just anything that tries to eat the vegetables, and do it just as best as you can, because you expire with the dawn." He stood a moment, pointing. He vaguely wondered if he was doing it correctly. Nothing was happening. "Why me?" he moaned suddenly, after another moment of frantic pointing, "What's the meaning of it all?" He suddenly remembered that he had to give a flick of the wrist to discharge the spell and slung the wand about from the elbow, just for good measure. A green ball of magical power slung out in an arc. He turned and staggered back into the cottage.

Behind him, the green ball of magical power fell onto a rock in the middle of the garden, sat a moment upon it, then dissolved and ran down the sides. A few drops slid down and touched the waiting skin of the red, ripening tomato. It quivered violently. It glowed with a green light. As the glow faded, the tomato and a part of the vine popped off the rest of the plant and landed neatly on the ground. It had enough vine about it to form the reasonable facsimiles of arms and legs, and on one side of its globe something like eyes and a mouth appeared, though, in the twilight, they were hard to see. It looked around, surveying the garden about it. After a moment's gauging of the situation, it began to stalk purposefully through the garden.

When it reached the edge of the cultivation, it turned right and began to march around the perimeter. Along the way, it procured a splinter of wood from a stake and held it as though it were a spear.

"What are you?" asked a voice. The tomato turned, brandishing the splinter, "Who goes there?" it demanded to know.

A tiny person leapt out of the grass beyond the garden and landed with a flutter of wings on the dirt before the tomato and bowed low to it with a winsome smile on his little face.

"I am Dawton," he said.

"What are you doing here?" asked the tomato, the point of his splinter aimed at Dawton's chest.

"I am asking you what you are," explained Dawton.

"I am the garden guardian," declared the tomato, "what are you?"

"I am a pixie."

"I must ask you to go about your business," said the tomato, "I cannot allow any of these vegetables to be eaten."

"I see," said the pixie, "that you have a job to do, and I will not hinder it. I do not want these vegetables. I prefer wild nuts, berries, and honey."

"Oh," said the tomato, "Well, as I have a job to do, I must proceed on my patrol, something might want to eat these vegetables, and I cannot allow that."

"It sounds interesting to patrol with a tomato," said Dawton, "may I patrol with you?"

The tomato thought this over, wrinkling up its tomato face as it thought. "I suppose that would be okay," it said, at last.

"Very good," said Dawton.

Together, they marched around the perimeter of the garden. Along the way, Dawton acquired a splinter of his own from a stake by the wall of the cottage, just under the kitchen window. When they reached the spot where they had met, Dawton asked, "What is your name?"

The tomato thought about it and said, "I think my name is Tree."

"It's a pleasure to meet you, Tree."

"It is a pleasure to meet you, Dawton."

"Wonderful. It's a pleasureful night, just full of pleasureful things, I think."

And they marched. The twilight deepened into night, and the glow of the moon increased. The marching grew rather tiresome to Dawton after the third time around. He stopped and sat on a stone. "Tree," he asked, "How long have you been here? I've never seen you before."

"I've been here my whole life."

"And how long has that been?"

Tree thought this over. He had been pondering a great deal anyway, but had not been looking backward much. It was a new line of thought.

"I popped off the plant over there," he waved a leaf in the right direction, "beside the big rock, and walked over there," he waved the same leaf, "and found my spear there," he gestured with the splinter, "and met you here." He looked pleasantly at Dawton.

"Oh," said Dawton, "I see."

"It was dark," Tree added helpfully.

"You're very young," said the pixie.

"Young?" asked the tomato.

"Not old," explained the pixie.

"Right, I think I understand. I'm young which means not old."

"You're only as old as tonight. That's very young."

A thought occurred to Tree. He voiced it uncertainly, "Dawton, how old are you?"

Dawton had to think this over, "I'm about six summers."

"Six summers," repeated the tomato.

"Yep."

"Is that old?"

Dawton thought that over. It wasn't. It wasn't old at all. Everyone called him youngster, actually.

"No," he said, "but it is a lot older than tonight."

"Oh. I'm very young."

"Yes, you are."

"Dawton?"

"Yes,"

"We should keep marching. I have to protect the garden."

"Okay, we'll march some more," said the pixie, with a sigh.

They marched. Fireflies hovered in the air, blinking. Somewhere, an owl hooted. Tree jumped and brandished his splinter.

"It's just an owl. They eat bats and moths, not vegetables."

"Oh, thank you."

They marched, in step. Dawton found that fun.

"Dawton?"

"Yes?"

"How many nights are in a summer?"

Dawton scratched his head. "I think it's about a thousand."

"You're very old," said Tree, in awe.

"Everyone calls me 'youngster.'"

"Really?"

"It's true."

"If you are young, what am I?" He stopped marching and turned to Dawton looking him full in the face. Dawton, puzzled, stared back and then smiled broadly.

"You're brand new," he declared, "a newborn baby."

"Wow," said Tree, "wow."

They proceeded to march some more. "What's it like," asked Tree, "to be thousands of nights old?"

Dawton wrinkled his face up, thinking that one over, and replied, "I don't know. I don't remember all of it."

"I see," murmured the tomato.

They marched. The owl hooted again. A bat flew over their heads. Tree thought about his task and about the night and about the coming morning. He realized that he would not see the morning. That was clearly in his mind. He had a job to do until morning, and he had to do it well, and it was all he had.

"Why me?" he asked.

"Eh?" asked Dawton.

"What does it all mean?" asked the tomato.

Dawton shrugged.

They marched. Somewhere in the grassy patch across the road before the edge of the forest, a creature scurried.

"What is morning like?" asked Tree.

"The sun comes up," said Dawton.

On the road, the creature, a rabbit, paused in the moonlight.

"The sun comes up," repeated Tree, as if he knew what that meant, but really, he did not. After a moment, he asked, "What is the sun like?"

Dawton was pleased, because these were questions he could readily answer. He said, "The sun is round and bright, like the moon, only brighter. It's so bright it hurts your eyes to look at it. It's hot too, especially in the summertime."

"I see," said Tree.

"In the morning," said Dawton, "it isn't dark like it is now; it's bright."

"Bright," Tree repeated, "bright."

"Like the moon," Dawton explained, "only brighter. You can see things by its light, more than by the light of the moon."

Tree looked up at the moon. He looked at its sheen and the soft halo in the sky just around it. He looked at the slight illumination it gave and the shadows cast by its light. "The moon," he said, "the moon is beautiful."

The rabbit crossed the road and made its way carefully over the lawn toward the garden.

"Yep," said Dawton, "It's pretty pretty."

"Is the sun even pretty prettier?"

Dawton pondered that. "No," he said, "I like the sun, but I think the moon is prettier. You can't really look at the sun. It's too bright, but you can see more by it."

"I still wish I could get to see it," said Tree.

"You will," said the pixie, smiling, "it will come up in the morning. Maybe we'll be able to play somewhere else, then."

"No," said the tomato, "I won't get to see the morning."

"Why not?"

Dawton didn't get an answer. With a snarl of defiance, the tomato raised its splinter spear and charged across the garden toward a large, shadowy, pointy-eared shape. Stunned, he watched as the shape, a rabbit he saw after a moment when it jumped high to avoid the tomato's charge, hopped away over the lawn into the tall grass across the road. It took with it the splinter of wood, which the tomato had thrust into its left hind foot, as it sprang away.

Dashing for all it was worth, the little tomato made its way to the nearest stake and pried another splinter off of it. Dawton approached with his little mouth open in awe.

"You were very brave and fierce," he declared with great enthusiasm.

"I have a mission," said Tree, "a job to do, and I only have tonight to do it, so I have to do it just as well as I can."

"Wow," said Dawton.

"But, I wonder," said the tomato, leaning in and whispering, "I wonder, why me, and what's it all mean?"

"Oh," said the pixie.

"And, I wish I could see the sun. The sun seems to me to be very important."

"Well, in the morning," began Dawton.

"No, I won't see the morning. I know that. I won't see it. I won't. I only have until then."

"What happens?" asked the pixie.

"I expire," he said, surely.

"What's that mean?"

"I don't know, but I'm a little scared of it."

"Don't be scared," said the pixie, putting his hand on the leafy part that Tree used like a hand.

"I am a little, though," said Tree, "but I do have my mission." It stood as tall as it could and held its splinter spear high.

"Let's patrol some more," suggested Dawton, "maybe that rabbit will come back, and we'll have some fun."

"Was that a rabbit?" asked Tree as they resumed their marching in step, "I thought it was a varmint."

"What's a varmint?"

"A thing that tries to eat the vegetables. I thought you were one, at first."

The pixie giggled. "No."

They marched around the garden several times, stoically sticking to their purpose, before Tree asked again, casting his gaze to the sky above in supplication.

See this, Dawton thought he knew what was on his friend's mind and asked, "What's what mean?"

The tomato stopped and scratched itself thoughtfully on top. "I just have to ask," it said, "Maybe I mean why am I doing this job instead of being a pixie, like you."

"Why is your name 'Tree' when you're clearly a tomato?" suggested Dawton.

"Why do I only have tonight?"

"Why do you talk when the other tomatoes don't?"

"They don't?"

"Nope, they don't."

The pair walked on and passed the tomato plant from which he had sprung. There were other tomatoes upon it, but none of them were as close to ripe as Tree, and none them showed any signs of animation or speech.

"They don't," said Tree, wondering.

"I never saw a tomato talk or walk before tonight," said Dawton.

"I wonder why not."

"Me too."

Tree extended his leafy appendages toward the plant and asked again, "Why me? What's it all mean?"

"Rabbit," shouted Dawton in an excess of excitement, pointing his splinter spear across the garden.

"Ya!" shouted Tree, dashing around the tomato plant and toward the offending creature, his splinter ready to thrust. Dawton took to the air and sped across with his splinter ready as well.

The rabbit had been craving the cabbage all day and had stayed hidden all day, waiting for its dinnertime, and avoiding a fox. When it had arrived, after nightfall, it had been assaulted, most unexpectedly, and gone away with an unsatisfied craving, and a splinter lodged in its paw. It had nothing to show for its day of patience and would have to face the next day and the fox on an empty stomach if it did not succeed in finding food. It might have looked elsewhere, but it was craving the cabbage. It was feeling hungry and belligerent on its return.

When the pixie and the tomato charged it, it fought. It leapt at them a little awkwardly for the remnants of the splinter in the one paw, but it leapt at them nevertheless, and it tumbled the tomato away from it with a shoulder block and nipped at the pixie with its large, sheering teeth. Dawton, fortunately, veered nimbly away, but poor Tree was all a tangle under the new blueberry bush. The rabbit knew well that tomatoes are edible too, and lunged to devour it. Pixies are nimble though, and they are fast fliers. Dawton had turned round in a space smaller than a man's fist. He dove, splinter thrust ahead, at the rabbit and embedded it in a soft, fuzzy ear. The rabbit actually cried out in pain, altered its course and hopped away from the garden again, its left hind foot throbbing, and its right ear bleeding.

"Whoopee!" cried Dawton as he alit beside the tangle of tomato vine and blueberry shoots, "We're dragon slayers."

"Really?" asked Tree, trying to extricate himself, "What's a dragon?"

"It's a great, fire-breathing monster. Let me help you."

"Okay. So, varmints are rabbits are dragons?"

"Well, almost."

"Okay."

They stepped away from the blueberry and resumed their marching.

"That was fun," said Dawton.

"I have been successful in my mission twice, now, thanks to you. It's good."

"Glad to be of service," declared the pixie.

They marched, full of a sense of accomplishment. At length, upon passing the tomato plant for the severalth time, Tree again stopped and looked up to the sky, imploringly.

Dawton brandished the new splinter he had procured and said, "We're heroes."

"And that's great," said the tomato, "but I still wonder, and I still long to see the sun, and I know I shall not, and I long to have thousands of summer nights, but I shall only have this one, and I must be satisfied with this mission and this night, but somehow, I want more."

Dawton thought a moment and asked, "Want to go play in the woods? That's always fun."

"Really?"

"Yes, really."

They both made a step toward the woods, but Tree's other vine leg simply wouldn't budge. "I have to complete my mission," he said, sadly and resumed his patrol.

"Oh," said Dawton, "well..." He stood for a moment, flightily imagining the joys of the woods, then sighed, then grinned, and rejoined Tree.

"We'll do the forest tomorrow," he suggested.

"You can, but I can't," said Tree. He wasn't accusing or jealous, but he was very sure of the facts of the matter.

"Really?"

"This night is all I have," he said.

"You keep saying that."

"It's the truth."

They marched in silence.

"Are they real?" Tree asked, later.

"Are what real?"

"The things I want: the sun, more nights, reasons?"

"Sure, I've seen the sun and more nights. They're real, for sure."

"What about reasons?" asked the tomato urgently.

"Um," said the pixie. "Um."

"Please, are they real?"

He scratched his head. He scrunched up his face in the effort of thinking, and finally, he shrugged his shoulders and said, "They must be real, because you want them."

The tomato considered that, and while he could find no flaw in it, he was not much comforted. He thought a moment and said, "I want real things...."

Dawton nodded and smiled helpfully. Feeling better, Tree smiled back at him. They resumed their marching.

Across the road and over in the woods, the rabbit was dead. The wounds, which had been inflicted upon it by the tomato and the pixie, were hardly fatal, but they had slowed it down, especially the wound in its foot. The fox had come, drawn by the scent of its blood, and caught it at last and was devouring it even then. It was a new creature, a new varmint, that was waddling unconcernedly by the fox as it licked its chops over the grisly remains of the rabbit. It was an armadillo that was waddling out of the woods and through the tall grass on the other side of the road and across the road toward the garden.

The armored monstrosity was not interested in vegetables. It was an eater of ants, beetles, grubs, and spiders, and it was drawn by the scent of the newly tilled earth at one end of the garden in which the wizard had recently planted several squash. It paused on the road, sniffing around to regain the scent it had lost in a momentary shift of the breeze.

As they marched, Dawton thought the little tomato looked so sad that he took one of his leafy appendages in his hand and said, "We're friends."

In his scanty knowledge, the word "friends," was not present, so he asked, "What are friends?"

"I like you," the pixie said, "and we play together and have fun. We're together, and it's good."

"Oh," said the tomato, mulling that over. He thought he understood, and he repeated the words, "Friends. Together. Good."

They marched on together, hand in leaf.

In the road, the armadillo caught the scent again, and

ambled on across the grass to the edge of the garden.

Dawton and Tree saw it approaching. Dawton paused to say, "Wow!" but Tree charged ferociously at it, splinter spear at the ready. Dawton remembered himself and charged too. The armadillo was not cognizant of the creatures coming its way. In its eagerness to dig for grubs and ants, it shuffled on, knocking the tomato aside without noticing. Tree tumbled on his vines and tangled up once again, this time in a squash plant. Dawton bravely dodged and thrust his splinter spear at the side of the armadillo but did no damage. The splinter broke without piercing the monstrosity's armor. The armadillo, still unaware of his assailants, began digging into the ground, searching for grubs, in the process, damaging the roots of a nearby squash.

Dawton flew over it, avoiding the clods of earth being flung behind it, and landed by Tree, helping him out of his tangle.

"I say," said Tree, "It's not eating vegetables."

"What?"

The tomato pointed at the armadillo. "It's not eating. It's digging."

"Oh, that's good, because I stabbed it in the side, and my splinter broke without hurting it. I don't think it even knows we're here."

"Well, I suppose we should continue our patrol."

"Yeah, I guess," said Dawton.

They marched on. Dawton acquired another splinter.

Behind them, the armadillo uprooted the first squash completely in its quest for tasty things in the ground.

"Do you suppose," asked Dawton as they approached the armadillo again, and saw the devastation it was making in the patch of squash, "that it hurts the plants to have them out of the ground?"

"I don't know," said Tree, "I'm only supposed to stop things from eating the vegetables."

"Oh," said Dawton, "Okay."

They marched by the armadillo, giving it a wide berth as it continued to fling earth about. It noticed them but paid them no heed. Its mouth was full of grubs.

"I don't like it," declared Dawton.

"Don't like what?" asked Tree.

"That armadillo is tearing up the garden," declared the pixie, his tone outraged.

It was true. It was very true.

"Well, maybe we should ask it to stop."

"It's an armadillo," explained the pixie, "It won't understand."

"I see," said Tree.

"We should stop it," declared Dawton, "Aren't we dragon slayers?"

"You said we are."

"Okay, let's stop it."

"But I have a mission," protested Tree.

"You won't have to leave the garden."

"But."

"It will be fun," said Dawton, and Tree lit up in excitement.

"Okay," said the tomato, "let's do it."

"We need a plan," said Dawton.

"Right," said Tree, wisely. "What's that?"

"We'll bash it with rocks, since splinters will break!"

"Hm," said the tomato, scratching its top, thoughtfully.

He picked up a pebble, the largest he could find at hand, and hefted it at the armadillo. The pebbled bounced off. The armadillo went about its business of tearing up the soft ground and uprooting plants.

"I don't think I can pick up a rock that is heavy enough," said Tree.

"Maybe together," suggested the pixie.

They looked around and found a very large pebble, at least two inches in diameter. Together, they carried it over close to the armadillo and threw it as hard as they could. It landed a bit short.

Huffing, Dawton said, "I don't think this is going to work."

"Well," said Tree, "At least it hasn't noticed us yet. I don't want it to breathe fire on us."

"What?" asked Dawton.

"You said that dragons breathe fire."

"Oh," the pixie laughed, "I was exaggerating. This is just an armadillo. It's not really a dragon."

"That's good," said the tomato, "I think fire would hurt."

"Fire burns," agreed Dawton with sudden enthusiasm.

"Right," said Tree.

"Let's go get some."

"Why?"

"To fight the dragon!"

"Oh," said the confused tomato.

So they ran until they reached the far end of the garden, and then Tree had to stop.

"Where are you going?" he asked.

Dawton stopped and looked around. "I don't know," he admitted.

"Where will you find fire?"

The pixie was perplexed. He cast about for a moment, his eyes searching, and then they settled on the window of the cottage, from which there came a slight glow from the fire set in the hearth there.

"There," he exclaimed, and rushed toward the house.

Tree watched him fly away through the window, and then, conscious of his sense of duty, resumed his patrol for varmints. He walked by the monstrosity of the armadillo twice before the pixie flew out the window of the house with some flaring thing in his possession. When he alit on the ground before Tree, Dawton was bearing a stick, one end of which was a hot ember. He said, "Quick, let's make it bigger."

"Okay," said Tree and waited.

Dawton looked at him, urgently.

Tree waited.

"Quick, get twigs and things to burn," he explained, setting the stick down not far from the armadillo.

"Okay," said Tree, and he gathered what bits he could inside the garden.

They piled twigs, dried grass, and leaves on the ember. Dawton fanned it with his wings, and soon the pile caught and blazed. Nearby, the armadillo paused in its digging and looked at the fire. It had, by that point, uprooted all but one of the newly planted squash.

Dawton and Tree stood back basking in the warmth and pleased with the results.

"Now what?" asked Tree.

Dawton started and recalled the task at hand. "Now," he shouted, "we attack!" He seized a burning twig and rushed at the armadillo with it. Amazed, it took Tree a moment to do the same. Dawton stopped before the creature, shouting and waving the burning twig. The monstrosity lunged at him, waddling forward so fast that he barely had time to dodge aside. Tree bravely stood his ground to protect the last squash, but it was already turning and chasing after its first target. Dawton took to the air to avoid its lumbering rush. Tree hurled his twig at it. The burning ember struck leathery hide and bounced off, unnoticed. Dawton began diving at its eyes, which did have an effect. The armadillo began turning every which way trying to escape. Dawton, in his enthusiasm shouted, "Come on, Tree, we have it confused, now is the time to strike."

Tree went back to the fire and grabbed two burning twigs. He rushed into the squash patch, his vine legs almost spinning in his haste. "Be careful, Dawton," he called. The pixie laughed, and continued diving at the armadillo's eyes. Tree whacked at its tail as it passed, but missed and was swept off his leafy feet by it instead. He rose to rejoin the fray, a burning twig in each leafy hand, but paused to think. The monstrosity was so much bigger than they, and its leathery armor was so impervious, that Dawton had the right idea. They needed to strike at vulnerable parts, vital parts. Too short to go after the eyes, as Dawton was, he would have to go after its nose. He waited, watching, as Dawton drove it this way and that, never quite getting its eyes, and never quite driving it out of the garden either, indeed, the flighty pixie seemed to be having too much fun to think practically about the situation.

"But getting it out of the garden would be best," thought Tree. He waited. Dawton swooped and turned and laughed as he waved his little torch in front of the monstrosity's eyes. Suddenly, when the great beast was facing Tree, with its nose only inches away, he lunged and thrust both twigs into its snout.

"Look out," shouted Dawton, diving close in to strike again at its eyes. The beast shrieked and jumped straight up. Dawton collided with its leathery hide and bounced off. Stunned, he fell into the cabbages. The armadillo landed, snorted out the now extinguished, but still hot, twigs, and waddled off at an amazing pace, away from the garden.

Tree stood up. Dawton was nowhere to be seen. He looked around, knowing he should resume his patrol, but wondering what had become of his friend.

"Dawton?"

There was no reply. He began to march again, calling out for the pixie and looking for a new weapon. He pried yet another splinter off a stake under the kitchen window, and followed the trail their repeated marching had made around the perimeter of the garden. Above him, a bat flitted by with an owl chasing after it. Fireflies blinked under the stars, and the moon was getting close to the tops of the trees on the horizon.

As he called out, he wondered what could have become of the pixie. He had been there just a moment before the end of the combat. He had even called a warning. Could the armadillo have eaten him when it jumped so high in the air? Was its belly finally full, and that was why it had left? He stopped in his tracks, stunned by the thought.

"Oh, Dawton," he said, "You were such a good friend. I liked you. And now you're gone." He sighed and marched on. He had, after all, to do his duty, regardless of how he felt. He stopped by the tomato plant from whence he had sprung and asked the sky again, "Why me? What is the meaning of it all?"

A groan came just after the question, but it did not come from him or, he realized after a startled moment, from the tomato plant either. It came from a cabbage a quarter of the way around the big rock. He brandished his splinter spear fiercely and investigated, wondering what might be over there, eating the cabbage.

It was Dawton, of course, and beside him, his now-extinguished, little torch.

"Oh, friend," said Tree, "what is the matter?"

Dawton made no response.

"What do I do now?" asked the tomato.

A moth fluttered by.

He shook Dawton by one shoulder. The pixie moaned but did not awaken.

Unwilling to abandon his friend, and unable to abandon his duty to guard the garden, he stood a moment in indecision, then, impelled by the duty, he resumed his patrol. He cast frequent glances back at the cabbage and, when the cabbage was hidden by the other plants, at the rock above it. An idea occurred to him.

When he returned to the spot where Dawton was, he gently lifted the pixie and climbed on top of the rock. As he had suspected, he could see the whole garden from the top. It was a good guard post. He set Dawton down, gently, and held his hand while scanning the garden for signs of varmints. He stayed thus as the stars slowly wheeled by and the moon sank beneath the trees. No more varmints seemed interested in the vegetables, but he stayed vigilant. Later, when the moon was just a vague glow behind the trees, Dawton awoke, rubbed his aching head and looked up at the tomato in wonder.

"I say, Tree, there you are, and here I am, and I wonder how we got here?"

Tree looked down at him and smiled as much as his ill-defined features allowed.

"I found you in that cabbage," he explained, "and put you up here so I could watch you and the garden at the same time. I was afraid I had lost you before I found you, and so I didn't want to go away from you."

"Oh," said Dawton, "well, that seems fine to me." He sat up next to his friend.

"I can see the whole garden from here," said Tree.

"Yes," yawned the pixie, "but you could see it better from up there." He pointed up at the windowsill.

"I suppose I could, but how would I get there?"

"I could fly you up there."

253

It seemed a fine idea. He assented; "Let us do that," and the pixie took hold of his leafy hands and lifted him up with much whirring and straining of wings to the windowsill.

"I can see it all better from up here," said Tree, looking the garden over. He looked down the sheer wall and asked in sudden worry, "You will fly me down if a varmint tries to eat the vegetables, won't you?"

"Naturally," said his friend.

So they sat on the windowsill together, enjoying the breeze, which was nicer up a little higher, as they were.

"What is that?" asked Tree, pointing east.

"What's what?"

"It isn't so dark over there anymore."

"Oh," laughed the pixie, "the dawn is nearly here."

"Then the night is almost over?"

"Yep, we'll be able to play in the woods after you expire."

"I don't think so," said the tomato, "and I'm afraid." His leafy appendages trembled. He stood up, looking east, eager for the light, hungry for the light, but terribly afraid. He glanced at the garden. It was no further disturbed; he looked at the pale, beautiful, dreadful light in the east. He squeezed Dawton's hand, and the pixie cried out, snatching his hand away.

"I'm sorry," he said, "I'm very sorry."

Dawton looked at him curiously, worriedly, then said, "It will be well if you just hold my hand without squeezing it so." He stuck his hand out again, and Tree took it more gently and, though he held it tightly, did not squeeze it painfully again.

"It will all be good in the end," said the pixie, "you'll see." He didn't know why he said it, other than that he wanted to reassure his new friend. "There isn't anything to be afraid of."

"I wish I knew what it meant to expire," said Tree, "and

why this night is all I have."

"How do you know that?"

"I just know it. I don't know how."

They looked east in silence for a time. After a bit, Dawton softly whistled a tune he knew to stave off boredom. Tree, trembling less for the comfort his friend's touch brought him, looked eagerly and fearfully at the growing light, yearning for its source.

"Is it truly true?" he asked at last.

"Is what truly true?" asked Dawton.

"Are all those things I wish for real, the sun and more nights and reasons?"

"Of course they are."

"They are all real?"

"I think so."

"The sun and more nights are not for me, Dawton," he said, looking earnestly at his friend.

"Truly?"

"Truly, but reasons might be for me. Tell me they are real, and that I'll find them."

"Reasons are real, and you will find them."

"Thank you."

The sun peaked over the horizon a moment later. Tree gasped in awe, and the tomato sagged down to the windowsill, the leaf slipping out of the pixie's hand.

Dawton looked closely and sadly at his friend. "Tree?" There was no response. "Tree?" he asked again, poking the tomato gently. He looked closely in the new light and saw that what had passed for facial features had disappeared. He stood straight, sighed, said, "Maybe he'll be back tomorrow night," and flew away in a whir of wings, a little less cheerful for a time and forever more thoughtful than he had been, before that night. Behind him, on the windowsill, the tomato ripened under the warming influences of the morning sun.

Around an hour after sunrise, the apprentice awoke with a bad hangover and stumbled out to the well to drink a lot of water, after which he went in to find some food that would not offend his surprisingly delicate stomach. He did not then notice the state of the squash patch in the garden.

He ate. He cleaned. He opened his books up to where he had been the day before and plunged desperately into his studies knowing full well that he had squandered the day before, as far as his studies were concerned. When he went to the well for water again, near noon, he noticed, at last, the state of the squash patch. It was then that he wept.

After he'd had a cleansing but otherwise useless cry, he began replanting the squash as best he could and watering them with the silver can that never ran out. Then, truly desperate, he went in to see if he could find a spell to rejuvenate plants. It was thus that the wizard found him a couple of hours later, poring over his books and praying that his master had not noticed the state of the garden.

"Well, boy, put the donkey cart away," was all that his master said.

He obeyed with alacrity.

The wizard, stiff and aching from his long cart ride, entered the kitchen, sat down by the window, and noticed the tomato.

"Oh, my," he said, absently seeing at the same time the evidence of his apprentice's desperate efforts in the squash patch and wondering whether he should dismiss the boy or give him hooves and another chance.

"This is a tasty-looking tomato." He picked it up,

plucked it from the bit of vine still attached to it, brushed it off, and took a bite. Juices ran down his chin. He wiped with his handkerchief, and he sighed. He'd worry about the boy after a snack and a rest.

"Oh," he said, "now that's a tomato."

About The Authors And Artists

Scáth Beorh: Scáth Beorh is a writer and editor. He may be reached at lambs.kingdom@yahoo.com

The Black Rabbit: Illustrator and storyboard artist from Atlanta, Georgia, The Black Rabbit's illustrations dabble in ethereal romanticism. He is currently finishing his first published art book, *Through the Woods*, aiming for early 2016 release. www.facebook.com/theblkrabbit

H. David Blalock: H. David Blalock has been writing speculative fiction for over 40 years. His work has appeared in novels, novellas, short stories, reviews and commentary. His work continues to appear from multiple publishers. Find out more at his website, www.thrankeep.com.

Tracy Davidson: Tracy Davidson writes poetry and flash fiction. Her work has appeared in various publications and anthologies, including: P*oet's Market 2015, The Binnacle, Modern Haiku, A Hundred Gourds, Mslexia, Journey to Crone, The Great Gatsby Anthology* and *In Protest: 150 Poems for Human Rights.*

Sarah Doebereiner: Sarah Doebereiner is a short story author, novelist, and poet. She graduated from Wright State University in 2010 with her BA in English. Sarah lives in central Ohio with her husband and two small children. She enjoys writing everything from micro-fiction to novella length works.
https://www.facebook.com/sarahadoebereiner.com

D. G. Driver: D. G. Driver is a Young Adult author of *Cry of the Sea, Whisper of the Woods*, and P*assing Notes*. She lives near Nashville, TN, and when she's not writing or working,

she's singing in a local community theater musical. Learn more about her at www.dgdriver.com

E. M. Eastick: E. M. Eastick worked as an environmental professional in Australia, Britain, Ireland, and the United Arab Emirates before becoming a writer of no-fixed genre. She currently spends most of the year in Colorado.

Rick Eddy: Born and raised in Buffalo, NY, Rick Eddy has been writing poetry and short stories for almost 40 years. Through his writings he has sought to explore moral and spiritual issues in this complex and challenging world.

David Elliott: David Elliott is the author of two books of poetry, *Wind in the Trees* (AHA Books) and *Passing Through* (Nightshade Press), and has been published in many journals including *Parting Gifts, The Cape Rock, High Plains Literary Review,* and *Passages North.*

G.L. Francis: G.L. Francis is a Midwest writer of speculative fiction and nonfiction essays, artist, tinker, and jane-of-many-trades with too many interests.

Karin Britt Gall: Karin Britt Gall has been writing fiction and nonfiction from Central Ohio for over 25 years. She lives with her husband and attack cat Smokey. Her work has appeared in anthologies, articles, magazines, and newspapers both in print and online. She recently completed a spiritual memoir and a cozy mystery for which she is seeking representation. Blog/Author Page: In Other Words (https://karinsgall.wordpress.com/)

Peter Goulding: Peter Goulding's work has been published in four continents by badgering editors until they capitulate. He has self-published many books of

alleged humorous verse, because nobody else will. He has just completed his first novel and plans to read another one soon. He has no practical talents at all.

John Grey: John Grey is an Australian poet, US resident. Recently published in *New Plains Review, Perceptions* and *Sanskrit* with work upcoming in *South Carolina Review, Gargoyle, Owen Wister Review* and *Louisiana Literature.*

Robyn Groth: Robyn Groth has an M.A. in linguistics and is a fanatic of lifelong learning and autodidacticism. She is fond of form, mythology and cephalopods. She lives in the Midwest with her husband and three sons. Her work has been published in *Blue Monday Review.* Read more at www.robyngrothwrites.wordpress.com.

Ann Hart: Ann Hart was born into a tomato and literature loving family. She has lived in Georgia (eating tomatoes fried and green), Arizona (eating tomatillos), and now resides in Illinois enjoying heirloom tomatoes and great poetry. *Tomato Heirloom* is Ann's first published poem.

Amanda Rotach Huntley: Amanda Rotach Huntley is the owner of Line By Lion Publications, LLC and the author of *Hunter the Horrible* and *Charlotte and Daisy.* Ms. Huntley lives in Louisville, Kentucky with her four children.

Katie Irish: Katie Irish is a Freelance Writer living in Hartford, CT. Her work as appeared in *34th Parallel Literary Magazine, Connecticut Gardener Magazine, Life in the Finger Lakes Magazine, The Ithaca Journal, Natural Awakenings Magazine,* and *Edible Nutmeg Magazine.* She lives with her Siamese cat, Cleopatra.
Her website is http://www.katiejirish.com.

Robert Iulo: Robert Iulo's work has been published in *Gastronomica, Museum of Americana, Hypertext* and others. He's had a special feature published in T*he Mississippi Sun Herald* about his volunteer work on the Mississippi Coast after Katrina. He lives in New York City. For more information go to http://robertiulo.naiwe.com/

Lora Keller: After earning a creative writing degree in 1979, Lora Keller was a scriptwriter, public relations executive and educator in Milwaukee, New York and Kansas City. Now when she's not writing poetry, she runs three small Milwaukee businesses. To connect with Lora and more of her work, visit her website: lakeller.com.

Wendy Kennar: Wendy Kennar is a freelance writer who finds inspiration in her eight-year-old son and from her memories of her twelve-year teaching career. Her writing has appeared in several publications and anthologies, both print and online. You can read more of Wendy's writing at wendykennar.com.

Richard Koreen: Richard Koreen is a retired teacher living with his wife Diane on the shores of Lake Winnipeg. His stories reflect a very unserious, often madcap perspective. He hopes you enjoy this offering. For him retirement is a process of continually re-inventing himself. Who knows who he'll be next year.

Robert J. Krog: Memphian, Robert J. Krog, is the author of *The Stone Maiden and Other Tales, A Bag Full of Eyes*, and numerous works of short fiction from Alban Lake, Ink Monkey, and Dark Oak, two of which have won Darrell Awards at Midsouthcon. He co-edited *Potter's Field Five* from Alban Lake. http://www.krogfiction.yolasite.com

Richard Leavesley: Richard Leavesley was born, raised and lives in Central England and has been writing for small-press publications for over twenty years. Most recently his poem *Leviathan* was published in the horror anthology Fossil Lake II.

Gerri Leen: Gerri Leen lives in Virginia and originally hails from Seattle. She has stories published by: *Daily Science Fiction, Escape Pod, Grimdark*, and others. She is editing an anthology, *A Quiet Shelter There,* which will benefit homeless animals and is due out this year from Hadley Rille Books. Website: http://www.gerrileen.com.

Randall Lemon: Randall has lived in the vivid landscape of his imagination his entire life. He was a director, an actor and a world-class roleplayer. Earlier in his career, he wrote articles for magazines but has now turned to fiction in 19 published short stories and 1 novel. Find him on Amazon.

Mark L. Levinson: Over the years, Mark L. Levinson has provided Israel's English-language newspapers with political commentary, book reviews, humor, and even a bit of reportage. He once regularly blogged on the puzzling points of technical writing but, having somewhat rerouted his career, now blogs on the puzzling points of Hebrew-to-English translation: http://www.elephant.org.il/translate

Nicole Lim: Nicole Lim is an artist, children's book illustrator, and self-proclaimed ice cream connoisseur from the Philippines. Most of her illustrations are drawn digitally and revolve around nature, fantasy, and whimsical themes. See more of her work at www.rinianart.com

Sam Matteson: Sam Matteson, physicist, professor, poet, essayist and storyteller is an unexpected writer who combines a realist worldview with a deeply felt sense of the spiritual in everyday life. In addition to scores of publications in scientific journals he has authored many published poems, essays, and short stories.

Samantha Memi: Samantha Memi lives in London. She is the author of the chapbook *Kate Moss & Other Heroines*, and the story collection All In Letters Bound In String. http://samanthamemi.net

Catherine Moore: Catherine Moore's work appears in many literary journals such as *Tahoma Literary Review, Cider Press Review,* and *The Southampton Review*. She won the Southeast Review's 2014 Gearhart Poetry Prize and had work selected for the 2015 Best Small Fictions anthology. She is the author of two published chapbooks.

Heidi Morrell: Heidi's work has appeared in magazines, anthologies, among many: *East Coast literary Review; Poised in Flight,* Hurricane Press; *Emerge Literary Journal; Poetry Pacific; Rotary Dial,* Canadian; *Outside In Lit Magazine; Mothers Always Write;*—Fiction: *Blue Skirt Press; Oval Magazine, Ink Monkey Press; Dual Coast Magazine,* and a Chapbook from Finishing Line Press.

Violet Nesdoly: Violet Nesdoly lives near Vancouver B.C. and has had poetry published in *Time of Singing, Your Daily Poem,* and others. She has published two poetry books, *Calendar* and *Family Reunion*. She enjoys trying out new poetic forms and writes often about nature and faith. Read more about her work at VioletNesdoly.com.

Lucas Olson: Lucas Olson is a graduate of the University of Massachusetts Amherst. His work has previously appeared in B*eorh Weekly, Sugard Water Myth + Magic*, and *The Golden Key*.

Rao Vandana Parankusam: Vandana is from India. Tomato Pergu Pachady is a typical South Indian dish usually served in the hot summer months. It is one of her favorite tomato recipes.

John Pierce: John Pierce is a teacher from the Texas Hill Country. Some of his recent work has appeared in Right Hand Pointing, Valley Voices, and Ometeca.

JM Prescott: JM Prescott resides in Nashville, where it's normal to play Frisbee in front of the Parthenon. She is an avid reader and has written several books. Jo is a member of the Nashville Writer's Meet-up. She likes to travel, design jewelry, knit, and hike in the mountains.
http://www.authorkatedonnelly.com

Herika R. Raymer: Herika R. Raymer grew up consuming books—first by eating them, later by reading them. After finally being published, she continues to send submissions, sometimes with success, and currently has a collection of stories in the works. She also does semi-pro editing. A participant of the voluntary writer/artist/musician cooperative known as Imagicopter, Herika R. Raymer is married with two children and a dog in West Tennessee, USA. Her website is at: herikarraymer.webs.com

Betty Rocksteady: Betty Rocksteady is an author and illustrator with a love for the strange and macabre. Keep up and keep in touch at
http://www.facebook.com/bettyrocksteadyart

Laura Rushing: Laura Rushing is a copywriter, Slytherin, and vintage cookbook collector from Atlanta, Georgia. She likes her tomatoes three ways: pureed in spaghetti sauce, sun dried on a pizza, and eaten plain with a sprinkle of kosher salt.

Melissa Z. Savlov: Melissa Z. Savlov has been publishing her creative writing since 1993. Her work has appeared in *The Best of Foliate Oak, The Wall, Happy, COMBAT,* and *The Chinquapin Journal.*

Wayne Scheer: Wayne Scheer has been nominated for four Pushcart Prizes and a Best of the Net. He's published numerous stories, poems and essays in print and online, including *Revealing Moments,* a collection of flash stories. (http://issuu.com/pearnoir/docs/revealing_moments). Wayne lives in Atlanta with his wife.

Holly Schofield: Holly Schofield's stories have appeared in many publications including *Lightspeed, Crossed Genres,* and *Tesseracts.* For more of her work, see http://hollyschofield.wordpress.com/

Tania Simcock: Since childhood, Tania Simcock has been known to live in a dream world. She expresses herself through artwork, music, cakes and fantasy writing. Her current goal is to publish her Fantasy Series, a budgeting book and a novel of short stories.
Website: http://www.taniasimcock.com/main/

Bret James Stewart: Bret James Stewart is an author, poet, playwright, and game designer living in the forested slopes of North Carolina. He spends his days dreaming about nonsense. Check out his website:
http://www.bretjamesstewart.com

Alarie Tennille: Alarie Tennille was born and raised in Portsmouth, Virginia, and graduated from the University of Virginia in the first class admitting women. Now in Kansas City, she misses the ocean (and long tomato season!). Her poetry books, *Running Counterclockwise* and *Spiraling into Control*, are available on Amazon. alariepoet.com

John Vicary: A contributor to almost fifty compendiums in his career, John Vicary is the submissions editor at Bedlam Publishing and also co-founded the editing business The Letter Works. He enjoys playing piano and lives in rural Michigan with his family. You can read more of John's work at keppiehed.com.

Sarah Susanna Wood: Sarah Susanna Wood is a writer and volunteer who lives near White Rock Lake in Dallas. She taught college English for sixteen years in community colleges in the Dallas area, and was a technical writer for eight years. Currently, she volunteers at East Lake Pet Orphanage and writes in her spare time.

Christopher Woods: Christopher Woods lives in Texas and takes photographs—http://christopherwoods.zenfolio.com/